THE COUNSEL OF THE CUNNING

A *ROGER VICEROY* NOVEL

STEVEN C. HARMS

SUSPENSE PUBLISHING

THE COUNSEL OF THE CUNNING
by
Steven C. Harms

PAPERBACK EDITION
* * * * *
PUBLISHED BY:
Suspense Publishing

Steven C. Harms
COPYRIGHT
2021 Steven C. Harms

PUBLISHING HISTORY:
Suspense Publishing, Paperback and Digital Copy, November 2021

Cover Design: Shannon Raab
Cover Photographer: shutterstock.com/ Kanea

ISBN: 978-0-578-93379-5

ALSO BY STEVEN C. HARMS

Roger Viceroy Series
GIVE PLACE TO WRATH
THE COUNSEL OF THE CUNNING

PRAISE FOR
THE *ROGER VICEROY*
SERIES

"Steven Harms rocks it in *The Counsel of the Cunning*. Murder, treachery, drugs, and a deadly trek through the Guatemalan jungle. My kind of story."
—William Nikkel, Amazon Bestselling Author of
Deadly Tide

"The suspenseful, edge-of-seat writing is captivating to the very last page, in this choice pick for connoisseurs of the genre."
—*Midwest Book Review*

"A must read crime thriller about revenge and race relations that is reminiscent of Truman Capote's *In Cold Blood*... Highly recommended."
—Bestthrillers.com

"A rare mystery book that is a true page-turner, even to the seasoned readers of the genre."
—*Thriller Magazine* (Starred Review)

"*Give Place to Wrath* will leave the reader wanting a quick release of a second book in the series."
—Sheila Sobel, *Killer Nashville*

"Knit together so well that towards the end of book I was on the edge of my seat and couldn't turn the pages fast enough."
—*Readers' Favorite*

"Cleverly plotted and anchored by an inventive and ingenious murder mystery, it will capture and hold the attention of readers in the span of time it takes to finish the novel. A good starting point for what is shaping up to be an interesting series."
—*Book Review Directory*

"Don't miss this one! It is a well plotted, complex mystery that mystery thriller fans will love…an absorbing and very satisfying novel. Be sure to put this one on your list. You won't be disappointed."
—*Mystery Suspense Reviews*

"A riveting debut mystery thriller…"
—*Underground Book Reviews*

He frustrates the plans of the crafty,
so that their hands cannot accomplish
what they had planned!
He catches the wise in their own craftiness, and
the counsel of the cunning
is brought to a quick end.

Job 5:12-13 – An Israelite's commentary in the Book of Job

THE COUNSEL OF THE CUNNING

STEVEN C. HARMS

CHAPTER 1

A howler monkey screeched, its shrill pitch adding to the endless cacophony.

Dr. Catarina Amador watched the animal move through the trees until it vanished in the dense canopy below, then drew a last puff on her cigarette, crushing the butt with the heel of her worn-out tennis shoe. Her eyes shifted to the ancient ruins sprawling in every direction; eroded, gray slabs of rock covered with vines, others crumbled beyond recognition.

Her prison.

Atop the temple mount, the slight breeze and mid-morning sunlight provided a respite from the enclave of stone ruins and paths that weaved through the jungle of whatever country she was in. To the east, the sun reflected off the lone glimpse of the river, catching her eye. The faint sparkles shimmering off the surface forever calling her home. Six years and counting. But each passing moment chipped away at her will, replacing those pieces with an ever-increasing hopelessness. She had become mostly devoid of thought save for the world-class talents she employed for her captor.

The youngest daughter of a large family from the slums of Mexico City, her intellect and scientific acumen made her a prodigy. World-renowned in academic circles by the age of fourteen. At fifteen she began her studies at Johns Hopkins University in Baltimore; flying through, she graduated just five years later with a PhD in biomedical engineering. Her human molecular manipulation thesis elevated her into the scientific world's stratosphere. Upon graduation, blank check offers from a hundred different companies and research labs spanning the globe filled her mailbox. All she had to do was pick one. Her parents had come to Baltimore for the graduation and to help with the decision. Over dinner, the list was pared down to four opportunities in the western hemisphere. When the evening came to a close, they parted company—her parents back to the hotel and Catarina to a local establishment to celebrate graduation with her peers. She was never seen again.

Sighing, she took a few steps forward to look out over the plaza area, resting her arms at chest height on the massive stone wall encircling the space. Standing just over five feet, her stature matched her frame. A lithe body and long, black hair kept in a ponytail most days accentuated her stunning facial features. A foot taller and she would have graced magazine covers instead of medical journals.

She peered down at a bird-faced stone sentry near one of the plaza's entryways and the eyeless human statue set a few yards to its left. A variety of bizarre figures were sprinkled throughout the ruins. She felt the strangest ones were the two tall snakes, standing erect at twice her height with human feet, holding large blackish orbs of polished rock in their massive jaws. Positioned on either side of "Main Street," as she had nicknamed it, they guarded a small but steady waterfall spilling in front of a steep rock wall. The falls travelled over the rock above creating a wall of water ten feet high, cutting off the path with no way forward. A five-foot-wide chasm stood between the path's end and the water wall. She once had peered into it. No splash sound, the rushing water just disappeared into an eternal abyss. Beyond the water wall was the forbidden canyon and the treasure of the ancient ruins.

She closed her eyes tight and bowed her head, reflecting on the moment she first penetrated the water wall, not knowing what was on the other side.

Two men had tossed her over the chasm where she landed on hard ground and found herself in a dank cave, lit only by a torch on each wall. Soaking, she followed the orders she was given and took ten steps forward to a turn in the cave, which led to the opening on the other side. About sixty feet ahead was the jagged mouth of the exit, perfectly outlined by the sunshine stabbing through on the other side. Picking her way carefully towards it, the temperature warmed until she was standing at the cave's exit. She took the final step, ducking slightly into the beyond, and took in the wonderment of her surroundings.

It was a smallish canyon with sheer, steep sides and thick vines growing in bunches among the rocks. Clinging in arbitrary clumps was a fruit she had never seen before, displayed in a spectrum of light green to black and every variation in-between. Above the canyon the jungle had formed a natural ceiling of branches; not overly dense, but enough to provide a protective layer yet still allow the sun to push through to the polished, black-stained stone floor in various spots.

And there, in the middle of it all, stood a man of some years with his hands clasped behind his back. Wearing a panama hat, unassuming slacks and a floral print button-down, the hat's shadow cut across his face making his mouth the only discernible feature.

He gestured to her to come and sit at a small wooden table to his left. She had walked with slow, unsure steps towards him. What would he do? Was this the end? As she neared, his persona became clear. A man of Hispanic descent, well-manicured, with an air of self-assurance that clung to him like an invisible but tangible layer.

Once she sat, the man took his own seat and lit a cigar, drew a few puffs, and spoke.

"Good afternoon, Dr. Amador," he had said. "Welcome to my kingdom," he added, with a sweeping hand gesture.

"Where am I?" she remembered asking, as if in a dream.

"Where you were *born* to be."

"Who...who are you?" she asked.

Her mind's eye recalled the memory of his response at this particular moment. A smile. Cryptic.

"My name you will never know. But take heart. You are here to lead a significant advancement in a little science project I have a vested interest in. You, Dr. Amador, will be its shining star." Then came his explanation for her kidnapping and what he wanted.

He began with a cloaked apology for his men taking her off the streets of Baltimore and blindfolding her for two days.

Her memory replayed the horrible experience. Someone coming from behind as she passed an alley. A hood suddenly coming down over her face. A vice-grip hand that quickly covered her mouth. The man whispering something in her ear—a throaty, aged timbre—before hustling her into a vehicle. Once inside, he let go but ordered her to be silent as she felt the unmistakable hardness of the barrel of a gun being pressed against her temple. She recalled the vehicle speeding up, taking a number of tight turns before zooming along a straight path, then slowing to a stop and taking a final turn. The last slice of recollection was a breeze touching her arms as she was pulled out of the vehicle, being carried up a flight of stairs and into an enclosed space, as the sound of an airplane's engine roared to life. For a brief moment the hood was removed, but an instant later, a man she assumed was her captor, sprayed something in her face. That was it. Her recollection of a hazy, in-and-out consciousness was the only vestige of the bridge between boarding that plane and coming off it some amount of time later. Once again hooded and placed back in a vehicle for a short ride, she was then in a helicopter—the sound of its rotors were unmistakable. She remembered the flight being incredibly long. Upon landing, the same throaty voice said something she couldn't understand and then her hood was removed.

The bright stab of lush greenery walling in a sunlight-splashed landing pad pierced her vision. She recalled squinting, trying to discern the environment. The warmth of the climate immediately registered. Baltimore and her parents were the first thought that came to mind and then the understanding that they and the city were now thousands of miles away.

Two different men, not so gently, had taken her arms and steered her to a pathway that directly led into what she then was able to realize was a tropical forest, and finally to the waterfall and the eventual meeting with the man in the panama hat.

With another puff of the cigar, he then presented her with the whole tale of what lay ahead.

She was to develop a new drug, and he had stated that her opportunity to use her intellect and talent when it came to molecular manipulation was going to be unfettered. "Anything and everything is at your disposal," he had said with firmness and a hint of delight.

Next was a tour of the compound and her new living quarters—a luxurious penthouse adjacent to the ancient temple featuring a grand view. It was stocked with a closet full of clothes, toiletries, a hot tub on the small balcony, a desk, books for reading, and a computer to be used for her research. Following that came an introduction to the world-class lab with five qualified scientists, also prisoners. Her operation to run. Her scientists to lead. A deadline of three years.

Included in the "tour" was a modern, plain brick building housing more prisoners, each given a simple cell. Haggard-looking people. Further on came the trails, the statues, the ruins. Another cement block building looking completely out of place, with a large "F" scratched into the door, and behind it the three men and one woman chained to the wall. Final stop, a spherical hut off the southwest corner of the plaza, secured by barbed wire and an armed guard.

"Sometime in the coming weeks I will escort you here again," the man had said in a different, almost reverential tone. "The treasure inside is truly priceless. Perhaps the single greatest discovery in the long, brutal history of this ancient empire."

His final comment echoed in her mind, reverberating, before she eased her eyes back open, fluttering them as they adjusted to the bright sunlight atop the mount. The present day resumed its rightful place in her awareness, which she reluctantly gave into.

It was an off day from the lab. No scrubs. Worn-out gray cargo shorts and an equally frayed white halter top draped her body. Utility and comfort for the task ahead. Eleven harvesters with large baskets strapped to their midsections came up beside her: seven adult women, three men, and one five-year-old girl. She looked down and winked at the child, giving her a soft pat on the head.

"Hello Isabella," she said. The girl giggled as she always did and hugged her leg.

STEVEN C. HARMS

Dr. Amador savored the indulgent moment before a cocked rifle cracked the air behind the group, making them all spin around. Atop a small, three-walled structure on the back edge of the temple mount, stood an enforcer, and next to him, the man with the unknown name. The king of the ancient empire. Panama hat and all.

"Time for the harvest," he said in his now familiar deep voice. "Thank you for your continued service. Business is prospering as planned." He tipped the hat before disappearing. The group stared back; prisoner slaves in the heart of ancient ruins whom the outside world didn't even know existed.

"Let's move," the enforcer screamed. "The Tat," as they had come to call him, had markings covering his skin, save for his face. As the group moved, Dr. Amador loitered just enough to ensure she was the last one in line down the familiar steps. Three more enforcers stood ready at the bottom to escort them to the canyon—two positioned twenty paces away on the plaza and one at the base of the steps. When her foot touched the plaza, she shot a sideways glance to the enforcer who stood there. He was a relatively short man, fortyish, with half his right ear missing and raven black hair fashioned in a bowl-cut. Her pet name for him was "Mrs. Lobe," a play on words that he found amusing. He caught her glance, blinking both eyes simultaneously before grabbing her elbow and shoving her forward to pick up her pace. The Tat joined him as they crossed the plaza.

The trail to the canyon was directly across. Wide at the start, it narrowed to single file after the first bend near a statue of a half-man, half-bird figure. Two enforcers led the group down the path, with The Tat and Mrs. Lobe bringing up the rear.

As Dr. Amador passed the statue she stumbled, taking her over the path's edge and down a steep incline into a heavy cluster of ferns; landing awkwardly, she yelled in pain. The Tat screamed at her, sending down Mrs. Lobe. Once there, he roughly lifted her upright and then hoisted her up the hillside, pushing her in the small of her back while she used her hand in his as a leverage point to climb. When she reached the trail, The Tat grabbed her neck and moved her quickly to catch up with the group.

They were out of sight around another bend when Mrs. Lobe

18

reached the path from his climb back up. He looked around for a moment before opening his palm to look at the flash drive Amador had given him. One more glance around, he then pulled out a satellite phone and punched in a message before heading down the path to rejoin the work party.

At the receiving end, a man in cowboy boots stared at the words.

DOC DID IT. IN HAND NOW. I'LL COME WITH THE NEXT SHIPMENT.

CHAPTER 2

Roger Viceroy sat decidedly higher in his desk chair than Anthony Strongsmith, so whenever his boss made eye contact in between his excessive gestures, the difference in height made it appear like he was thoroughly engaged in the conversation. In reality, Viceroy stared just above the top of Strongsmith's head at his own smiling image emanating from a framed candid photo of himself and Governor Kay Spurgeon hanging on the opposite wall. As the meeting wore on, he found himself stealing more looks, drawn to it by the subject matter being discussed. The photo had been taken years prior, at some event he couldn't remember, and gifted to him by the governor. There was a warmth captured in that moment, a random snapshot of two people holding each other in high regard. He hadn't seen her since her resignation in the wake of her former husband's murderous scandal.

Going on three years. Hope Canada has been treating her well. All things eventually come to cease. He let the thought trail off.

"I'm sorry," Strongsmith concluded. "I wish I had better news. Didn't mean to hit you with this on a Friday afternoon, but I didn't want to ruin your entire week." He loosened his tie and reached for his leather overcoat laying across the opposite chair. "Think things through. I'll need your final decision a week from today."

Viceroy stood and nodded; shoulders somewhat slumped.

"Don't know what to say. I'll try and get back to you before then."

"And like I said, if you need me to—"

Viceroy shook his head. "No, no. I'll speak to everyone first thing on Monday."

"Fair enough. I can come back middle of next week if you change your mind." Strongsmith grasped his hand and gave him a shoulder pat, exiting in silence.

Viceroy waited for the familiar sound of the front door to close at the end of the hallway before he shut his own door. *Wow. Didn't see this one coming.* Looking around at the few framed photos on the walls, he sank into his chair, placing the soles of both feet against the front edge of the desk. He had an impulse to call in Regina Cortez and Trevor "Silk" Moreland, his two assistant detectives, but decided against it.

The second hand clicks from the miniature grandfather clock on the desk's corner was the only sound for a good ten minutes. He watched as the hand made a small shimmy each time it moved. At 3:20, he calculated it was time. Another appointment. This one private. Donning his coat, he quietly exited out the front door.

Regina watched him skirt by her office, then gave it a minute and stepped into the hallway. Silk was already there, his 6'5" frame leaning against the wall looking at the closed front door. The two shared a glance. Silk audibly exhaled and returned to his office, ducking as he always did to clear the door jamb. Regina turned to Viceroy's assistant.

"Tough day," the assistant said.

"I'd love to follow him out there, but I won't."

"He probably could use someone, but you know him."

"Yeah, I know him. The thing of it is, he'll never let us see him that vulnerable."

"Oh no, never."

Regina reentered her office, closing the door behind her.

Outside, Viceroy pulled out of the parking lot and caught the freeway three blocks down.

CHAPTER 3

A tricked-out SUV drove around the mall. The driver, a young man with long, brown hair coiffed to fit in with his fellow lacrosse teammates, slowly rolled his twenty-first birthday present along the perimeter. He called it 'The Black Beast'; his friends just referred to it as 'Jake's sled.'

Practice time was starting at 5:30 and the drop was scheduled for 4:30. Plenty of time. But he knew to be punctual. Never early, never late. Two clients this time. He checked his watch again as he steered his baby to a spot far enough away that other vehicles wouldn't ding him, and headed inside. Looking around as he walked, he tried to see if he could spot the watchers.

He weaved his way down the long concourse to the escalator taking him to the vast second floor food court. Each drop was different. This one seemed odd to him, almost whimsical. He knew their eyes were on him as he reached the landing, then headed to the deli. Despite the crowds, the line was short. After placing the order for two submarines, he sidled down to the pick-up counter trying to casually blend in while he waited.

When the order was delivered, he turned towards the seating area, nudging one of the sandwiches to the tray's edge to create a small space where he set his cell phone. The text popped up immediately.

TURN LEFT. GO DOWN FIVE COUNTERS TO THE PIZZA STAND. TURN RIGHT. HEAD TOWARDS THE PLANTED PALM TREE.

The next text message hit as he neared the tree. Seating himself at the closest table, he pulled out a Ziploc he had stuffed in a pocket, then removed the toothpicks from each sandwich, skewering two berries from his bag before stabbing them back into the buns. The next command had him walk the entire length of the food court to a booth at the far end, nearest the down escalator, where a man and woman sat calmly waiting and sipping on soft drinks. Jake's text included a name.

"Liesl?" Jake asked.

The woman looked up at him. He recognized her condition and empathized. The drug's toll on her clearly in late stage. Disheveled, droopy clothes, and bloodshot eyes. Her long, blonde hair hung in stringy disarray from the unstoppable outpour of sweat. This was in complete contrast against the diamond-studded watch loosely hanging from her wrist, and the Aston Martin car key next to the napkin holder.

"Yes," came the reply in a raspy tone.

Jake put the tray down between them and returned his eyes to the woman. Rich, yes. He wanted to ask her a question, but when he looked up to gather his thought, he saw a woman of slight build, dressed in tight-fitting monochrome black workout clothes staring him down six tables away. He blinked, then swung his eyes to the male across from Liesl.

"They got your half-a-mil," he nodded to him. "Enjoy," he snarked and moved to the down escalator.

"Next time make it turkey," the man shouted to Jake.

Liesl Sandt scrutinized the sandwiches and skewered berries then turned, spying a family a short distance away. The father, maybe early-thirties, was using his cup to play a peek-a-boo game with the little girl sitting across the table from him. A pang of pain rolled through Liesl's heart as she watched the innocence of the girl laughing and playing along. *All the money I could ever want, yet here I sit in the food court of a mall. Because I have to. They own me. Dad would be so disillusioned. My life's a damn shameful wreck.*

"Well?" her friend asked, interrupting her train of thought. She looked to him as he held his skewered berry like a treasure to behold.

"It'll change your life. Bon appétit," Liesl said, joining him in a faux toast.

They both bit in and Liesl felt the berry's effects rapidly spread through her body, providing much-needed relief from the final few days of suffering stage three anguish. The drug's potency ran through her, erasing the pain and replacing it with vitality. Most important, her heart rate calmed to a normal beat.

"Oh, I forgot to tell you. The first time's the worst," she stated as she watched her friend heave once then fling the tray across the food court, just missing an elderly woman. The outpouring of words and maniacal ranting ensued. He screamed out anything that came to his mind, unfiltered, waves of run-on sentences, sweating profusely as his volume went unchecked while his arms jerked and flailed. Mall security descended on him quickly.

Hastily stepping in, Liesl said, "Sorry, sirs. Sorry. He's my friend. He has Tourette's. He's going through an episode. I'll take him out of here. It probably wouldn't be wise for you to do anything to him in this condition."

One of the guards stared down Liesl, then escorted the two out the nearest exit they could find. By the time they reached the Aston Martin, the crazed ranting had ceased.

"That was a *rush*," the friend said.

"Yeah," Liesl said. "Welcome to the club. You'll feel like Superman for the next three or four weeks, but remember, once your heartrate starts climbing, it'll be time. Here," she added, handing him a business card. "Call that number when you need the next one. And don't put it off. If you wait too long, you'll find yourself on the ground unable to move while your heart races faster than you ever thought possible. I know. It happened to me. Screed takes no prisoners."

She fired up the engine and sped out of the parking lot, heading back to the estate.

CHAPTER 4

Viceroy situated the sack chair in the exact same spot as last year. A completely clear sky maximized the sunshine and provided a bearable late afternoon temperature of thirty degrees. Most of the sun's rays made their way through the stately oak towering sixty feet above him. Half the dried, brown leaves still clung to the branches as they do every winter in a northern climate, dancing every so often when a breeze passed through.

He had changed in the SUV upon arrival and now sat in jeans, hiking boots, and a dark blue and green flannel button-down poking out from the neckline of his coat. A baseball cap and winter gloves rounded out the look. With his feet half-buried in the snow, his back was turned away from the trunk of the tree, facing the objects of his destination. Every so often a fallen leaf would tumble across his line of sight, skipping atop the frozen surface. A car passed by slowly, off in the distance, the sounds of the tires accentuated by the crusted snow and ice being crushed underneath the roll.

Fifteen minutes ticked by. He looked at his watch, then back to the objects, then again to his watch. When the hands registered 4:25, he gently opened the lid of a cooler and opened the Joel Gott Chardonnay. The brand was specific and important to him. He poured himself a full plastic cup while keeping an intent eye on the time. At exactly 4:29, he offered a silent statement then took a healthy gulp, letting the wine warm him. There he sat for another ten minutes sipping away. With the sun setting, the dim light slowly transformed everything in his vision to a muted grayish color.

I'm still one pissed off guy, but you know that. If you want me, come and get me. In the meantime, I want you to hurt. I want you to hurt until you can't escape the pain. Until your every moment is bathed in misery. So, I'm done being your dealer, pushing your crack. He snapped his head up, looking at the sky. *Yeah, that's right. The whole Jesus thing. You hearing me?*

An uncontrollable muffled wail escaped his lips as he stared down at the two slabs of marble. One final toast, then he packed up the chair and cooler and turned to go back to the SUV, glancing one last time over his shoulder. The two blocks, one etched with the name Debbie Viceroy, and the other with Baby Viceroy, looked back at him as if to say 'goodnight' as the dim light relented to complete darkness, and the chill of a winter evening set in.

CHAPTER 5

The smell of coffee permeated Viceroy's kitchen.

He had selected the strongest caffeinated option he could find. Strongsmith's meeting the day before nagged him through the previous evening. The idea of moving to Chicago wasn't particularly desirable and moving to St. Louis even less. The cemetery visit also beleaguered him well past midnight. Despite his best intentions to sleep in, his body clock awakened him at 6:30. Half his body wanted the bed, the other half wanted to do something…anything. The second half won out, so he found himself at the coffee maker with the first half screaming for coffee.

Thirty minutes later the doorbell rang.

Viceroy rose from the kitchen stool, pulled the drawstrings tighter on his sweatpants, walked towards the front door and looked through the peephole. A neatly dressed elderly man stood in view. He paused, weighing the option of ignoring him when the bell rang again, this time twice. Viceroy opened it quickly. Staring him down was the man he had seen, and to his right was a second one, even older.

The first guy appeared to be in his sixties and the other, leaning on a cane, was probably closer to eighty. Both two inches shorter than himself. *Guessing 5'8''*. The oldest man's face was quite rounded with an undersized nose and sported a full head of blazing white, wavy hair atop his head. His slightly heavy frame buoyed a navy blue cashmere overcoat. The other man stood perfectly postured with both arms at his sides, one hand holding a satchel. No coat but wearing dark brown gloves. His thin, salt-and-pepper hair was slicked back, and a well-manicured handlebar mustache bisected his face.

"Can I help you?" Viceroy asked.

"Hello, Roger," the oldest one said, his breath visible in the cold air. "We've been wanting to meet you for a long time."

Distinct gravelly tone. I know this guy. Can't place him.

The man adjusted the position of his cane.

"You're wondering who we are and why we're at your door on a chilly Saturday morning. But as you can see, I'm not a quite a pillar of strength, so might I play to your sense of kindness and ask that we continue introductions inside? I assure you we are here to talk about something that I have no doubt you'll find fascinating."

Viceroy eyed them for another few seconds, then let them through, guiding them to the small living room and two wingback chairs on either side of the fireplace.

Viceroy asked, "Coffee? I just brewed a cup. I can make more."

The older one said, "Thank you for your hospitality, but I'll pass."

The other man waved off the offer.

Viceroy retrieved his coffee then took a spot on the couch directly across from them.

"You've got about two minutes to tell me who you are and what you want," Viceroy said, taking his first sip.

"Ah, where is my head? Introductions. Of course, of course. My apologies," the older man said while bowing. "The gentleman to my left is Kendrick Winston; my manager, so to speak. As fine an individual as you'll ever meet."

"Good morning," the man said holding a stiff posture.

Faint English inflection. The name…I know this guy too. Where? When?

"And I can see you're wracking your brain over who we are," the older man continued. "It's been a long time since I've been in the public eye."

He let the statement hang in the air just long enough before

28

using his cane to stand.

"Jürgen Sandt. I'm pleased to finally meet you in person," he said with nod, then sat back down, adjusting the crease in his pant leg as he resettled.

Viceroy lowered his cup and stared at him. Jürgen Sandt. Former United States Senator and last heir to the once mighty Sandt Brewing Company. A Milwaukee legend. One of its few billionaires. Viceroy knew the history. Jürgen Sandt's great-great-grandfather started brewing beer in the late 1800's, and became an integral player in the city's legacy as "Beer Capital of the World." The Sandt Brewing Company was America's number two brewer from the turn of the century until the Great Depression, after which the company survived but lost its hold. In the ensuing years, its market share slowly declined until a young Jürgen Sandt sold the family business to an investment group and then launched into a stellar two-decade career of public service. He became Washington's most influential senator but vacated his seat upon the untimely death of his wife in order to tend to his family.

As for the other man, Viceroy's memory clicked. Kendrick Winston, Sandt's long time communications director and spokesperson throughout his Senate years. The handlebar mustache and the unique name was hard to forget. Viceroy only needed the context of Senator Sandt to place him.

Viceroy walked over to shake both men's hands. "Senator Sandt, I'm so sorry I didn't recognize you. It *has* been a long time."

"Please, call me Jürgen. While it may be proper to forever reference me as a senator, I prefer to leave my political title retired. Twenty years of Washington was enough, even for me."

"Will do, Sen—I mean, Mr. Sandt," he said as he repositioned himself on the couch.

"Jürgen. I insist."

"Fair enough."

Sandt said, "So, onto the question of why would Jürgen Sandt be sitting in my home? To answer that, let's go back to yesterday. Anthony Strongsmith informed you of the shutdown of the Midwest Region Special Crimes Unit due to budget cuts, actionable as of March. Despite your agency's successes, including the prevention of the assassination of former Governor Spurgeon and the arrest of her criminal husband a few years ago, they're apparently not enough to sustain the continuation of funding in these challenging economic times. Your options are to join him in Chicago as he transitions over to the FBI, or take a similar position at the bureau's field office in St. Louis."

"How do you know this?" Viceroy asked.

"I know this because I am who I am. Money, power and being Jürgen Sandt comes with, well…opportunity."

"Apparently. So, you're here to give your opinion on which option is best?"

"Absolutely." He leaned forward with both hands on his cane. "Neither."

"What are you saying?"

"Neither one, Roger. Your talents are better served elsewhere."

"And where might that be?"

"In my direct service."

Viceroy said nothing for a noticeable moment before replying. "I'm not quite sure how to respond to that but I'm not a security guard and probably wouldn't be too good at it."

"On the contrary, I believe you'd be good at most anything. But that isn't what I'm here for."

"Okay. If you're thinking chauffeur, I'm probably not your man either."

The comment prompted a laugh, a hearty outburst that made the old man's entire body bounce around. "That'd mean I'd have to fire Robert and I don't think Mrs. Williams would take too kindly to that. Robert's been expertly driving me around for thirty years so, no, you're way off base. Let me be direct." He gathered himself and pointed his cane to underscore his statement. "I want to hire you and your team to become my own detective agency. Roger Viceroy, Regina Cortez, and Trevor Moreland." Turning to Kendrick, he added, "What's his nickname, again?"

"Silk, sir."

"Yes, of course. Silk. Jerry King would have been included as well, but he'll be telling you of his retirement on Monday. And to make sure you understand the magnitude of the offer, all your salaries will be quadrupled, fully covered health insurance, and other details that we can provide at such time as would be appropriate. Oh, and one more thing, although this one is just for you. You would be moving to my estate where you'll live free of charge. The original gatehouse has been recently renovated and sits on a quiet corner of the property. We stopped using that entrance twelve years ago when the current grand entry was built."

The room went silent as the old man pulled out a hanky and blew his nose. Viceroy took a few long gulps while keeping his eyes affixed on the man in front of him. *The demise of MRSCU. FBI options. Jürgen Sandt offering me a job. This is crazy. Is this for real?* The seconds ticked by in silence while the famous billionaire and Winston sat still. *The molecules. Always.*

"Jürgen, I'm honored you think that highly of me and my team. It appears your offer would keep us together, which is enticing. Sorry to hear Jerry will be retiring; although, it's extremely awkward that you know this, and I don't. But I need more clarity."

"Sure. What exactly?"

"You said the word 'agency.' What do you mean?"

For the first time all morning Jürgen paused and glanced over at Kendrick before answering. "Well, there are many things governmental bodies just can't do. Legalities, politics, sensitivities, protocols, funding—as you now are experiencing—and other impediments. Sometimes life's challenges require different avenues. Wrongs can be righted if there's a clear path forward. What I'm trying to say is you three would become my stealth investigative agency serving on a variety of fronts. There are fires burning both home and abroad, both personal and public, that could benefit from three elite firefighters, so to speak. And don't make the mistake of thinking I'm simply exploring an idea or placating a wild fantasy in my old age."

"This isn't your first time having this sort of conversation."

Jürgen leaned back in his chair and grinned. "That's exactly what I like about you. Your perceptive skills are admirable. The answer is: 'No, it isn't.' Others have gone before you."

"Then why me and why now?'

"Oh, that's easy. You possess a skill set of unquestionable

excellence, but also a certain truth that is rare. Loss. It breeds perseverance. And frankly, I could also use your other two detectives. For years I've kept it to one person, but the world's become a more complicated place. And to set the table, my last firefighter disappeared eight months ago. If you accept, you will pick up the trail he left. If you decline, then this as far as our conversation goes."

"Candidly, the FBI isn't too appealing so...I'm listening."

"Excellent. Then let me begin by telling you the trail. He disappeared trying to find my son Bertram."

"*What?* What do you mean? He was declared dead, what...five or six years ago?"

Jürgen nodded.

"I don't understand," Viceroy said.

"Well, I think it would be helpful to recap my son's story." Jürgen laid the cane across his lap and gripped it every so often as he spoke. "You may recall he was on a mission trip to Guatemala a decade ago. Bertram was always very religious, dedicating his life to the poor both here and abroad. Admirable. I was a proud father, to be sure. He found his life's calling in doing mission work, which his mother encouraged, rest her soul. Before the Guatemala trip, I think he'd been on a dozen all over the world. He poured himself into his faith but over time became detached whenever he was home. It was as if something changed, making him uncomfortable around wealth. For a time, he lived in a small, rundown apartment in a rough neighborhood on Milwaukee's northwest side, passing his time helping the homeless or spending entire days at a church in prayer. His mother and I finally convinced him to come home for safety's sake, which he begrudgingly did about a year before Anna died. Good thing, too. I was still shuttling between Milwaukee and D.C. and his mother needed him. Cancer can be a terribly swift disease, and my daughter Liesl was beginning her drug habit right about then. Tough times. Anyway, Bertram went to Guatemala with a group of people from a downtown church. And then they all disappeared, as you know. His team was doing outreach in the rural mountains in the northern parts of that country. Vanished, every last one of them."

"How many were there?"

"Thirteen. All adults, except for one young man. Joaquín was his name. I remember how excited Bertram was that he was going because he spoke both English and Spanish, so they wouldn't need a local interpreter. I provided the plane to take them down there. The least I could do. That was the last time I saw him."

"I'm sure that's been rough."

The old man put forth a brave smile as he continued, "Five years and a multitude of search parties into those mountains, not to mention a vast amount of dollars to the Guatemalan government, proved futile. Their people said there was no trace to be found... so I let him go."

He paused for one final memory, then changed demeanor and pulled himself up in his chair.

"But a father's heart is forever tied to his children. Complete closure never came. Over time I couldn't shake a gnawing feeling that he was still alive. It got so strong that I finally sent my firefighter down there two years ago. Last June he called to let me know that he might have a credible lead, but he wouldn't expound. I never heard from him again. There's no report of his death, absolutely nothing informative from my Guatemalan contacts. He also vanished without a trace. That's the background story. And I got to the point of accepting once again that my son was dead and that my firefighter had met the same fate. But you see, sometimes what we believe as truth can become a rather abrupt turnabout. Kendrick, please," he said, gesturing to his aide.

Kendrick grabbed the satchel, a faded green color with frayed seams, and unbuckled the straps, passing a small rectangular wooden box to Jürgen, who lifted out a torn piece of white cloth with a red border, inviting Viceroy over for a closer look.

The cloth was two inches wide, torn about five inches down where its silk shreds limply lay. A red cross was embroidered down the middle. There were words on either side of the cross once forming a sentence starting down the left side, then underneath what would have been the bottom of the cross, and then up the right side. The only legible words were the first two on the left, 'Therefore go,' and the last one on the right, 'Spirit.'

Jürgen lay the cloth down on the end table and, without looking at it, said, "It reads, 'Therefore go and make disciples of all nations baptizing them in the name of the Father and of the Son and of the Holy Spirit.'" He looked up at Viceroy. "I should know. It was the bookmark I gave Bertram right before he boarded that plane."

"But that could be anybody's. How did you come across it? And that particular bookmark is probably sold at lots of bookstores."

Jürgen walked to the kitchen door overlooking the backyard. "I came across it from that satchel. It was hung from the gate of my estate one night about a month ago. Robert discovered it and brought it to me."

"That doesn't mean—"

"It means everything," Jürgen said as he spun back around. "The satchel belonged to Theo Gandy." The old man pulled out a chair and sat, all the while keeping eye contact with Viceroy. With deliberation he placed the cane on the table and in almost a whisper said, "He was your predecessor."

Viceroy slowly lowered himself onto the armrest of the sofa. Jürgen's gaze was unblinking.

"I'm going to say this with as much care and deference as I can," Jürgen said before clearing this throat. "I lost my son, Roger. I'd do anything to have him home and restore this man's broken heart. You of all people can understand the depths of such a loss. We share a common thread. And perhaps now you can understand why I appeared on your doorstep this morning."

Viceroy turned to Kendrick who simply leaned forward as if to underscore the magnitude of the moment. He looked once again at the cloth. *I don't know.* The cloth stared back.

'Therefore go'

You tyrant. Not again.

CHAPTER 6

"Here they come," the driver said as he and Mrs. Lobe leaned against the front hood of the semi-truck watching three men and a beagle detector dog approach.

The driver wiped a bead of sweat off his upper lip, then used the same shirt sleeve to wipe his forehead. Mrs. Lobe pulled his sunglasses down to see the inspection team in full sunlight before pushing them back up.

The semi, full of fruit, was parked at the U.S. Customs and Border Patrol inspection site in Brownsville, Texas. Emblazoned on both sides of the truck was the company logo—Guata-Fruto—in its trademark bright yellow script with an equally bright orange outline around each letter. Imagery of fruits filled the remaining space.

"Hot as hell," the driver said to the inspectors. "About time."

"Sorry," the gray-haired one replied. "Today's a busy one."

All three held clipboards. After opening conversation, Mrs. Lobe walked to the rear and opened the doors of the truck, pulling the ramp out and setting the one end on the ground. Two inspectors walked up with the dog while the gray-haired guy stayed with the driver, escorting him to the office to dispense with the paperwork. As the two inspectors began, Mrs. Lobe stepped away and placed a cell call to the head of U.S. logistics, the cowboy named Conrad with an incredibly long, hard-to-pronounce last name. Instead of fumbling it, everyone simply called him The Lisp.

"Where are you two? Don't tell me you're still in Mexico," The Lisp answered after the first ring, lisping the 'esses.'

Mrs. Lobe spoke in a quiet tone, turning away from the semi. "Customs is jammed up. Never seen it this busy before. They finally just started the inspection. Guessing we'll be an hour or two, assuming one of these guys doesn't want to perform a full anal on the truck."

"Well, you better haul ass. Orders are the shipment leaves tonight and we gotta unload you first."

"We'll be there, but I'll call you back if there's a problem."

The Lisp clicked off.

Mrs. Lobe turned back to the truck, watching the dog go crate-by-crate while the inspectors wrote on sheets of paper and forms, flipping to the next one on their clipboards after each stop. The process was halfway done near the front wall when the dog began to bark at a crate in the corner.

"Damn," Mrs. Lobe said under his breath.

The inspectors turned to him and waved him up. Mrs. Lobe grabbed the crowbar by the door as he climbed in.

"Open this one," the guy wearing glasses said.

Mrs. Lobe popped the top to expose a crate full of almost ripe blackberries. The guy put on gloves and gently dug around the fruit, looking and feeling for any oddities, while the other one led the beagle around the crate to continue sniffing. After one complete lap the dog calmed.

"False alarm," he said.

Twenty minutes later they gave Mrs. Lobe a stack of carbon copies and left with the beagle. The driver returned, yelling at him to close it all up, then started the motor. Mrs. Lobe locked the doors down and joined the driver.

"All good?" the driver asked.

"We're good."

The driver nodded, put it in gear and headed to the highway, hugging the Brownsville Ship Channel leading to the Gulf of Mexico. Forty-five minutes of pavement behind them, they pulled into the outskirts of Port Isabel, weaving their way along the inlets until they reached the nondescript white-sided warehouse of Mitchell Industries and reversed the semi into one of the loading bays.

The moment they got out, The Lisp was standing there with his hands on his hips. He spat into his hand and wiped off a smudge mark on his jeans.

"Sam hell, where you been?"

"Sightseeing," the driver cracked.

"Funny."

The Lisp spun and headed inside to his office, each step of his cowboy boots clicking against the concrete. The two followed. Once inside, he shut the door and tossed his cowboy hat onto a corner of his desk, exposing his bald head, then leaned back in his desk chair interlocking his hands behind his head. His ripped arms and chest stretched his black t-shirt across his upper body.

"Trouble at customs?" The Lisp asked.

"No," Mrs. Lobe said. "Just took a while. Although there was one moment that damn dog started barking. Thought we were going to have an issue, but it passed."

The Lisp said, "Good. One of these times they're gonna tear one apart. I hope he knows to keep mixing up the placement."

"Come on, he's in charge of the world," the driver said. "Genius level. He's not going to ever get caught. My guess is he's got some CBP director on screed anyways."

"You're probably right," The Lisp said. "Customs and Border Patrol. Pain in the ass."

Mrs. Lobe started laughing. The comment was funny under the circumstance, made funnier by the man's lisp.

"Zip it," The Lisp said. "Where they at? I'll get the crew working on it."

Mrs. Lobe said, "The screed berries are mixed in with the blackberries like usual. There's three dozen of them. Just look for the—"

"Bright yellow stems. Yeah, I know. Ain't my first rodeo. Where's mine?"

Mrs. Lobe flipped him an envelope. The Lisp dumped it out and gulped the berry, then put the $5,000 in cash back in the envelope and into a desk drawer, locking it.

"Those berries will be on their way to L.A. in the morning. Felipe's making the run," The Lisp said.

"I'll let the boss know when I get back," Mrs. Lobe answered.

"And what about the new shit?" The Lisp asked, looking at both, turning his head side-to-side for an answer.

Mrs. Lobe said, "The misters and bags are loaded into the false bases of each crate. Look for the red paint mark and just push hard and those bases will open easily. They're loaded, so just be careful when your team handles them."

"Okay. They're supposed to ship tonight. We got a van hitting the road by midnight. Mickey's doing the run. He's gotta courier something to Florida and up the east coast before he lands in Milwaukee."

The driver excused himself to the restroom down the hall.

Mrs. Lobe and The Lisp stared at each other for a moment.

"I'm still with you on this," The Lisp finally said. "The good doctor is risking her life. We're doing the right thing."

"If we're found out, we're all going to be executed."

"I know. But he's gone to madness."

The Lisp held Mrs. Lobe's gaze for a moment and then nodded a silent approval of their discussion. Mrs. Lobe reached into his secured pocket, grabbed the flash drive, and dropped it onto the desk. The Lisp took it.

"When you headed there?" Mrs. Lobe asked.

"I'm planning to be there a week before the event."

The Lisp rose and extended his hand, exposing the branded 'F' on his palm. Mrs. Lobe looked at it compassionately, having gone through the same agony. They shook, then Mrs. Lobe exited back to the semi to oversee the unloading of the fruit.

The Lisp closed his door once again, shut off the lights, and in one swoop pulled his cowboy hat down over his eyes and kicked his legs onto his desk.

By 9:00 p.m., the driver and Mrs. Lobe pulled the semi away for the long haul back to Guatemala.

At 10:30 p.m., The Lisp opened his office door to the dark and empty warehouse. He unlocked the door leading to the exterior loading bays, punched in the code, then stepped through. The van arrived five minutes later.

Mickey stepped out; his long, red hair coiled up in a man bun.

Within minutes they got to work on the bases of the empty fruit crates stacked against the southeast wall.

CHAPTER 7

One of Jürgen Sandt's private jets headed toward the guest waiting area.

A little over three weeks had passed since Viceroy accepted his offer and four days since he moved into the gatehouse. Kendrick sat next to him reading the morning news on his tablet. Viceroy pondered how often the man must've been in that exact chair in his career. He looked around one last time before the jet arrived to admire the lengths to which Jürgen had outfitted the small building.

The satchel he had left with Silk to figure out how and who had placed it on Sandt's front gate. The three detectives had all viewed the surveillance video two evenings prior. Around 3 a.m., the individual was caught on camera in full cover: black clothing, gloves, shoes, and a strikingly odd mask. He or she had darted into view, hung the satchel, then quickly exited. No car or headlights were caught in the periphery of the video angle. The only scrap of identification was the mask and markings on the sleeve that was caught in the pool of light from the gate area. It looked like an 'S' or a '5,' with a small arrow below it. The grainy nature of the nighttime shot made it hard to know with certainty. They all thought the decal was simply a corporate logo of the manufacturer, like a Nike swoosh. When the individual turned, the mask came into full view, a snake head with mouth agape as if it were about to bite.

Regina's assignment was the entire history of all previous efforts to find Bertram Sandt, taking a deep dive into every report on file over the last decade, all of which was delivered to them in four large file cabinets from Jürgen. The tedious task of piecing together the timelines and whatever details they had was hers to master. Some reports had come from the Guatemalan government in Spanish, making Regina the only one of the three able to interpret them.

Viceroy's self-assigned task was a discussion with a man named Cesar Quintero, a highly regarded Guatemalan national and unofficial political and industrial lobbyist in Washington D.C. Due to the prior search failures, Viceroy insisted to Jürgen that all normal channels be bypassed. It was Viceroy's instinct that the Guatemalan government was either incompetent at best, or a conspirator to Bertram's fate at worst. He demanded a complete covert operation to avoid detection that the hunt was restarting. Jürgen consented, but not without some pushback. He implored Viceroy that his connections to the Guatemalans were at a high level and that his sources down there would be of great benefit. In the end Viceroy won on the merits of his strategy, but he ceded to Jürgen this one exception. Quintero had become a trusted Sandt family ally over the past twenty years and had some familiarity with the case. Viceroy knew the man's connections and knowledge of Guatemala would be assets, if he could be trusted. The trip to D.C. was to find out.

The jet, a four-seat Lear, pulled up to the building and idled while the two men swiftly boarded, taking seats across from each other as the lone flight attendant took their coats. Within minutes it rocketed down the runway.

Once airborne, she let Kendrick know that Mr. Sandt was on the line. He punched a large button on the speaker sitting atop the center table.

"Hello and good morning, Mr. Sandt," Kendrick said.

Jürgen said, "Good morning, Kendrick. Thank you for escorting Roger on his inaugural flight as an official employee. And a hello to you also, Roger." His tone more accentuated through the speaker, adding with a self-mocking, "And welcome to Sandt Airlines."

"Thank you, Jürgen. Truly the only way to fly."

"Indeed. You're on my little guy, the Niña. I named them all after Columbus's ships. Shouldn't take you but an hour to get there."

"Well, it's going to be hard flying the regular way from now on."

"Hopefully, you'll never have to. Listen, I forgot to tell you about a distinguishing personal characteristic regarding Cesar and thought it appropriate to call you before you meet him."

"Certainly."

"The poor man has a bum right arm. He can't really use it at all so, when you meet him, extend your left hand. It will avoid what could be an awkward moment."

Viceroy thanked Jürgen for the heads-up as Kendrick said his goodbyes before excusing himself.

Alone in the cabin, Viceroy looked out the window as they flew over the endless sea of clouds below and the sun's dazzling highlights on their billows. *Heavenly. Nice try. Beautiful, but you gotta bring more than pretty pictures to the table.* The thought reminded him of his former pastor and friend, Greg Oxenhaus, and more vibrantly his life's love, Debbie, a rush of sadness on both counts. Debbie, who he'd never see again, and "Ox," who he hadn't seen in seven months, by his own choosing. *Move on.* He popped in his earbuds and hit play.

In the restroom, Kendrick pulled a small tin container from his pocket and flipped open the lid, exposing two neon green pills. He poured a cup of water from the sink and swallowed one. The reassuring tingle in his fingertips was a relief. He looked down at the lone pill in the tin. *Cutting this way too close.* He glanced in the mirror and twisted the left side of his mustache back into perfect form before rejoining Viceroy in the cabin.

CHAPTER 8

The gatehouse, a two-story Colonial Revival on the grounds of the Sandt estate, was built in 1911 as the temporary original residence of Volker Sandt, the founder of the dynasty. Built first while the grand mansion was underway, finishing that in 1918. The entire property was three hundred forty acres of forest and rolling meadows called Emilina—in a nod to his parents, Emil and Lina Sandt. A meandering brook and woodland separated the two buildings; all that could be viewed from the gatehouse was the very tops of the eleven chimneys of the mansion located three hundred yards away. A paved tight road with a bridge spanning the waterway connected the two buildings as it gently wove through the woods.

Silk pulled up next to the security gate and flashed his access card across the electronic reader. The gate and its large steel bars with an old English "E" welded to each one parted down the middle and rolled slowly open. He drove up the small incline, then down the backside to the gatehouse parking area, heading inside with two coffees.

With the enthusiastic approval of Jürgen, Viceroy decided the best option for their offices was the gatehouse's lower level; a space he determined he would never use, plus it afforded convenience. Still under renovation, the three detectives had set up shop. All three working spaces had one window facing the gate and small parking area, with half walls separating each other's area. The two on the ends also had a side window. Silk had the middle one, with Viceroy's office space to his left and Regina's to his right as he sat oriented towards the gate view. Against the back, Viceroy had a giant wallboard installed.

As Viceroy taxied down the runway, Silk backed in through the doorway and headed to his space, the smell of fresh paint still strong. A drop cloth and two used paint cans sat against his half wall. He draped his coat across the half wall and peered over to Regina.

"Black, no sugar," he said as he extended a cup. She was situated behind her new desk with a computer screen almost blocking her entirely. "Just like me."

"You're one amusing man," she said, standing to take it from him.

"Whoa. You look like sh…um…you don't look so good. You sleep here or something?"

"Yeah," she said as she took off the lid and gulped, then added with a nod of her head to the leather couch in the corner of her space, "right there."

"Comfy. But why?"

"Didn't plan to, but once I got started on Bertram, I couldn't stop. It's like a great mystery novel, only better. I called it quits around three and woke up at seven. I did my best to freshen up."

"What'd you find out?" Silk asked, taking the lid off his coffee.

"Have a seat. It's a long one."

Silk walked over to a chair off her desk corner.

"Where to begin? Good-looking man," she began as she pushed a box overflowing with photos to Silk. "He would be thirty-eight today, so add ten years to those pics."

"Wow," he said as he pulled out one photo and held it up for a better look. "He's taller than I expected."

"I hope you're right."

"Huh?"

"It sounds better than 'he was taller.'"

Silk held Regina's look for a second, then returned to the photo. The shot captured Bertram with a warm smile, kneeling and surrounded by equally cheerful black children outside a bamboo hut dressed in faded jeans and a simple gray t-shirt. His longish blond hair awash in the sunlight created a dreamlike glow about him, an angelic image particularly in context of what Silk assumed was one of his mission trips. Physically, he was lean but muscular and bore an unmistakable resemblance to his father.

"Yeah," he said as he returned the photo to the box, "I hope I'm right too. What else can you tell me?"

"Everything Sandt relayed to us about him seems to be spot on from what I can gather in all these files. Nothing in them would counter what we know already. If he's alive, and so far, I haven't found anything that would sway me with any certainty, but if he's in fact alive, well...the world will be a better place."

"Okay."

"I mean it," she added to make her point, "Bertram Sandt is far more than an heir to a massive fortune and I'm glad to play a part in bringing him back."

"Well, his return would balance out his sister's contributions at a minimum."

Regina playfully lobbed a pen at him.

"So, what else?" he asked.

"Some really interesting stuff."

"Let's hear it."

"It's all rather bizarre, and a lot of dots need to be connected, but I got as far as Bertram's last known position in Guatemala. The short of it is their mission team landed at Mundo Maya Airport in Flores on Sandt's plane. There, they met up with a pastor named Federico Bustamante, a seemingly well-regarded man with a church in the city. He founded a missionary operation down there into the remote and rural areas in Guatemala, forming alliances with a few American churches about five years before Sandt's disappearance. One of those was Emmaus Road, Bertram's church on Milwaukee's northwest side. After arrival, Bustamante led the group and they spent about a week on the road making scheduled stops at a few villages, heading west through the country. Gandy had him tracked to El Ceibo near the Mexican border. Apparently, that was an unplanned stop on their mission before heading northeast towards the mountains."

"Unplanned?"

"Yeah. The report says due to weather. They apparently needed shelter."

"And why the mountains?"

"The ultimate purpose of their mission trip was an outreach to the villages around the base of those mountains."

"Okay."

"From reading the reports filed by the Guatemalan government investigation, the mission team spent two days in El Ceibo staying at the only church in town, camping inside the building. The morning of the third day the group left Bustamante's church bus at the village's school and headed out of town in three pick-up trucks driven by mystery men. They made it to their base point; a village with no name at the foot of one of the mountains. That's been verified. They spent a day there and then embarked eastward on a trail towards the next village, never to be seen again."

"What about the pick—"

"The pick-ups were never found in the ensuing investigations, nor their drivers. In fact, the townsfolk of El Ceibo claim they didn't know who the men were."

"You're sounding skeptical."

"Follow me on my instinct here and fast forward to Gandy. I'm pretty sure he was in El Ceibo when he called Sandt that night about a credible lead. But, at the mandate of the Guatemalan state police, Gandy was always to be driven around by someone on their staff. The official final report also says that Gandy was dropped off at El Ceibo and that the police escort was scheduled to return two days later, giving him some time to sniff out what he could. When the police escort arrived back there, Gandy was gone, also vanished. Fair enough. But now we have a satchel and a bookmark. A message seemingly from Gandy. If the assumption is that he's alive and found Bertram Sandt, it's too far to walk from El Ceibo to the mountains. He got a ride. I'm guessing it was in a pick-up that knew exactly where to take him."

Silk leaned forward in thought, pressing his hands together, interweaving his fingers, resting his chin on his extended thumbs.

"What do you think?" Regina asked.

"I think that finding Theo Gandy just got a little more essential."

CHAPTER 9

Kendrick shook hands with Viceroy through the car window and watched the detective walk down R Street towards the Guatemalan embassy. The driver pulled away as he dialed the office of Senator Clay Czerwinski to let him know he was running late.

Czerwinski was going on three decades in office and although Jürgen had his battles with the man, they became respectful adversaries. Kendrick had many a row with him on behalf of his boss, but those policy fights were always followed up with a free dinner on Czerwinski at his favorite spot in Georgetown—a five-star surf and turf called Poindexter's where the senator's irascible demeanor vacated after a few bourbon shots and a prime rib.

As the car neared the capitol building that old burning feeling of patriotism and politics stirred in his gut and Kendrick asked the driver to pull over so he could walk some of the way. The trip to "The Hill" had been a daily commute for much of his career. His parents had migrated to America from London when he was ten, becoming a U.S. citizen at eighteen, going on to achieve a doctorate in journalism and communications at Columbia before his first job at the Washington Post. Six years later he did an exposé on the sale of Jürgen Sandt's brewery empire. Following an interview with the billionaire, he found himself in his employ and never once looked back.

Kendrick crossed over to a walkway weaving through the Capitol Grounds on his way to the Russell Senate Office Building, a familiar tree-lined stretch of concrete. He strolled up the slight incline then down towards Connecticut Avenue to cross. The grounds and sidewalks were moderately heavy with tourists and the normal hubbub of government business. When the light turned, he began his walk across and was met halfway by a noisy cabal of schoolchildren on a field trip. He maneuvered his way through the crowd and then felt a jarring bump on his right shoulder causing him to lose his briefcase. He quickly retrieved it and turned to face the culprit but all he could spot was a large man in a long, black leather coat hurriedly walking the opposite way.

Kendrick shook his head and finished crossing the street then turned right towards the building entrance. A half a block later, he stopped. Sprayed on a tree a few paces from the entrance was a freshly painted neon green slash; still glistening, a few drips still ran down the bark in the cracks. He knew what it meant. Setting down his briefcase, he began a methodical circular turn. With so many pedestrians he didn't know where or who he was looking for and his eyes darted wildly from face to face trying to find the messenger. A loud honk from a taxi interrupted his scan and he naturally looked that way. Across the street staring him down was the man in the leather coat standing next to a park bench, large sunglasses blocking his face.

The man gestured holding a camera and mimicked taking a picture then pointed to the roofline of the Senate building, moving his finger back and forth.

Cameras, Kendrick thought. *Got it*. Kendrick nodded to him.

After the exchange, the man looked down. At his feet was a small cardboard box. He looked back up to Kendrick and then nudged the box over to a park bench with his foot. Kendrick followed that move with his eyes, understanding the box was for him. The man shot a look back to Kendrick one last time before turning away, disappearing up the sidewalk.

Feebly grabbing his briefcase, Kendrick walked to the crossing, keeping his eyes affixed on the cardboard box.

CHAPTER 10

The earthy aroma of Guatemalan coffee drifted through the lobby of the embassy. Viceroy spied the decorative pots and strolled over to them across the tiled floor, catching a nod from the cute staffer at the front desk that had checked him in. With a full cup of medium roast in hand, he began thinking again about what to expect from Cesar Quintero, other than a man with a bum arm and a thick, black mustache.

Jürgen had reiterated his unwavering conviction that Quintero would not only keep the new search for Bertram secret, but that he could help behind the scenes should assistance be vital while in Guatemala. Viceroy's research on the man provided some information that he found educational but not necessarily different from what Jürgen had outlined to him. Photos on the internet were scant with just two head-on photographs. Viceroy pressed Jürgen to never disclose the satchel and bookmark to anyone, not even Quintero. Jürgen agreed.

Viceroy started back across the lobby to take his seat, but spotted Quintero walking down the center stairs from the second floor. At first glance the man was all that Viceroy envisioned from the photos, but with additional distinguishing features.

Quintero's right arm hung loosely at his side as he thought it would. The large mole above his right eye was more pronounced than the photo he had seen, and a pair of wire rims sat agreeably on his face. *Two distinct additions.* The mustache was more prominent in person as well and accented his black hair, brushed back in one swoop across the top of his head and ending in a neat ponytail. *Didn't see* that *in the photo.* He was in generally decent shape for his age, sixty or so as Viceroy had learned from Jürgen, and impeccably dressed in a silk suit complemented by a colorful pocket square accenting his tie, cufflinks, and alligator shoes that matched his belt, adorned with an oversized gold buckle. In its center was a large circle with two inverted thin gold triangles extending from the top, not quite touching the bottom arc. The triangles were embedded across a smaller black circle. He held a casual posture all the way down, extending his left hand when he hit the last step.

"Welcome, Mr. Viceroy," he said with genuine warmth.

Viceroy took note of the man's rather high-pitched voice and one front tooth outlined in gold. *His accent's obvious.* He took a step forward. "Please, call me Roger."

"Roger it is. Thank you for meeting me here at the embassy. My schedule is such that my travels are frequent, and I find that the embassy is a convenient place when I'm in Washington. Let's head upstairs. There's a nice room where we can chat."

The two ascended and entered a sitting room just off the landing. "This is Ambassador Pachuca's favorite room and he lets me use it when I have the need. Please take a seat," Quintero said and gestured to one of the large, brown leather chairs while he took the twin directly across. "I see you are already enjoying one of my country's best products. Do you need a refill?"

"No, thank you," Viceroy said, setting the cup down. "It's very good coffee, though."

"I'll have some delivered to you. I understand you are in residence at Jürgen's estate now." Viceroy raised an eyebrow. "Jürgen told me last night when we talked. He just wanted me to know in case it came up in our conversation."

"Yes, he's letting me reside at the gatehouse. A great gesture on his part."

"A common occurrence from him."

Viceroy nodded. "Mr. Quintero, my thanks for meeting with

me today. My compliments on your English."

"Thank you and, as well, call me Cesar. America is a land of many things, great universities being perhaps at the top of the list. My family ran a simple clothing business in Guatemala and one day I met an American benefactor while selling him a poncho in our shop. I was fifteen at the time. By my next birthday I was in a prep school here in D.C. and learned your language quite well, and then had the good fortune to attend Princeton."

"Well, again, my compliments. I wish the nature of our conversation would be something other than what it is, but Jürgen was adamant that I meet with you."

"He's a dear friend. It's a heavy heart for me as well. Bertram haunts me. His disappearance in my country is a blemish on Guatemala. And after ten years, it's still fresh. Jürgen Sandt is one of my most cherished relationships in life and finding his son would have been, well…a gift I wish could've been given."

"Sounds like you believe he is…" Viceroy paused, wrestling with whether to be direct or indirect.

"Dead?"

Viceroy looked him in the eye trying to discern if he said it for shock value or to raise the specter of another futile search. "Yes. Sounds like you believe he's dead."

Quintero reached for a small painted box on the end table nearest him and pulled a thin cigar from within, offering one.

"No thank you. I don't smoke."

"Nor should I, but if you don't mind?"

"Not at all," Viceroy said with a small wave of his hand.

Quintero lit it and leaned back in the chair, crossing his legs. "Perhaps the second-best product from Guatemala, depending on one's point of view," he said while admiring it between his fingers. "I find a cigar to be wonderful medicine during difficult chats." He took a long puff before returning to the subject at hand. "Yes, I'm convinced he's dead, somewhere in the jungle. I told Jürgen as much a long time ago, but he can't accept that reality. I can't blame him. He's a father with unlimited resources."

"Why do you think that?"

"Theo Gandy asked me the same thing and I'll tell you what I told him. The Guatemalan government did everything in its power to find him and *all* the missionaries. It was an exhaustive search in very rugged terrain over a long period of time. A rainforest does not readily give up its secrets. I know because I assisted with the coordination of the first one. With the help of Jürgen's money, we were able to do far more than any other search and rescue operation. But at the end of two years, we had nothing. No trace. Not a shred of clothing or a footprint, let alone an eyewitness from one of the villages that would stand as a plausible explanation. They literally vanished, as you know."

Viceroy added, "Made even stranger by Gandy also vanishing in the same region."

Quintero took another long puff then leaned forward. "I couldn't agree with you more. You want my guess?"

"Absolutely."

"Bertram, the mission team, and Gandy are all up there resting in the hands of God. Their fates due to the mountain people, the Chizecs."

"*Chizecs?*" Viceroy asked, now sitting forward.

"Descendants from an ancient indigenous tribe of Guatemala. They were only discovered within the last half century or so. They live a life of exile, not wanting to assimilate into modern day. On occasion some of them come down to the surrounding villages to barter and the like, then return up to their mountain homes. They sustain themselves and the Guatemalan government has given them protected status, so much so, that their habitat is off limits without special permit. It's also a no-fly zone, believe it or not."

"What's their habitat?"

"A very large tract of the rainforest. I don't even know the size but it's a vast number of square miles. The belief is that the Chizecs aren't necessarily unfriendly, but they are extremely wary of outsiders. Over the decades there have been one or two incidents of violent encounters."

"I didn't find anything in the reports, no mention about the mission team acquiring any specific permit, nor anything about the Chizecs. As I understand it, the team was doing mission work targeting some of the villages around the foothills."

"No, you wouldn't have," Quintero said with a slight shake of his head. "The Guatemalan pastor leading the mission would have been the one to get the permit but that never happened."

"Why do you think the Chizecs are involved, and were they spoken to during the initial or subsequent searches?"

Quintero brushed off a bit of small ash that landed on his knee before responding. "Let me find a way to explain. There is no main city of the Chizecs. Each family lives separately, alone in odd dwellings, and they only come together as a people for special religious ceremonies held at some secret spot deep in their territory. Some of them walk for many, many miles to get there on those rare occasions. The thought is those ceremonial moments have something to do with the alignment of the stars, but that's conjecture. We spoke to a few in the initial search, but the language barrier made that challenging; plus, there's no census of their numbers, making it impossible to locate them all. There are Chizec scholars in Guatemala but even they do not fully comprehend them."

"Was that in the report?"

"At the insistence of the government, no, it wasn't. Drawing attention to the Chizec people in light of the disappearance of a famous American's son was not a public path forward."

"What's your theory then on their involvement with Bertram?"

He let Viceroy's question hang, walking to the window and puffing a few times on the cigar before he answered. "I understand from Jürgen that his son's passion for his faith was not a timid thing. My theory is that the villages probably told the mission team of the Chizecs." He turned back around to finish his thought. "They became a shiny object that a young zealous missionary couldn't resist. I believe he took the team into the mountains in search of them. A group of outsiders in their midst may have scared one of them enough to, well...take measures."

"Interesting theory. A hard one to prove. Impossible, really, without physical evidence." Quintero reseated himself. Viceroy continued. "I'll be figuring out a way of exploring it once I get down there, but I'll probably need your help."

"That's why Jürgen sent you to me. Of course I'll help. And if I perceive correctly, you'll want to explore my theory *undetected*?"

"That amongst others."

"That's the sort of help I'm probably most adept at providing."

"Good. I'll have to figure out a way to enter under the radar."

"Might I ask, why the secretive investigation?" Quintero asked.

"There've been two prior searches. The first one produced nothing. The second produced scant information and ended abruptly eight months ago with the investigator presumed dead. One common denominator is the Guatemalan government. Apologies."

Quintero stared at him, leaning on the armrest with his elbow while a thin line of smoke danced from the cigar towards the ceiling. "I see, and I understand. Let me think on a way."

"I'm sure between the two of us a strategic plan will emerge. Jürgen trusts you and, by extension, so do I."

Quintero reached over to his knee and gave it a friendly pat. "Good. Trust and communication are going to be essential. Gandy went a bit rogue down there. I don't know what happened to him either, but maybe he did indeed meet the same fate."

Except for the satchel and bookmark screaming otherwise. "Let's hope not. He may still be alive."

"Perhaps," Quintero said.

Through the window, the late winter sun cast a subdued splash across the D.C. landscape. Viceroy spotted the top of the Washington Monument above the tree line and it prompted in him the thought of the absolute power within the inner workings of governments and the entanglements of influence, both foreign and domestic. His detective receptors were still engaged in neutral on the man in the other chair. *Friend or foe? Throw a curve ball.*

"I'd like your opinion on another possibility," Viceroy said.

"Sure."

"This one seems a little out there, but I need your take. Jürgen mentioned a name that had been whispered to him at one time during the first search. He couldn't remember who said it, but apparently it was someone in the Guatemalan government. He said it was strange, but he wanted me to know about it. There's not a mention of it in the reports that I've reviewed. One of my detectives is pouring over them but nothing's come up yet. I'm hoping you might have some knowledge of who this person is."

"What's the name?"

"The Ghost of Guatemala."

Quintero chuckled, crushing out the nub of his cigar in the ashtray. "That name," he said as his amusement subsided, "is a... oh, how do you Americans say it? Is a...an...urban legend," he said, finishing with the snap of his fingers.

"Tell me."

"Hmmm. How to explain the Ghost of Guatemala? The name has been around for decades. I wouldn't put any stock, and I mean *any* stock, into chasing that fairy tale."

"Why not?"

"It would be a grand folly of an undertaking. There are some who believe the Ghost is real, but he's never been seen, and no photo exists although there is a rumor of one down at Federal headquarters in Guatemala City. Whether that's true or not, the photo's treated like your Area 51. Legend has it he was orphaned as a young boy somewhere in the wilderness of Guatemala, although no one knows where. Some say in the very mountains you and I just talked about, while others say he was born in the south, closer to Honduras. There are those who believe he was a full-grown man who rode in from neighboring Belize on the sails of a hurricane, and still others who claim he is a direct descendant of Montezuma taking up residence in the forests of Guatemala. Folklore says he's a giant standing some seven feet tall. The most consistent tale is that he was orphaned and came to grow up in one of Guatemala's many jungles. Perhaps the simplest answer is that the Ghost is our twisted version of Tarzan. When he was old enough, he somehow emerged from the wilderness and rose to establish the most powerful drug empire in the country through murder and bribery."

"Assuming for a second he's real, why would he care about a small missionary team from America?"

"My point exactly," Quintero shrugged. "I wouldn't waste any thought on that question. The Ghost of Guatemala doesn't exist."

"You're not one of the believers?"

"Decidedly not. The Ghost is a catch-all for criminals and bad actors of every sort. A convenient manifestation to explain away unsolved crimes and scare people."

"Did Gandy follow that trail at all, as far as you know?"

"That question I don't have an answer for. Gandy never brought up the name and I had no cause to."

"Fair enough. I'd like to get down there the first week of March, but I need to ensure my name isn't on an entry list."

"Smart, *very* smart," Quintero said. "Maybe you should consider a bit of a wild idea."

"And what would that be?"

"I just now thought of this, but if you could figure a way to ride along via a U.S. military visit, I could make sure you are lost in the shuffle upon arrival."

Viceroy scratched his cheek, thinking about the possibility.

Quintero continued, "Both Jürgen and I know someone quite high up in the U.S. Army. Perhaps he could be of assistance if Jürgen asked."

"Who would that be?"

"General Grady Hammaren. Well connected, and a mutual friend who would probably do anything he could to help Jürgen."

"Let me chew on that and I'll get back to you," Viceroy said, checking his watch. "For now, I'm going to have to take my leave, but I'm sure we'll be talking as things develop."

"Of course, of course. My private cell is the best way to reach me. I'm rarely at my office."

Quintero escorted him downstairs and out to the sidewalk. Air a bit colder than usual met them as they stood directly across from one another. Viceroy let a passer-by scoot past and out of earshot before he spoke.

"Thanks for your time," Viceroy said. "Jürgen will be pleased we met. I hate to say this, but I can be rather anal sometimes, just ask my staff, but our conversation is to remain unconditionally confidential. Jürgen said that wouldn't be a problem."

"Rest assured that is understood completely."

"Good. By the way, that's an interesting belt buckle."

Quintero looked down and replied back with some pride, "Yes, it is. It's from a goldsmith in Guatemala City. I just like the unique design. It caught my eye and I had to have it."

"It suits you."

With that, Quintero nodded and went back inside. Viceroy headed towards the National Mall on foot. After six blocks the plan took form in his head.

Regina, full dive into the Chizecs. General Hammaren angle? If he would arrange for a couple of stealth paratroopers and a transport plane to match, it may work. Going to need Jürgen for that. Then talk to Ox and break your self-imposed exile. Going to need a mission team. And find out if Princeton has a record of Cesar Quintero and who his American benefactor was. Stealth every step of the way.

At the embassy, Cesar Quintero exited the back door and into the rear passenger side of an idling sedan with tinted windows. It edged onto the street then found its way to the freeway, heading for Dulles International Airport.

CHAPTER 11

"There are two letters in the alphabet I want you to find. The beauty of it is, they're next to each other so you don't have to burn any brain cells locating them. One is 'n' and the other is 'o.'"

Kendrick sat in the chair watching Senator Clay Czerwinski battle in his trademark navy blue pinstripe suit. The last few wisps of hair on both sides of his head floated in unison above his glasses' temples with every gyration. The man was forever overweight; not quite obese, but continually heading in that direction.

The ebb and flow of the senator's orations made it evident the conversation wasn't going to end soon. Kendrick took the opportunity to focus his nerves as he stared at the contents of the cardboard box now laying within his briefcase, positioned on his lap with one side flipped open blocking Czerwinski's view, while his right hand subconsciously touched the tin in his front pocket.

The moment outside and the task now before him pulsated. When he reached the box, he had set it on the park bench and took a seat. Pulling back the two cover flaps, he saw three objects, each labeled sequentially one through three. The first item was an envelope with the word "INSTRUCTIONS" in a large font typed across the middle. He opened the envelope to expose a postcard with a simple message typed on it. 'REMEMBER, CZERWINSKI IS THE KEY. IF HE RESISTS REFER TO ITEM #2. YARLING

NOW SUPPORTIVE.'

Kendrick knew the meaning of the words. Dr. Alicia Yarling held the powerful position of Commissioner of the Food & Drug Administration and his politicking with her had been terse and ineffective for almost a year. The idea of her pulling a one-eighty meant only one thing. *Rather unfortunate,* he thought. But it still made him shudder. Czerwinski was the final piece. His influence and power-broking would bust open the dam.

The second item was a small aerosol sprayer or some sort of mister. He couldn't tell exactly. The tag on it read, 'ONLY PUMP IF NEEDED. ANYWHERE NEAR HIS FACE.' Kendrick had set it aside, almost afraid to touch it but knowing he would have no choice if the situation called for it.

The third item was small but vitally important to him. It was a replica of the tin in his pocket, only larger. He lifted it and gave it a shake, but to his chagrin there was no sound. Another instruction card on the inside bottom of the tin read, 'COUGH IN LEFT HAND IF SPRAY USED; RIGHT HAND IF NOT.' He took a moment to gather himself then placed the items in the briefcase and headed back across the street to the senator's office, where he now sat.

Czerwinski let out a final discourse then slammed the phone. Kendrick laid his briefcase on the chair next to him and half shut the top to keep the objects out of view. *And now the battle,* he thought and tried not to think about the consequences of leaving the building without Czerwinski's support.

"Menderhoff wants my vote on his bill," Czerwinski shouted, pouring himself a drink from a side credenza as he kept talking. "Who the hell does he think he is? And, goddammit, who does he think I am? Some pasty-faced freshman?" He took a large gulp and sighed, leaning against the credenza then realizing Kendrick was seated. "Oh, sorry for all that. The guy has a four-point-oh in asshole-ology."

"Good to see you, Clay," Kendrick said.

Czerwinski laughed, slapping Kendrick on the shoulder as he retook his seat. "Those are the calls I won't miss. A year and a half to go, Winston. Then the only way you'll see me is on a beach on an island of naked women."

"Well, that's an incentive to come see you."

"Shit. In all these years I never saw a beauty on your arm. Don't patronize me," he added. "Oh, did you want a drink?"

"No, but thanks."

Czerwinski took another gulp and leaned back. "How's Jürgen?"

"Amazing. He'll be seventy-nine in August and still going strong."

"And Liesl?"

Kendrick shrugged his shoulders. "Not much to say. She's still residing at the mansion, but Jürgen tells me he doesn't see her much."

"What a waste. Inheriting a shitload of money and she becomes an addict."

"Yeah. Unfortunate."

"And here you are back to push this thing across the finish line."

Kendrick held the mister a bit tighter, having grabbed it once the senator had sat back down. "Yes."

"Why? Why in the name of Abraham f-ing Lincoln do you want this so much? Hell, Winston, you don't even know anything about it or the problem it's supposed to cure."

"Clay, c'mon, you know why. Yes, I have a piece of the company but it's because I believe in them. Maybe I bleed for Liesl and her drug problems, but my heart is in the right spot on this. Jürgen lost Bertram and I'd like to think what I'm pushing for will ensure he won't lose his daughter as well. It's not just some sort of speculative venture, it's a humanitarian investment. And we know a lot more now than we did even a few months ago."

"You and Quintero are like the good cop, bad cop for Christ's sake. Why can't Cleveland Labs or Barker or some other American pharm bring this to market? And while we're on that subject, what the hell market are we talking about? It's not like we got people using screed all over the country. You keep making it out to be an epidemic."

"More and more cases are popping up. And as for bringing it to market—"

Czerwinski interjected, "Yarling will never approve it, that's the whole point. And I'm too old to go to war on this."

"Clay, relax. The political seeds are already planted and are in the process of blooming."

"Quintero?"

"Well, yes, he's a passionate persuader, but I think this is moving forward on its own merits. You know full well the only way to get that drug gets into the country is to grant it orphan status. Medicamento won't share their patent and Yarling won't move on *that* unless she knows she has the backing from *you*. She's a doctor first and a politician second. She doesn't have the stomach for a major battle. The American pharmaceutical industry is going to push back hard, and you know it."

Czerwinski took off his glasses and wiped them down to buy a little time, then poured another drink before walking over to his office door and shutting it completely. "Yarling's a feisty one. Last we met she was saying what I'm spouting. You're telling me she's flipped?"

"Yes, I have cause to believe that."

"Goddammit, Winston, you know I'm going to call her the second you leave my office. Is she or isn't she?"

The postcard said as much.

"Is."

"That's a hunk of meat to choke down. Figured she was in Barker's back pocket. Look, you keep asking me to help green light a drug to benefit a small bunch of rich idiots to profit a pharmaceutical company from Guatemala. Not a shrewd political position to be in. I know you've been away from the battle for a while but...for Christ's sake."

"You're gone in eighteen months. Your final term is ending on a stellar career. Future votes are no longer a consideration. Should some political enemy want to sling the mud, they'll have zero reason to. The utterings and motives of Senator Clay Czerwinski hold incomparable credibility, and you know that. Besides, there's always bleeding hearts in the media that I can call on for help if you needed it. In the name of compassion, you pushed it through. One death would be one too many."

Czerwinski smiled. "You're good, Winston. Sometimes too good. I envy Jürgen."

"Clay, the simple fact is, it's far more powerful than heroin, really than anything, and starting to spread. The fear is its moving to the streets now and no longer just a drug for the wealthy."

"And Oval...whatever, is the cure?"

"Ovalar. Not a cure. A combatant drug that mitigates the effects of screed as I've outlined before. That, too, is a permanent need for a screed addict. A daily pill, but without it, they have no hope of living a normal life, and without a control drug like Ovalar, they'll die."

"How can one berry do all that damage?"

"I don't know if anyone has all the answers. Someone's growing them in Central America and distributing in the US. I'm asking you once more today to make sure Ovalar gets through quickly and unimpeded by the pharm lobby. Yarling will green light it, if you can commit. It's going to save lives."

"Okay, let's play a little chess. If—and that's a big goddam 'if' I'm throwing out there—*if* I agree to your wishes, you still got Newcastle downstream. How're you handling him?"

"I'll leave Newcastle up to Dr. Yarling. That's her boss so let's assume she'll have that covered."

"Garrett Newcastle is a lot of things, but rubber-stamping shit that flows to him isn't his style. You don't get to be Secretary of Health and Human Services by being a total lap dog."

"Well, perhaps, but let's assume—"

"You're pushing my buttons, Winston. Assuming makes an ass out of you and you. This town devours agendas like candy. You either get me some intel that Newcastle is on board with Yarling or I'm staying on the sidelines."

Kendrick hung his head. *This is crashing fast.* He looked at the mister in his hands and started thinking about how to do the deed now that the moment seemed upon him. His mind landed on a lunge rather than some sort of faux need to get up and walk around the desk. *One final plea.*

"There's nothing I'm pushing for that would be illegal. I just want you to clear the decks so it can get fast-tracked. I wish the answer was that Medicamento would share or work with one of ours, but they're holding firm. If Cesar Quintero can't sway their minds to do so, no one can."

Czerwinski sat in silence staring him down. Kendrick waited, and waited some more, and then got the mister positioned in the grip of his right hand.

"I need more time," Czerwinski finally said. "The pharms have a lot of chips they'll want to play. You're going to have to give me another month, so I can massage this."

Kendrick curled his thumb and index finger ready to the squeeze position. *Lunge now.* His hand began trembling. *Now.* A bead of sweat trickled down the back of his neck and he could feel it run down his spine. *Can't do it.* He glanced to the door knowing Czerwinski's assistant was right outside. *They're waiting, watching.* He raised his eyes to look at the man. *I don't know what this is. It might kill him.* He sat forward in his chair getting his legs anchored for the attack. *Lunge...now...*

"Excuse me, Mr. Czerwinski," the elderly voice said as she opened the door. "Very sorry to interrupt, sir, but the president is on line two."

"Thanks," he said as he picked up the handset, cradling it in both his hands as he addressed Kendrick. "Duty calls. The guy's a machine. As I said, I'll need some time. And tell Quintero to back the hell off. Say hi to Jürgen," he finished as he punched a line on his phone and spun his chair around "Mr. President...."

Kendrick's muscles unwound from attack mode. Uncontrollably, the mister dropped from his grip to the floor, letting off a tiny mist at impact. He panicked and snatched it, threw it in his briefcase and left, hurrying to the back exit of the building, and finding himself alone in a stairwell. A half a floor below him an exit door beckoned. He moved down the stairs gripping the handrail tight before pushing the door open into the rush of crisp air. Lowering himself to the landing, he concentrated on longer inhales and slower exhales.

People walked by, some in groups, others solo, each at a business pace. Most of them were texting or talking on their phones. The only one that noticed him was a young woman jogging by who appeared to sense he was in some form of distress. Probably a staffer or intern in the sea of government surrounding the building. She slowed, keeping her jog. Kendrick made eye contact and gave her a quick wink to let her know he was okay. She picked up her pace and was gone.

Kendrick watched it all as his heartbeat finally calmed to a manageable level. He sat there for a good five minutes until he felt a text buzz from his cell phone.

?

They're watching. How do I convey 'maybe'? Slowly he raised both hands and coughed straight forward.

RIGHT OR LEFT?

He stuck his left hand out with his thumb extended, then pointed thumbs-up and shook his head, followed by thumbs-down in the same manner, and then returned it to a neutral position and held that for a moment before slowly lowering it. A long time ensued. More people filled the sidewalk as the late afternoon meant working hours were coming to a close. Among them was a tall man in a black leather coat and sunglasses approaching from the north. Kendrick spotted him. Another text.

LEAVE MISTER. GO SOUTH 2 BLOCKS TO BUS STOP

Kendrick set it on the landing and went in the direction he was told. The next text hit in unison upon his arrival at the bus stop.

SIGN POST, HALFWAY DOWN

Six other people were waiting for the bus, but Kendrick didn't care. He looked over the bus stop sign and there, lodged in the u-channel post, was a small tin. He stuck his finger in and dislodged it and heard the rattle of something within, giving him hope.

WE'LL BE IN TOUCH

He hopped on the bus that pulled up and took it to wherever it was going. Alone in a window seat at the back, he opened the tin and sighed relief at the thirty neon green pills all neatly stacked and aligned in five rows. Closing it gently, his emotions ebbing, he called the driver.

Four blocks down he got off, texted Viceroy to tell him where they'd pick him up and waited for the limo.

CHAPTER 12

Two questions ping-ponged inside Silk's mind. First, can someone become completely invisible? And, second, is someone ever fully and truly underground? The volleys started at breakfast, picked up pace mid-morning through the noon hour and, like all tight matches do, careened into a heated battle with both questions holding serve. By dinner he knew the two were mutually exclusive. For if the answer to the first question wins, the hunt for Bertram Sandt loses. Badly. Therefore, he knew how to solve the problem by utilizing one action and one action only.

Dig.

Silk sat behind the wheel and watched as an elderly Black woman stumbled across the slushy street wearing disheveled clothes and a raggedy knit cap. She mumbled to herself as she walked, almost falling when she tripped on the curb. The streets were quiet and dusky. A lone streetlight cast an eerie pall on the intersection ahead. The woman continued into an empty lot where the grass held the blanket of snowfall from the night before. He lost sight of her when the gloom of the neighborhood swallowed her into darkness. Ahead, along the north side of the road, a single pick-up truck was parked at the liquor store; on the other side, a line of cars sat in front of a strip club. Every so often a vehicle would go by, slowly.

Time had taken its toll on the old neighborhood. Years ago, he drove down his childhood street saddened to see the boarded-up windows and crumbling front porches, a depressing legacy of his youth. The businesses were all but gone leaving a meager landscape of dismal economic endeavors. He checked his watch a second time. *Where you be, Cass?*

Cassidy Jeffers. Silk's best friend from his boyhood years and through his stardom at Marquette University, they remained close until the fateful day when the bullet ripped through Silk's leg, altering the course of his life. Cass was involved. His bullet didn't hit Silk, but his actions were as culpable as the real trigger man. Their relationship transformed from friends to animosity to unintended interaction until finally, fifteen years later, to a reconciliation of sorts. Silk was the one cop that Cass would never begrudge. Over time, Cass became a surrogate eyes and ears for Silk on Milwaukee's streets. He ran a small fiefdom in the old neighborhood and Silk understood street news was truer than any other source and always spread like wildfire to every corner of the city. Cass might have some answers.

A sleek, silver, two-seat Mercedes stopped at the corner just inside the pool of light. It idled there for a minute before the passenger door opened. Cass got out and tapped the roof for the car to pull away. He drew a cigarette and lit it underneath the light pole exhaling a large puff of smoke, the signal that it was clear to approach.

Silk stepped out into the night, moving slowly towards him, his large athletic strides unmistakable to anyone from the old neighborhood that saw the silhouetted man moving down the sidewalk. As he neared, Cass took another long drag and welcomed him.

"Trev," he said with a nod.

Silk towered over him as they clasped. It had been eight months and a few extra pounds, but Cass's flashy clothes hadn't changed at all. A maroon ascot accented the black, three-piece, sharkskin suit with a matching and neatly placed maroon pocket square. The shoes reflected the light emanating from the pole. A thin scar from a long-ago knife fight ran down Cass's left temple.

"You ever wear jeans?" Silk asked.

"It's after 8:00. Showtime."

"Of course. You're looking good, man."

"Keepin' the ladies interested at least. How 'bout you? When you settlin' down?"

"Not sure, but not anytime soon. No one's on the radar."

"Trev, you coulda' had any girl you wanted. Hell man, prob'ly a harem. I thought Doris was the one."

Silk looked away as he responded. "She exited. Took a job in Atlanta."

"She still doin' the news?"

"Yeah. TV is where she belongs. She knew it. Atlanta's a whole lot bigger than Milwaukee."

"Hmmm. Women. Can't live with 'em, can't live without 'em, and you sure as hell can't regulate 'em."

"You've been saying that since we were ten."

"Words to live by."

Silk looked around the intersection as he spoke. "Thanks for meeting tonight."

"Walk with me," Cass said as he turned and headed in the direction of the strip club. He puffed a few more times on the cigarette then tossed it into a grate along the curb. "Word is you're livin' the dream with the beer man."

"Yeah. I'm in private practice now. Same boss. The agency was shut down, but we all got hired by Jürgen Sandt."

"Treatin' you well?"

"Money's not an issue, if that's what you're asking. So far, no complaints."

"He ever find that son a' his?"

"No. But we're trying to help him. He still thinks he's out there somewhere."

They turned a corner and headed down a street lined with old tool and die shops. The buildings were all one-story and most seemed to be out of business to Silk as he passed by. The Mercedes turned the corner to follow, keeping back a good block as they walked.

Cass said, "His daughter used to show up 'round here sometimes. We'd always get her some shit—the good stuff, not that garbage they sell on the west side."

Cass stopped at one of the buildings and nodded for Silk to follow him to the back. A single exposed light bulb above a metal door was the only thing on when they rounded the corner of the building. Cass pounded in a pattern. A small slot opened about eye level and then the door opened. Three large men, two of them teenagers, greeted them as they stepped into a small lobby space.

Silk heard the click of the deadbolt behind him as the oldest one said, "Look out America, it's Silk Moreland."

"Guys," he responded, looking over the three. "If this is an ambush, I'm going to be disappointed."

"You don't remember me, do ya?" the oldest one asked.

"I'm sorry but no, I don't."

The man turned to the two teenagers as he spoke. "This is the man. Dropped forty-two on my head my senior year." Both teenagers looked at the legend standing in front of them. "Isaac Crabtree," he said to Silk, then with a wave of his hand added, "My sons, Clevon and Ellis."

"Pleasure's mine," Silk said.

"Alright, alright," Cass jumped in, "I told ya the boys could meet him, but we got some biz to take care of."

The teens shook Silk's hand then left. Cass flicked on a switch lighting up the entire inside of the building. The place had been gutted and decked out with a mahogany long bar against the left wall and a small stage at the far end complete with curtain and sound board in front of it. Plush pile carpet covered the rest of the space with a dance floor in the middle. Rich-looking tables, chairs, booths, and high-tops dotted the perimeter. Silk turned his gaze to Cass, who just shrugged and moved to one of the tables.

"Opened it in September. 'CJ's', but it's a private club, Trev. No listin' anywhere, if you know what I mean."

"Got it."

"Bass Ale's, Isaac," Cass said as he and Silk took a seat.

Silk said, "The tab on this can't be cheap. Didn't know the old neighborhood was this lucrative."

Cass smiled. "Depends on the quality of what you're sellin', and I ain't sellin' to kids or addicts, just those with lots of cash."

"You're testing my honor and my loyalties."

"Promise ya, Trev. Nothin' happens in here. I don't allow it. Streets only."

Isaac returned with a tray of three ice cold beers and a large bowl of snack mix.

Silk said, "Deal is no boys in blue on your ass and a lifetime membership to CJ's. How often you open?"

"Already got a few cops as lifetime members but you got yourself a deal. Open Fridays and Saturdays from ten 'til dawn," Cass said as they clinked the beers and toasted their arrangement. "Whatta ya got? You said somethin' about a guy you're lookin' for."

Silk pulled out an envelope, flinging it on the table. Cass spilled out three pictures. The first two were duplicates—one in color, the other black-and-white—each the head shot of a Black man with pockmarks just below both eyes and deep-seated cheeks. A neatly trimmed Van Dyke-style beard accented the lower half of his face in contrast to his bald head. The third picture was a candid side view shot.

Silk said, "His name is Theo Gandy. Used to work for the Secret Service, then was with Sandt for several years. He disappeared. But there's reason to believe he may have resurfaced, possibly here in Milwaukee. I'm trying to find him."

"I gotta tell ya, I don't recognize him," Cass said as he passed the pictures to Isaac. "Don't look familiar at all. Been no talk of some guy like that roamin' the streets either."

"He's on the shorter side. His file says he's 5'8"," Silk said.

"You're not goin' to tell me why you're lookin, are ya?"

"Can't."

Cass leaned back and began munching on the mix. "Isaac, you seen that guy at all?"

Isaac shrugged his shoulders. "No, but if we can keep the pics I'll get 'em out to the boys; maybe someone's seen him."

"That'd be great," Silk said. "Any way you can get the word out to the rest of Milwaukee?"

"I'll see but we don't hold meetin's, ya know? Why don't you use the cops? They see more people than we do."

"Too dicey. This one's sensitive. If you think you spot him at any time, call me. Don't talk to him and don't approach him."

"We gotcha covered, Trev."

"I mean it, Cass. This guy could be dangerous and may have some pretty nasty connections."

"Alright, alright. We'll be all snoopy and shit about it. Black ops. Got it. Now, maybe you can help me with somethin'?"

"If I can."

"Some weird drug is startin' to show up on the streets. Nothin' widespread, but random hits here and there. We had one near here in December, and I heard a' four or five more since then, mostly on the south side."

"What do you mean?"

Cass pulled out a small item, placing it on the table. "Yer lookin' at the delivery method. Street name is screed."

Silk picked up the item to look at it closer. "What's the drug do?"

"From what I'm hearin' it's the most powerful narcotic on the planet. Hooked immediately if ya' breathe it in. I'm guessin' that little thing sprays it right at ya. Isaac here found it at a certain location that made what I just said crystal clear."

"That's like a…weapon," Silk said.

"You're damn straight. Those that use it go fuckin' nuts for minutes, then fly high for weeks. Isaac's cousin was on that shit."

"Where'd he get it? Can I talk to him?"

Cass glanced at Isaac who lowered his head before he spoke.

"He's dead," Isaac murmured.

"I…I'm…I'm sorry. How'd he die?"

Isaac began to speak then looked at Cass. His face contorted into a combination of anger and sorrow.

"Follow me, Trev," Cass said.

All three went out a side door into the night. In silence the whole way, Cass took Silk down five blocks to an abandoned street of homes and then guided him into a house. Cass used his cell phone as a flashlight, being careful to pick their way towards the rear of the house. He stopped at a small room just off what would have been the kitchen, pipes still attached to the walls, but the sink and cabinets long gone. Cass raised the phone to shine into the space.

Isaac said, "This is where I found him. He was layin' on the floor by that window breathin' so hard the house rattled."

"From running?" Silk asked.

"No, sir. Not at all. From the drug. He kept shoutin' 'screed' and was floppin' back and forth on the ground. Then he just stopped and looked up at me, frozen sorta."

"Did he say anything else?"

"No. He just lay like that. And all of a sudden, he stopped breathin'. Died right here."

"My condolences, Isaac."

"There's more," Cass said. "That sprayer was laying next to him."

Silk crossed his arms and surveyed the whole room as best he could with the light provided by the cell phone. He settled back on the spot where the body had laid and walked towards it, staring down and imagining the man in severe anguish. Another senseless drug death. It's what took his parent's lives as well. Both cocaine overdoses, his mom first. Two months apart. Within three weeks after his dad's death, he applied for the police academy.

Silk turned to Cass and extended his open hand.

"I'll see what I can do."

CHAPTER 13

Pastor Greg "Ox" Oxenhaus was home on a late Thursday evening.

The last sip of a chocolate protein shake lay pooled in the bottom of a glass next to a mangled granola bar wrapper a few inches away as he sat still at his kitchen table. A blinking cursor visible on his laptop screen flashed its beat, waiting for the next key stroke when his cell rang. He was four bullet points into an inspired idea and was finishing the fifth, so he let it ring, not even glancing at it as his fingers tapped out a final thought. His mind subconsciously tracked the rings as he furiously perfected the words and then picked it up just before it would have stopped. He didn't see the caller ID, he just said hello.

A silence answered.

"Hello again, this is Pastor Oxenhaus."

He could hear some breathing, but no words came. Ox held the phone away to see what the ID displayed, then slowly brought the phone to his mouth to speak again.

"Roger?"

"Yeah, Ox. It's me."

"I, uh...I...wow. Hi."

"Hi. Listen, this is a little difficult. I know I was the last person you expected to hear from, but I'm hoping we can talk."

"Sure. Yes."

"Can we do it in person?" Viceroy asked.

"Yeah. I told you my door was always open. Anytime, anyplace, anywhere. I, uh…I just didn't think it would be this random, I guess."

"It's not random. A lot has happened. I'd like to see you."

"You okay? Anything wrong?"

"I'm fine. You?"

Ox moved to his favorite living room chair and sat; the vibe more conducive than a linoleum-floored kitchen. "I'm great. Really great. But the church misses you. A lot. But I think you know that."

"Yeah, I um… I was hoping you would say something like that."

Ox grinned. "So, what's up?"

"Beer and a dinner? It's on me. But I'm hoping we can meet this week."

"You name the night. I'll be there."

"How about tomorrow, if you can make that work?" Viceroy asked.

"You bet."

"6:30?"

"Sounds great. Where?"

"The Farm and Fork. Where else could we do this but there?"

"You're right. See you then."

The phone clicked off and Ox headed straight to the shower, tossing his clothes wherever they landed on his bedroom floor. *Roger Viceroy. Thank you, Lord.* The warm water felt immediately cleansing, more so than usual.

CHAPTER 14

Ox plopped his greasy napkin down and pushed away the plate. A smidge of tartar sauce and crumbs were all that remained.

"That's my record," he said, leaning back on the barstool. "Five," he added with a muffled burp.

"Five more and you'd be on the wall," Viceroy said as he nodded to the 'Ten Plate Triumphs' plaque hanging next to the kitchen door.

"Five more and I'd be in the bathroom. She needs a plaque to honor 'Five Plate Failures.'"

Viceroy smirked. Ox made a fist and pounded his stomach with an audible exhale. They were sitting at the upstairs bar of what used to be a monitor barn on a dirt road. The entire building had been renovated to mimic a farm theme, including miniature pitchfork silverware and a farm-to-table menu. The ambience had quickly made it their favorite restaurant to talk in the aftermath of Debbie's death.

Ox spun his barstool slightly towards Viceroy.

"Okay, so where we'd leave off? I think I was telling you it was hard to take when you shut down and left."

Viceroy took a long swig, then stared straight ahead while he replied.

"I know. I'm sorry. I really am. I just needed to, well, I don't know…I went inward. I was angry. Still am, more than before.

The hardest moment was when the doc told me about the baby. Everything gone in one instant. I'm having trouble squaring that up." He took another swallow. "I just needed to unplug. I can't get to a place of acceptance knowing a drunk seventeen-year-old kid took my family away. You tried," he said, now making eye contact, "but I still can't find the answers. Two seconds on either side of that moment and he ends up in the lake and Debbie doesn't. It's haunting knowing she tried to get out after the car plummeted through the ice but she couldn't. Can you imagine her final seconds?"

"Roger—"

"I know, I know. Look, you did exactly what you should've. It's on me. I can't get over the hurdle."

Ox nodded but sat still. *Let him talk.*

"I have something to tell you. A secret. Something that happened about a week after I stopped talking to you. I wanted to call, but, well…it was just a very private thing, so hear me out. Debbie used to leave me notes around our condo. Usually scripture on little folded up pieces of paper that she would hide or place on or around things she knew I would discover. Uplifting messages about love and encouragement, that sort of thing. It was her way of speaking about her faith and it was fun to find them every so often."

"I'm sure you miss that."

"I miss a lot of things. Anyway, that morning I decided to get back into the habit of running. You know, a few miles two or three times a week. I figured it would be a new routine to get me out of the condo more often. I found the old pair of shoes I used to run with and sat down at the edge of my bed to put them on. Laced up the left one, grabbed the right and there, in the heel, was one of her notes. I froze. In fact, I dialed your number right then, but hung up before it rang through."

"Why?"

"Something happened that sort of rocked me."

"And you want to *now* talk about it?"

"Yep. Just recently something else has happened along the same lines."

"I'm listening."

"A long time ago you once told me about God's voice. Do

you remember? How you believe God speaks most often in quiet wisdom?" Ox nodded. "Listen…I pulled her note out of the shoe and just stared down at what she had written. It said, 'Many waters cannot quench love; rivers cannot sweep it away.' I love you.' It's scripture."

Viceroy went silent.

Ox said, "That gives me chills. Um…I know I'm supposed to have some spiritual response for you right now, but…."

"Yeah. My reaction exactly."

"This whole time you've been thinking you heard the voice of God?" Ox asked.

"One that was so loud it knocked me for a loop. And since then, I can't shake it. There's no way the circumstances of her death and the content of that note was coincidence and, if that's true, which I believe it is, then God knew before she ever got into her car that night. He knew. He knew the accident would happen. He knew she was going to die that night and in that way. He inspired her to send me *that* message before she got in her car. It's too damn freaky not to align that way, and He could've stopped it. He could've prevented everything."

"That's why you're so angry."

"Pretty much."

"But yet, you called me and here we are."

"Yeah, I did."

"You said something else happened."

Viceroy raised his hand to the bartender for another round, then motioned Ox to grab his beer the moment they were delivered. He found an open corner table.

"Privacy," Viceroy said as they seated themselves, facing the corner with their backs turned against the main floor of the restaurant. "Listen, I'm going to need you to trust me, even though I cut us off."

"My faith remains."

"I think you know we were shut down?"

"Yes, that much I knew. I heard you were involved in some PI work somewhere in town."

"It's a little deeper than that. Me and the team are working for

Jürgen Sandt."

"Really?"

"He's hired us to find his son."

"*What?* Are you kidding?"

"You sound like I sounded the day he showed up at the condo."

"You took the job then?"

"Yeah, just a short time ago. He moved me to his estate. I've got his guesthouse and Silk and Regina have stayed on. I'm living there and using the lower half for an office."

"I guess things have changed. What prompted all this tonight?"

"I can't divulge too much detail, but there's reason to believe Bertram Sandt may still be alive. There're some circumstantial things that could be interpreted to support that possibility. It's what drove Jürgen Sandt to seek me out and hire me to find him."

"Where?"

"Guatemala, where he disappeared."

"And you're going there to investigate."

"Yeah."

"How much are you buying that he's still alive?"

"I'm all in. Not a shred of doubt."

"The evidence is that strong?"

"No, the evidence is thin. As I said, circumstantial at best."

"I'm not getting it."

"Confidentially, one of the things brought to me was the discovery of a bookmark that Jürgen claims was his son's, and I believe he's telling the truth. It's damaged, but the part of it that remains was a cross with scripture around the edges, only it's rather torn and there's only a few words legible."

"Another note from God."

"You should be a detective."

"What's it say?"

"It says 'Therefore go.'"

Ox took a slow sip, shifting his eyes out the window into the darkening evening. Viceroy leaned back, looking at the floor when he spoke.

"I had to accept. And I'm going to need your help. But, if you pass on it, I'm going to find a church that will. That's not a threat.

Don't take it as such."

Ox took a larger swallow, then another, while his head made small affirmative nods to himself.

Ox said, "Over the years I've been cautious embracing any claims about definitively hearing God's voice. People can deceive themselves or be manipulated into believing it. But God does talk to us, through His word, through prayer and worship, through circumstances, and even through the supernatural. The fact that this has happened to you twice, and each time the words connected to a specific significant moment in your life with even more unique circumstances, well, I land on a 'highly likely' vote of affirmation. Scripture says most times God speaks in terms of principles and commands. You're two for two."

"So…?"

"So, my answer is, whatever you need."

Viceroy smiled, almost in relief.

"I've arranged for a cargo plane to escort a mission team from a church to fill it. It's heading to Guatemala as soon as possible. I'm assuming you have connections in Central America that can find a use for a small group wanting to help the poor and do a little evangelizing. And, I need to hitch a ride."

Ox downed the rest of his beer, then turned over the mug and placed it on the table. "What exact date would you like to leave?"

CHAPTER 15

The salad chef went about her business in her prep area at Poindexter's on a busier than usual night. The place was packed, the kitchen in overdrive. Orders were coming and going fast. The shout from the head chef to "pick up the fucking pace if you want to keep your job" rattled the whole crew, but his added comment across the entire kitchen saying "and I'm talking to you, too, Sheila" while pointing a skewer in her direction, furthered her already frayed nerves.

Her shift had started with a visit from a tall man in sunglasses who surprised her the moment she exited her car in the employee parking area. It lasted maybe one minute, but the instructions and the threat of non-compliance was clear.

As the evening wore on, she kept a detailed eye out for the specially marked order from the new waiter; a young Hispanic, stoic, neatly groomed, and the one the tall guy instructed her to look for. He had appeared a few times throughout the evening at her station, but each order dropped off thus far was missing the distinct mark she was told would be the signal. Finally, at 8:10, he swung by to pick up the salads for one of his tables and casually gave her his next order, then disappeared to deliver her creations. She picked it up and saw the four Greek salad orders with a red smiley face next to one of them.

She made a visual sweep of the kitchen just to make herself feel better. Nothing was out of the ordinary. The usual chaotic rhythm of the kitchen staff was in full drive. She grabbed three bowls plus the one bowl with the small chip in its rim and went to work.

Inside the restaurant the waiter approached a corner table and asked if anyone would care for another drink while their dinners were being prepared and to tell them the salads would be out shortly. The famous senator lifted his glass and ordered a second bourbon.

Once the waiter delivered the drink, he returned to the kitchen. Sheila looked at him as he stood across from her prep table. She hesitated, swallowing hard and shifting her eyes to the four salads she had beautifully constructed laid out on the chopping block patterned tray for him to take. He looked them over but couldn't discern which one was the definitive bowl. He flashed his eyes up to her and, without saying a word, conveyed his annoyance. In response she reached down and turned the salad bowl with the chip counter-clockwise until it was facing him. She had positioned the berry he had provided her earlier in the evening against the side of the bowl. Satisfied, he nodded to her but grabbed a nearby fork and used it to entomb the berry into the greens, then slid the tray onto his forearm and exited to the dining area.

At the other end of the kitchen a tall man entered dressed as a chef and walked towards her. Same man from the parking lot. But for the sunglasses covering his face, he was outfitted as they all were, including the Poindexter's script across his toque. He walked deliberately, never wavering from his path in the direction of her prep area. No one noticed. He blended in. Sheila took a step backwards and froze against a counter as he reached into the front pocket of his apron. In slow motion, he pulled back the pocket of her apron, dumping an object in before exiting out the opposite door. Once clear, she looked down and cautiously pushed back her apron pocket lip to view the item, praying it was benign. A large wad of bills neatly rolled up lay within.

The young waiter returned and dropped off the tray, then wheeled and exited out the back door as the four patrons seated at the dimly lit corner table began the salad portion of their meal.

Across town, Garrett Newcastle lay dead in his driveway, slumped against his steering wheel with fresh cracks in his windshield emanating from the small hole where the bullet had passed through and lodged in his temple.

CHAPTER 16

Silk was in his office, one hand holding his cell phone to his ear, the other using a mouse to scroll through a report displayed on his screen.

He was talking with Lori Coate, a longtime friend from Milwaukee PD's crime lab, someone he worked with during his tenure and stayed connected to over the years. She was a twenty-year lab veteran, it's most senior analyst and usually the one called on for expert opinions during trials. A mother of two and soon-to-be grandmother. Caucasian with brown hair cut medium length and a wit to match his.

Coate said, "So listen, whatever the hell this is, it's not coming up. You can see that from the report."

"Dead end then?"

"My ass it is. I'll cross-check the results with other labs and the Feds. Don't go jumping off a cliff. Dead ends only apply to my hair. I'll be in touch when something hits."

Silk thanked her for the clandestine assistance and clicked off. Her lab report stayed open on his screen. He scrolled back to the top to review what he was just told one more time.

'All traces of known narcotics are non-existent.'

'Variation form of MDMA (Ecstasy), crystal meth, LSD, and desomorphine (krokodil) inconclusive.'

'Global database exhausted. Zero analogous identifiers.'

'Analysis unstable due to trace sample size and time lapsed.'

There were an additional few paragraphs of scientific language explaining in further detail the processes and results.

Which basically means the drug's a new one. A killer. An unknown.

He pulled on his jacket and dialed Viceroy as he exited to his Jeep.

"Silk," Viceroy said.

"Hey. Just a reminder, me and Regina are meeting Cass at his place in an hour to talk to the girl that he says can identify Gandy. One of his son's friends. Didn't want to interrupt your plans unless the lead's credible, but just checking to see if you're coming?"

"Yeah, I'd like to be there. Give me thirty minutes. Finishing up a dinner with a friend."

"Okay. Meet me at Brew City Bowling; you know that place on Capitol and 38th. I'll tell Regina the same and we can jump in my Jeep. A storm's maybe blowing in so no sense we all drive down."

"Yeah, I know the place. See you there."

Silk called Regina and Cass and pushed back the time a bit, then drove to the bowling alley, a forty-lane enterprise that managed to fill up every night and overbook on the weekends. The place maintained its magnetism as a hang-out despite its wood paneling and stucco walls. Cheap beers and tradition more than anything else. Plus, it was the main hub for street news.

The never-ending sound of balls crashing into pins boomed as Silk bee-lined it to the second floor. The smell of cigarettes was heavy as he reached the top step, which led into a carpeted, dimly lit bar frozen in time. The carpeting all but worn out with the high traffic spots down to the padding.

"Yo, Eddie," he said as he approached.

Eddie Browner. The bespectacled, middle-aged Black man behind the bar raised both hands like guns and playfully shot a dozen rounds into Silk. "Silky Smooth Moreland. How the hell are you?" he said as they clasped hands. "What can I get you?"

Silk sidled up. "Nothing. Still on duty."

"Just in the neighborhood?"

"Yeah, sorta."

"What's the occasion?"

"I only got about fifteen minutes, but I've been meaning to pay you a visit and thought I'd pop in while I'm in the area."

"I'm all ears."

Silk slid three photos of Gandy onto the counter.

"You see this dude around at all?" Silk asked.

Eddie squared up his glasses and studied the photos.

"Can't say that I have."

"Well, look, keep the photos and if you spot him sometime, give me a call. I got no reason to believe he'd show up here, but between this place and that other one you own, maybe you'll see him. You're still the man in these parts, so if he's around I know you'll know."

"You got it."

"And stay away from him. Could be dangerous."

Eddie reached around to his hip and pulled out a pistol.

"Ain't worried."

"I need him alive, brother, so just call me. And tell your street team the same."

"Who is he?"

"Can't tell you, but let's just say he's a high interest target."

Eddie held a stern gaze then burst into a laugh.

"You got it."

"Thanks, man. I gotta run. Meeting someone any minute." He strode out of the bar area as Eddie shouted back.

"You're welcome. Stay smooth."

Once Silk was down the stairs and out of sight, a muscular Black woman half Eddie's age rose from a corner table, and came over and around the bar. He gave her a kiss, then dialed a number from his cell.

"Yes?" the voice said.

"He's got a shadow."

CHAPTER 17

"Son of a bitch," Mickey muttered as he tried to keep the cargo van from sliding off the freeway. He was halfway between Chicago and Milwaukee on a lonely flat stretch in southeastern Wisconsin on the final and most important leg of his multi-state run with the drugs in tow. The Lisp had just called to check on his progress.

The previous evening he stayed at a Motel 6 in Fremont, Ohio, got high with a local who kept him active until well after midnight, and finally crashed a few hours before dawn. The snowstorm he headed into was unexpected, simply because he didn't get out of town until noon and checking the weather report never hit his radar. The front edge of the storm met him on Chicago's south side and picked up intensity every half hour.

A gusty squall blasted snow across his headlights and windshield like an insect attack, while the wind sheers battered the van's sides. His hands were cramping from trying to maintain a constant squeeze on the steering wheel.

A sign for an exit ramp abruptly appeared out of the snowy gloom and he opted to take it and ride out the storm. He swerved tightly, too tight, careening the van into the side rail, sending him uncontrollably down the ramp, spinning counter-clockwise and picking up speed. When it hit the bottom, it struck a curb and flipped, vaulting him through the windshield as the van continued to tumble five more times before coming to rest on its side in a frozen cornfield.

Mickey landed in a ditch full of three feet of snow about twenty yards away. The angle of his impact was shallow, the snow serving as a landing pad. His left side took the brunt of the impact. He heard and felt broken ribs the instant he landed, then slid another twenty feet before coming to a stop. Both ankles shot stabs of pain northward, the right worse than the left. His head and shoulders were mostly buried in the snow with both legs sticking out onto the side of the ditch. A small pool of red began to form around the snow nearest his head, absorbing the blood coming from the cuts and gashes to his face from being launched through the windshield.

He lay there while the vivid replay of what just happened flashed through his mind.

The boxes!

He tried to move. His left side screamed, but he brushed off the snow from his face, noticing much of it was clumpy with what he knew to be his blood mixed in. With a herculean effort, he crawled out of the ditch, every muscle recoiling in pain. He pulled himself forward enough to flop onto the shoulder of the road, then lay exhausted.

A light came out of nowhere behind his head and he soon heard a vehicle pull up and park, followed by the shuffling of feet through the snow.

"You all right?" the voice said.

Mickey looked straight up at the upside-down face of a bearded man wearing a parka with the hood tightly laced around his face.

"Son, can you hear me? I called an ambulance. I live just down the road and saw your accident from my window. Got here as quick as I could."

Mickey reached a hand up and the man grabbed it, gently pulling him to a sitting position.

"I thought you were dead," the man said. "You should be."

Mickey looked up at him again, then turned his sights to the cornfield to his left and the van with its back doors flung open and a trail of metal boxes spewed all over the crash site.

"What's your name?" the man asked.

"Huh? Um…name…um…Mick…Mickey."

"Well Mickey, you're one lucky guy. Name's Bob. Ambulance should be here in ten minutes, so sit tight."

Mickey turned the other way and saw the man's vehicle, a heavy-duty blue pick-up. He looked at it intently, then over to the totaled cargo van, back to the pick-up, and once again back to the van.

"Listen," Mickey said, "you and me are going to get those boxes into your pick-up. Quickly."

"What are you saying? Are you nuts?"

Mickey unzipped a pocket in his coat and drew his gun.

"Now."

Bob made a dash for his pick-up. The bullet Mickey fired buried itself in the side door. The man came to a halt and turned back around; arms raised.

"All of them," Mickey said.

With the gun pointed at Bob, Mickey struggled to his feet. Pain shot down both legs and he couldn't quite straighten his back or put any pressure on his right ankle, but all in, he was erect and in control. He gestured with the gun to walk to the pick-up, then sloshed his way to it himself and painfully joined Bob in the cab.

"Pull up to the van. Move."

Bob drove the fifty yards, his pick-up easily handling the off-road portion, and parked alongside the wreckage.

"Load. Sixteen boxes. Count 'em."

Bob did as he was told, swiftly packing each one onto the pick-up bed. All but one, the last one, had stayed shut.

Mickey watched Bob lift the final box and then saw him look over the debris of misters and sizeable translucent bags in the snow around it. Bob bent down to inspect but jerked up when he heard his pick-up pull away, stopping about the spot it was originally parked at, placing his hands on his hips in a sign of confusion.

From the darkness of the truck, Bob saw two small light flashes for a split second with simultaneous loud pops.

The second bullet hit its intended target and Mickey floored the pick-up, watching a twenty-foot high fireball rage from the rearview mirror, consuming everything in all directions. Everything.

CHAPTER 18

Silk, Regina and Viceroy waited at a high top at the back end of CJ's with the snowstorm winding down outside. The place was quiet and empty but for Cass yelling at someone on his phone as he walked back and forth near the stage. The conversation one-sided. Cass ended it by implying to the individual on the other end of the call that they wouldn't be getting paid until they returned some night with their band to play another two hours. Apparently per the contract.

"Sorry, Trev," Cass said as he pulled up a stool. "Musicians gone wild. Had to straighten 'em out."

A round of introductions and some small talk about their situation took up the next ten minutes.

Cass said, "So, yeah, she seen him."

Viceroy said, "That's promising. Is she here? Can we talk to her?"

"She don't like cops. Sorry, but that's just the way it is. She bailed."

"That's unfortunate."

Silk said, "You think you can arrange for just me to meet with her?"

"I can try. No promises."

Viceroy said, "Did she tell you anything about sighting him? Where or when?"

"A few nights ago at a bar her brother works at. 'Parently she was walkin' in to see him, and your man was walkin' out. Literally bumped into him hard, otherwise prob'ly wouldn't have noticed. He apologized and kept goin."

Regina said, "She's sure it was him?"

"She says so. Ellis gave her copies of those photos Trev gave me. Like, right after we had that meetin."

Silk said, "I need to know what bar. And her brother's name so I can talk to him."

"Tell ya what. Y'all give me some time to sort it out with her and I'll give you a call."

"Thanks. That'll work," Silk said, intuitively knowing Cass wasn't going any deeper tonight.

"Deal. Hey, you got any word on that shit you seen with me?" Cass asked Silk.

"I'm working on it."

The detectives thanked him again and exited.

"What was that about?" Viceroy asked as they climbed into the Jeep.

"He showed me something when I met with him before about Gandy. Some new, weird drug that's been showing up over the last few months on the streets. He asked if I would assist him in return and look into it."

"Do what you need to do," Viceroy said. "Just keep your eyes on our prize."

"Always," Silk said.

"I didn't mean to suggest you wouldn't."

"No problem," Silk said.

"I'm good too," Regina said. "Just looking for molecules."

Viceroy grinned. "You two are gold. Maybe because we're leaving in two days, I'm just edgy."

Silk patted Viceroy's knee and shifted into drive.

90

CHAPTER 19

Milwaukee was quiet. Six inches of snow had ground the city to a halt.

Theo Gandy sat in black jeans and a gray-colored mock turtleneck at a desk looking up at the moon through the skylight panes forty feet above him, the only windows the building had. All other lights inside the warehouse were off, except for his work station and the minimal floor lights on the second level.

"Welcome to March," he said to himself, his voice echoing in the cavernous space.

He tore open a FedEx box that had been delivered earlier, lifting out a rectangular slab of lightweight aluminum. Initial step was to check the serial number stamped into its side against the manifest he had displayed on the computer screen.

Next, he opened a nearby storage locker, locating a small white box, cross-checking the stamped code on it against the serial number on the slab, then sat down to finish the assembly.

He let fall two flash drives from the box onto a towel he had laid across the desk. He opened a small compartment door in the aluminum slab exposing a port deep within. With tweezers, he picked up one of the flash drives and inserted it into the port, making sure the connection was snug before closing and gluing it shut. He wished the whole thing had come assembled but understood the

91

logic of shipping the slabs and the flash drives separately. Less risk for damage to the drives and less chance of an inspection along the delivery route red-flagging a flash drive buried inside.

Satisfied, he grabbed his cell and inserted the other flash drive into the phone's port. Using one hand he held the slab aloft, then used his thumb on the other to punch in the nine digit code and hit 'send.' All the slab's sides immediately flew open. *All right, then.* He reclosed the slab's sides, setting it down, and placed the flash drive back into the box, then rehanging it in the locker.

Grabbing the slab, he hiked up the stairs in the northeast corner to the second level, reaching a twelve-foot-wide grated mesh walkway along the exterior walls of the warehouse twenty-five feet above the floor. A yellow safety rail guarded the interior. Ringing the second floor were bays. He walked to the bay number matching the serial code and approached an aluminum box missing its cover sitting atop a table. Five minutes later, he had the slab attached to the cover hinges. On his way back to the stairs he stopped, eyeing the empty bays on the east wall.

Sixteen left. The plan's coming together. April first. D-day.

He descended the stairs and sat back down at his work station computer and stared at the screen. The wallpaper he selected as his default was an image of a jungle. *She'll get it to me. She will.* He powered it down and went to a back room in the southwest corner, the only one in the warehouse. It used to be the shipping clerk's office from whatever company had owned the building previously, but now served as his living quarters.

Getting comfortable on the edge of his creaky bed with a family size bag of trail mix, he sat munching for a few minutes.

"Shit," he said out loud, noticing the time.

Running to the back corner door of the warehouse, he exited into a former dump zone of cement scrabble, now piled up with snow, and jumped on the rusty bicycle leaning against a massive block of cement. The snowy path was all downhill through an industrial waste field where it intersected with an old railroad track, tarred over years ago but with the rails still visible. From there he rode it to the gate and punched in the code. Ten-foot tall, dual steel doors swung away from the center. Staying focused not to wipe out, he kept the bike on the trail until it joined an intersection of city streets. Two blocks down he steered into a gas station.

Inside, he seized a beer and a meat stick, finding a corner near the front window after paying the attendant. Grabbing a plastic crate off a stack, he flipped it upside down and expectantly took a seat.

Ten minutes passed.

Then twenty.

His cell phone buzzed.

HAD AN ISSUE AT FREEWAY. THERE SOON.

Five customers and another twenty minutes later, a blue pick-up turned in and parked itself in front of the window where Gandy sat, engine still running. Mickey spilled out, falling to the ground, his long, red hair matted and crusted with blood. He tried to pick himself up but laid down again.

Gandy jumped to his feet, keeping an eye on Mickey through the gas station window as he hustled outside. *What the hell…where's the cargo van?* Once outside, he approached with caution, glancing to the pick-up every other step to ensure there wasn't a surprise coming from inside.

"Mickey?"

Mickey rolled over onto his back to talk.

"Yeah. Hey."

"What the *hell* happened?" Gandy asked, doing a visual scan of the bloodied human wreckage at his feet. He sat Mickey up and leaned him against the front tire.

"Had to get a new rig when I hit town. The other one blew up. Check the news."

"Where's the merch?"

Mickey pointed over his shoulder.

Gandy stepped to the back of the pick-up. "I count fifteen."

"Yeah, well, lost one in the fire."

"*Fire?*" Gandy asked, both hands flying open facing the sky. "Boss ain't going to like that."

"They'll make more. It's one box and some bags."

"And one major disaster. The news, you said?"

"The van's unrecognizable. Fireball. Killed a man."

"Fireball? What the hell happened? What *man* are you talking about?" Gandy asked, again waving the hands.

"Bob. Owner of this pick-up."

"We need to get the hell out of here. They're going to be searching for this. Fuck, Mickey. Just...*fuck*."

Gandy picked Mickey up under the armpits and dragged him around the front to the passenger side. Mickey screamed all the way as Gandy then lifted him and roughly threw his mangled body into the passenger seat. Scurrying back around the front of the pick-up and into the driver's seat, he slammed the door and hit the gas.

At the intersection he spun the front wheels onto the former railroad, feeling the tires rumble from crossing over the rails, closing the gate again once through. He passed by the bike trail and looped around behind the building to the warehouse lot and to the same door he had exited out of to reach the bicycle. As Gandy went around the front of the pick-up a text hit.

UNLOAD. THEN KILL HIM

He looked up and around, knowing the watcher was somewhere, then to Mickey inside the pick-up, slumped over, wracked in pain, moving in and out from foggy consciousness to being completely passed out. Gandy hesitated.

CHECK YOUR PALMS

He knew what the words meant, but did it anyway. The 'F' branded into both. The reminder of who he was in the scheme of all things.

He bowed his head and nodded, knowing the watcher had him in view. He unloaded the boxes, stacking them just inside the door as quick as he could while sweat and fear poured out of his body. Then the 'how' on part two of the instructions rattled around his brain. Shooting meant a dead body, which meant a burial, which meant impossible in the winter wonderland. Then it hit him.

He got back in and drove a mile down the lakeshore to a dilapidated junkyard. In his rearview mirror, the watcher followed. Pulling up to the gated entry, Gandy hit the speaker button.

"I can see you from here. Whatcha got?" the voice said.

"This here pick-up," he answered. "It's all yours. I don't need a payment. Just need a place for this to disappear."

"You kidding?"

"No. No bullshit. It's yours. But you have to take what comes with it."

"What you talking about?"

"Comes with a meal for your pit bulls. Bonus."

No answer came for minutes. Gandy saw two people get into a car at the run-down office building fifty yards away. It sped to the gate and skidded to a stop, then they continued the conversation through the cyclone fence.

"No bullshit?" the one guy with a few teeth missing asked.

"None, but make sure your dogs get fed."

The two junkyard guys looked at Mickey passed out in the passenger seat, then to each other.

"Okay," the missing teeth said.

"One more thing," Gandy said as he pushed the key through the fence.

"What?"

"I'd paint this another color as quick as you can and find yourself a different set of plates. I'm sure you got a few of those laying around here somewhere."

Gandy turned and began the arduous mile-long walk back. The watcher drove up alongside and he hopped in, riding in silence the long three minutes it took to return to the warehouse.

"Well done. You've earned a night on the town. Sometime soon," she said.

He got out and disappeared into his studio.

The watcher called in her report and then resumed her position, hoping her replacement would arrive earlier than scheduled so she, too, could get some sleep.

CHAPTER 20

The fireplace in the library of the south wing of the Sandt mansion was ablaze with soft flames and tranquil warmth. The library itself dated back to Volker Sandt's era. An opulent gold and red curtain, the colors of the old Sandt Brewing Company, framed a Palladian window at one end. Rich, brown oak served as the material for the unending bookshelves, the floor, as well as the crown and floor moldings. Three large animal skin rugs from the founder's hunting expeditions to Alaska were placed in strategic locations. The room had two areas for reading, one nearest the window and the other at the fireplace at the opposite end of the room.

It was there that Kendrick and Liesl sat in conversation absorbing the warmth, each working on their second glass of scotch. A grandfather clock in the corner went through its chime sequence followed by the eleven o'clock hour strike. They had been talking for a long time but mostly it was Liesl prodding or rattling on with opinions, sometimes loudly, while Kendrick stayed calm, trying to persuade her to see the bigger picture before the meeting.

"I'm not happy either," Kendrick said. "It wasn't supposed to get this rough."

"*Rough?* There's a dead cabinet secretary and a senator lying in a hospital who's probably going to kick it as well. We're way beyond rough."

"We're way beyond a lot of things. I'm sorry to have gotten you into this."

"Hey, no problem. What's a mere forty million and a life-changing addiction?"

"You'll get back the money. If Czerwinski comes out of his coma, he'll move on the approval."

"And Plan B?"

A long silence hung in the air, a few crackles from the logs were the only sounds. The library's acoustics amplified the awkwardness.

Liesl broke the stillness. "So there is no Plan B. They're going to continue to wait it out?"

"We'll know the answer to that when he gets here."

"We're both in deep shit. What if Dad finds out? What then? The Sandt name and empire come crashing down."

"Your father is completely unaware. Even if it comes out that you invested, we did it to help people overcome and manage an addiction to a horrible drug. If you admit you are a screed addict, like we discussed, we win the PR battle before it even gets going."

"I don't know. Dad can't find out. It's as simple as that."

"He won't."

"You better be right." Liesl took a finishing gulp. "Hey, one other thing. That guy at the gatehouse…what's the deal?"

"Your father hired him for security."

"I'll accept that at face value. I'm sure if I ask a few more questions it'll get hairy."

"Quite."

A gentle knock on the open doorway turned their heads.

The butler said, "Sir, there's a gentleman just arrived at the main gate. He won't provide his name but says he has an appointment with you."

"Yes, I'm expecting him. Please let him through and escort him here."

The butler exited while Liesl rose to get her third glass, giving Kendrick a raised 'here we go' eyebrow. Within minutes, the butler led the man in.

He stood in the doorway like a statue, fingers entwined at the waist of his three-piece charcoal suit, standing a good six-plus-feet with jet black hair groomed straight back and finely trimmed eyebrows against his light brown skin. A pointed nose served as a sort of prow ahead of his gaunt cheeks. The light emanating from the fire pronounced his extruding features but cast dark shadows in his facial crevices and the small gaps in his suit where the fabric wrinkled. The dancing light almost made him animated. Kendrick stood.

"Please sit, both of you," he said with a gesture. He took the remaining open chair by the fireplace, clasping his hands in his lap. "I don't know how you live in a climate such as this."

Liesl said, "We have the good fortune of four seasons. Glass of wine?"

The man shook his head.

"Whiskey, vodka, beer? Anything?"

"No."

Kendrick said, "Well, if you change your mind just say so."

"My mind is never undecided."

"Then, I guess we can just talk," Liesl said. "You two wanted this cozy little chat."

"My apologies for being late. The plane was delayed out of D.C. due to a mechanical issue," the man said.

Kendrick said, "No concern. It would help to know your name, however."

"My name is to stay unknown. Of more vital importance are the next steps."

Kendrick shot a look to Liesl, then sat back to let the two hash it out.

The man continued, "Your dismay at the recent events in Washington is noble but misdirected."

"Two men are dead," Liesl said.

"One."

"Okay, okay, technically one, but do you think Czerwinski is going to survive?"

"We have taken steps to safeguard he will."

Liesl smirked. "Fantastic. But unless you're a medical magician, how do you know? And, assuming for a moment he kicks it, I need to know your Plan B. Not too happy about Newcastle either.

Funding your company wasn't inclusive of murder. And, I got a few other questions on what the hell is going on. You're supposed to be the good guys in this. I need answers."

The man said, "Newcastle was a necessity. Time is of the essence now. More important than all else."

"Why?"

"Yarling told us he was never going to see things our way. He's from Ohio. Cleveland Labs would've been pulled in and most likely would've delayed everything."

"Yarling hasn't exactly been a cheerleader for the cause either. How'd you turn her?" Liesl asked.

The man sat stone silent.

"You people are out of control," Liesl said, raising her voice.

"Medicamento will not share this opportunity and Dr. Yarling is now in our corner."

"So, she's now on screed." More silence. "Are you in business with the other side?"

The man leaned forward. "Hardly. We don't know who the drug lord is or where they're growing them, but we have some of their berries. We intercepted a small shipment several years ago. How else do you think Ovalar came into being? We needed berries to figure out its properties and to find a cure. We're not close to that, but at least we have a manageable solution."

With that he reached into his coat pocket and slid a small tin across the coffee table to Liesl.

The man asked Liesl, "What stage are you at right now?"

Liesl looked at the tin and then over to Kendrick.

Kendrick said, "It's okay. I'm the one who told them you were on screed."

"Why did you do *that*?"

"Because I used to be."

"*What?*"

Kendrick said, "Sorry for not telling you before. I think tonight will be quite illuminating. Me and this gentleman have much to discuss with you."

"Whoa. Back up the tape. *You're* on screed? Since when?"

"*Used to be* on screed," Kendrick corrected. "It was all quite innocent. Two years ago, Cesar Quintero let me stay at his apartment while I was on business for your father in D.C. He was in Guatemala and I was going to be there for a few weeks, so he gave me use of his place. There was a small pack of berries in his refrigerator. Sealed tight. You know how healthy I try to eat, so I broke the seal and ate one. The rest is history. Came to find out that Cesar had been hooked as well just a few months prior during one of his trips back home. The berries were his six month supply."

"I don't even know what to say," Liesl replied.

"Stage?' the man asked again.

"Two. What's the tin?"

The man said, "The answer to all your questions. It's your first supply of Ovalar." Turning to Kendrick, he said, "Mr. Winston, perhaps it's time."

Kendrick rose and refilled his glass, trembling. Instead of returning to his chair, he took a position next to the fireplace and set down his glass on the mantle, crossing his arms and looking Liesl square up, then leaned against the stone edge and began.

"I'll get to any questions you're going to have but allow me to give you the entire picture before you talk. I, of course, have kept everything you're going to hear away from your father's ears. Rest assured he's completely in the dark and will remain so. Never would I compromise the Sandt name. Perhaps that's why I was targeted."

"Targeted?' Liesl asked.

"Prior to that trip I just told you about, I was approached by a representative from Medicamento here in Milwaukee. I was dining alone at Sullivan's, calmly sitting at a corner table and the hour was late. A man simply sat down and introduced himself. No name, just that he was with a pharmaceutical company from Guatemala and he needed to speak with Jürgen Sandt about some political assistance his company needed in Washington. It was an odd moment, but I listened along. It was then that I learned of screed and that it was starting to make inroads in the U.S. He explained what his company knew. The powerful berry and the ravages on its victims, which you can now attest to. The toll it has taken in Guatemala at the highest levels of their society. The fact that the business model was to hook those of wealth and then ransom their life. Pay up, as you did, or ultimately die if you don't. I wasn't going to help him that night. I simply told him to leave a phone number and I'd look into it. Instead of a card, he gave me a cell phone and instructed me to use it solely for communication with him. Of course, I wasn't about to get your father involved, and after a few weeks of back-and-forth, I stopped communicating. And then a month later, I opened Cesar's refrigerator. I've been trying ever since to help them. When you informed me of your addiction about a year later, my efforts redoubled. I convinced you to invest in the company to find the cure for both our sakes. Again, my apologies on not being as forthright as I should've been from the beginning. I was hoping the cure would be swift."

"With all due respect, Kendrick, Medicamento doesn't exactly strike me as a company with empathy as a virtue. You kill people," she added, looking at the man.

The man responded, "We do what is necessary at this time. Thousands will be saved in the end."

Kendrick said, "The result of their work is Ovalar, the drug I told you was coming. The fruit of your investment. I've been taking it for about seven months as a test. And now you're a beneficiary," he added with a nod to the tin.

Liesl opened it and stared at the neatly aligned rows of neon green pills.

The man said, "No more payments to the drug lord. No more berries. Take one a day. You'll receive a tin every three months until we find the cure."

Liesl said, "But again, you're in the murder business."

The visitor said, "We're in the solution business. The company has taken the brunt of this fight full on. We've had eighteen investigative agents killed at the hands of the people behind screed. We're in a secret war and unfortunately there will be collateral damage. This war has arrived in America. We are the only line of defense. If Medicamento were to bring in other pharmaceuticals by sharing our research and Ovalar, your approval system here would have tragic consequences. We are the exclusive and absolute solution and we are unyielding in our position. We just need it fast-tracked."

Liesl asked, "Are you saying the only way this works is you need it approved in Washington to bring it here?"

"Yes."

"Why are you two pulling me in? I don't get it. I didn't need to know any of this," she said, raising her voice.

Kendrick resumed his seat next to her, and said, "The war is moving to a new battlefield."

"What do you mean?"

Kendrick sighed and nodded towards the man.

"Miss Sandt, we believe the other side has very strategically put the pieces in place to deliver screed to the masses. And, we also believe the first strike will be here in Milwaukee."

"Hah. Really? What…are they going to force feed a berry to everyone? What the hell other drugs are you two taking?"

The man placed a small mechanism on the table.

Liesl said, "What am I looking at? What the hell is that?"

The man said, "We discovered this last June showing up in the slums of Guatemala City. They figured out a way to turn screed into aerosol form. We believe they were randomly testing its effectiveness on the poor. Trials with non-voluntary human test subjects. Stories from the streets started popping up about people going crazy and months later dying. The same effects as the berry. We started investigating. Fortunately, we were able to track one of theirs into an alley several months ago; after the bullets stopped flying, he was dead and we had a bag full of these. Fully loaded. Our labs confirmed what I just said."

Liesl held it in her palm and examined it. "Spray away and instantaneous addicts."

"Yes. And this is the one-on-one version of the delivery method. We don't know if they've advanced other means of delivering the aerosol. Something that would victimize many people at one time."

"The new battlefield," Kendrick said.

"Time is not on our side, Miss Sandt," the man said.

"Why? And what's Milwaukee got to do with it?"

"The man killed in the alley had an item of note inside the bag, a folder with a detailed map of your city. I also now know of a few deaths, like what happened in Guatemala, right here in your urban areas. That is how we believe Milwaukee is the U.S. target city. Why here? That, I'm afraid, we don't know. As for the question of time, the feeling is they are moving now with great speed."

"Why hasn't your government gotten involved? Pulled in the DEA here, the FBI, the Border Patrol, ICE?"

"Not possible," the man said.

"Why not?"

"Our president's brother, Omar Del Santos, was kidnapped seven years ago by the very people behind screed. A note was left inside his car that night. I was on the president's security team at that time. I *was*, Miss Sandt. The next morning, the president told me to take twenty agents and begin to hunt for his brother. Offline. Never was it to be public. He loved his brother above all else."

"What did the note say?"

"It was lengthy, and while I can't divulge everything, the short version was, 'He's gone. Do not seek him or he will die. If you ever make this public, he will die. If we discover you are disobeying this directive, we will kill every person you know. He is now a soldier for us.' And as for the directive not to seek him, please understand that President Del Santos could not bear losing him to a drug lord. You see, they are twins, Miss Sandt. And so, the undercover hunt began. Eventually we hired the services of the only pharmaceutical manufacturer in Guatemala to see if they could help us figure out what we were dealing with. Since then, my team has been under their employment."

Liesl said, "Look, I'm not trying to be flippant, but your president could've done a hell of a lot more, couldn't he?"

"I'm here in your library while you suffer torment from eating a single berry a year ago. Is that not answer enough?"

Kendrick said, "Liesl, since this war is clandestine, there's only so much President Del Santos can do. He won't publicly fight, so he can't publicly fund it."

She rose and walked to the other end of the library. Hands in her pockets, she stood staring. Moonlight blanketed the rolling hills outside. The stars were cold this time of year, seemingly more distant to her as well. *They need more money. What would Dad do?* Her father was fast asleep on the first floor of the east wing and she had half a mind to go ask him for advice. *Milwaukee…a battlefield of a drug war that must be stopped. If it becomes public that I'm involved, I don't care what Kendrick says. I'm history, so is Dad, and so is the empire. Disgrace. Scandal. Prison. Mom would've helped. And Bertram…dear brother. He wouldn't have hesitated.* She looked up at the moon and wondered if somehow, some way, he was still alive and looking at it from some place in the world. *His life forever lost in Guatemala. Maybe this is my penance for him.*

"How much?" she said, still gazing outside.

"Another forty million," the man said.

"Thirty. Kendrick will handle the transaction," Liesl snapped back.

The man walked to the doorway. "Miss Sandt?"

She turned, the tin in mid-air having been lobbed.

"Start tomorrow."

She caught it before it would have hit her in the face. The last and only sight of him was his exit through the library doorway.

CHAPTER 21

At 2:40 a.m., in room 1209 of the Georgetown Medical Center, Clay Czerwinski lay in a medically induced coma.

Twelve stories down, a man seeking to pay him a visit stood on the sidewalk outside the hospital's truck delivery bays.

Crouching, he aimed a laser pointer at the surveillance camera until he heard the almost imperceptible click of its disabled optics. Hugging against the inside wall and squat-walking, he eased past the security office, ducking under the bay window, then entered the far truck bay to the load-in dock, and then onto the stairwell.

Twelve flights up, he soundlessly opened the door just enough to sidle into the darkened corridor of the ICU unit. A shadow moved across the muted light emanating from a nurse's station to his left, but whoever it was stayed out of sight. He walked the other way, finding the target, then slipped inside.

Five doors down, Beth Llewelyn was on the final lap of her scheduled round, glancing at her watch before her stop at the patient in the southeast corner room. It had been a relatively quiet night partially due to a low bed count and no one in extreme condition, except for the large man in a coma that she was about to check in on. All she knew was that he was a senator, and the doctors had been adamant that the nursing staff follow a more rigid protocol with him until further notice.

He arrived from ER four nights ago as she was starting her shift. The doctors hadn't been able to stop the convulsing and the man's wild rants. Despite his physical condition he was overpowering, and the ER staff needed three extra aides to strap him to a gurney before wheeling him into one of the treatment rooms where he then suffered a heart attack. The ER team kept him alive, but it took every bit of expertise to do so and ultimately the coma was ordered to prevent further complications. Since then, the doctors still hadn't determined the cause of the man's convulsions when he first arrived. Tests came back empty for all known drug traces. Orders were to check on him in person every half hour.

She stifled a sneeze before quietly pushing open the door to the senator's room. A nightlight in the corner provided enough for her to go about her business. She got on her tip toes to check the bags. Each one seemed functionally proper, but she switched out a low volume one for a new bag. Grabbing the tablet from the credenza, she went around to the side of the bed furthest from the door and scanned the readings from the monitors, noting a very slight but noticeable uptick in his heartrate which she recorded and made a mental note to alert the doctors upon their arrival later that morning. Other than that, his condition seemed unchanged. Satisfied he was all right, she returned the tablet to its place and pivoted back towards the door, then muted a shriek.

"Shhh..."

Beth backed up, hands to her mouth. In front of the door stood a man, index finger to his lips. He was impossible to totally make out in the dimness; all she could discern was his above average height and her image reflecting in his sunglasses. Her calves bumped against the wall. Cornered.

"I'm not here to hurt you," he said in a whisper.

"What...what do you want?"

"I want what you want. A healthy recovery for him," he said, with a nod to the bed.

"Who are you?"

He took a step forward and unbuttoned his coat.

She swallowed, trying to slake her completely dry throat. "I...I don't know what you want."

He reached into his coat pocket and pulled out a small Ziploc bag, extending it to her.

"You want me to take that?"

"Yes, Beth. I want you take it."

"How do you know my name?"

"It's my job to know your name."

Her knees momentarily buckled; her voice unable to scream even she wanted to.

"Wh...why? Why should I take that?" she asked, trembling.

"It will save his life."

He held it out in the palm of his hand. She didn't move.

The man tilted his head, almost in disgust. "Dr. Crouse is going to bring him out of this coma. The senator's heartrate is climbing, as I'm sure you've noted on that little pad of yours, and unless that is stopped, he will die. Keeping him in the coma is too perilous."

"What does that have to do with me? I'm just a floor nurse."

He tossed the bag onto the corner of the bed.

"Dr. Crouse's task will be fulfilled tomorrow." He buttoned the coat and took a step back towards the door. "And now you also have one. Once fully out of the coma, you will find a private moment to give him those and instruct him to ingest one each morning. No variance. If he follows your instruction, he will live. This moment between you and I is to remain completely confidential. If our conversation this evening becomes known, then your son, Ryan, dies. These are the terms. They are non-negotiable." He held stock still for a moment then quietly exited down the corridor.

Beth stayed against the wall for a good two minutes before peeling herself away from her spot. Her shaking legs somehow brought her to the bed. She took the bag, holding it between her thumb and index finger like a piece of crime evidence. Moving into the stab of light from the hallway, the small, tin box reflected. Hands trembling, she popped open the tin.

CHAPTER 22

Jürgen Sandt stood with Viceroy on the private tarmac at the Milwaukee airport, a chilly wind tugging at their pant legs causing a snapping sound with each flap. The *Santa Maria*, the largest of the fleet, parked at attention just behind them.

Inside the jet, Regina sat alone in the last row, subconsciously caressing the small scar on her neck left by the bullet that had almost taken her life. A physical reminder of that day on the Capitol steps in Madison two years prior. She replayed what lay ahead.

The plan was to begin in El Ceibo and then continue into the land of the Chizecs, replicating Gandy's actions. Viceroy had scrubbed details with her based on all the reports of which she meticulously deciphered regarding Bertram's disappearance from Jürgen's files. After long hours and days of mental tennis between the two of them, plus Silk's instincts, Viceroy had landed on this path. She closed her eyes and put on her earphones to block out the buzz in the cabin.

The Bread of Life Church mission team was already settled in for the three-hour flight to Houston for a change of planes. Ox watched from his window seat the two men in private conversation on the tarmac.

"If he's alive, I'll find him. At the very least you'll have the answers to the mystery," Viceroy said, as Jürgen pushed himself away from the embrace.

"I trust you, Roger. Perhaps at this appointed time in your life, it's what you're meant to do. Never forget that. And," Jürgen added, "from time to time I'll have Kendrick check in on Silk, but don't hesitate to call me."

"Silk can be a little aloof sometimes, but tell Kendrick to check on him anyway," Viceroy winked.

Jürgen grinned before shaking his head and pointing a finger in Viceroy's general direction. "Now remember, General Hammaren himself will be meeting up with your group in Houston to transfer everyone to the cargo plane. Oh, for goodness sake, you know this already. My apologies, but it must be my excitement."

"No worries. General Hammaren has been a great help with every step in my planning." *Most of which remains confidential between the two of us.*

"We go way back. He owed me a chip or two and I'm glad he's throwing his considerable weight into this last best chance to find my son. I still don't know why you need a military cargo plane, but he'll have some of his best boys fly everyone from Houston into Guatemala. Oh, and Cesar will be with him and escort you through customs. Ah, again, apologies. That is known to you as well. I know we've gone over the sequence of the trip ad nauseam. Forgive my nattering."

An engine kicked in on the *Santa Maria*.

Viceroy said, "It's alright. We're all set. You hired me to do this. I don't know when I'll see you next, but I'd be shocked if I was on the return flight home a week from today. And thanks again for giving Pastor Oxenhaus the use of the plane. It provided both of us a means to a worthy end."

Viceroy turned away to the plane but felt a small tug.

Sandt said, "One more thing. You asked me a while back if I knew who Cesar's benefactor was who brought him to the States. I finally remembered something this morning. I think seeing the airport's name did the trick, General Mitchell International Airport. Cesar once said a man named Mitch Mitchell paid for his tuition at Princeton. Quirky name, so I don't know why I couldn't remember that and I'm not sure if that would be the same man he's referenced to you, but at least now you have a name."

Jürgen patted Viceroy's shoulder twice, then turned and walked to the limo. Robert helped him climb in and, with a tip of his cap, they drove away, disappearing behind the building.

A small, still moment of solitude enveloped Viceroy before he spun and hustled up the jet way stairs and took his seat.

'Therefore, Go.' I am. Hope you're happy, Viceroy thought as the plane slowly pushed back.

CHAPTER 23

A tinny buzz and background droning pervaded the interior of the U.S. Army cargo plane in flight from Houston to Guatemala. The plane had three sections, each separated by a heavy, drab, military green curtain with weighted bottoms.

Seated in the rear cabin section with Regina, Viceroy clicked off from the internet after reading a few articles on Mitch Mitchell. The information stated he died eight years prior from cardiac arrest. Drugs were suspected, but never confirmed. Mitchell owned a small but successful international shipping company in Port Isabel, Texas, dealing mostly with Central American clients. That fact made the Quintero story seem plausible. Mitchell had willed his business to an undisclosed individual and that's where the trail ended. After ten minutes, he emailed Silk with his final thoughts on the matter and asked him to dig deeper.

Viceroy peered through a small opening in the curtain at General Grady Hammaren, seated in the middle section. The two had connected on five occasions, once in person and on four lengthy conference calls developing the strategy and operational details to execute the plan.

Hammaren's thick forearms and chest stretched his beige, button-down shirt, while his sturdy legs punctuated with over-sized calves did the same to his pants. The only blemish on the man's physique was a paunch which Hammaren chalked up to age and genetics. The cabin lights highlighted his tightly cropped, silver hair contrasted by his black skin and the bald spot atop. He was in quiet discussion with Cesar Quintero. Two paratroopers sat ahead of and across the aisle from Hammaren, ready and awaiting his command. All the church passengers were in the forward cabin, kept out of sight by a set of double curtains.

For the detectives, each minute ticked by like a countdown to a timed explosion. Across and facing them sat Ox, having just taken a seat. The moment for the jump was coming soon. Ox whispered prayers under his breath, as Regina tried to control her nerves by thinking of her extended family back in Milwaukee. Viceroy could think of nothing else except Debbie and the note and the wooden box with the bookmark in his backpack.

Back in Houston, Viceroy and Regina had said their goodbyes to the mission team in the military hangar under the guise that the two of them had hitched a ride on Sandt's plane to attend to some business in Texas, disappearing down a hallway to an unused office. The Bread of Life group transferred from the *Santa Maria* to the cargo plane with Ox playing along, getting everyone boarded before excusing himself to a restroom.

Viceroy and Regina took turns changing into civilian, stylish, ankle-length black fatigues, hiking shoes, and tops—he, a gray polo shirt; she, a very Guatemalan blouse—and each wearing a jacket of non-descript appearance but over-the-top usefulness. Ox entered the office and took the moment for a silent prayer as Viceroy finished lacing up his shoes.

Hammaren pushed the door open. "My apologies for interrupting but the timing is critical."

Viceroy flicked his upper lip as the four quick-stepped it to the cargo plane, out of sight from the church members who were all now settled into the forward cabin. Ox and Hammaren boarded through the normal stairs leading up to the forward compartment, while Viceroy and Regina climbed the open rear cargo ramp and took their seats in the rear cabin. Two waterproof backpacks, full of everything they would need for the unknown venture into the wilds of Guatemala, sat next to their respective seats. He gave Regina a wink as the ramp's hydraulics kicked in, closing the plane tight as it cleared the hangar.

Regina leaned forward to speak, feeling secure knowing they had boarded without the mission team's knowledge and that their conversation would be buffeted by the noise and separation. "I'm scared."

"Of what we'll find in Guatemala?"

"That's the least of my worries. No, no…I'm scared of jumping to my death, but if we manage to live somehow, *then* I'll worry about what we'll find in Guatemala. I'd trade places with Silk right now."

"What's to fear? We're in the hands of the U.S. Army, best in the biz."

"Oh, you know, just the parachute not opening, my paratrooper accidentally unlatching me in mid free fall, landing on something that's going to hurt, like a tree or a fence or perhaps busting my leg on impact with the ground. You know, the usual rational fears of any virgin jumper who happens to have her first experience in a pitch-black nighttime landing to conceal her arrival on foreign soil."

She got that out, then relaxed as best she could and let the noise of the flight fill her ears. Viceroy retraced what they knew of El Ceibo, the scant intel on the mountain villages and the less than scant intel on the Chizecs. Quintero's information about them was confirmed by his research. At that point, Viceroy had switched gears and went online to while away some time with that one final read on Mitchell and his email to Silk.

The swishing noise a while later startled all three of them. Hammaren gathered them together with Cesar Quintero and the two paratroopers entering the rear cabin with him.

Hammaren said, "Okay, just to refresh. My troopers here will get you to the landing spot. You'll be about three miles from El Ceibo. Any closer and it might draw some unwanted attention. Roger, you'll be with Ben," he added, motioning to the male. Both troopers were outfitted with their parachutes and tandem harnesses. "Regina, this is Emily, your bird for the jump. We've got about fifteen minutes." The two paratroopers repositioned themselves against opposite sides of the plane adjacent to the rear cargo ramp door. "Regina, get harnessed. I need a minute with Roger."

Hammaren pulled Viceroy closer to the curtain where Quintero was standing. Ox stood a polite distance away.

"Listen," Hammaren said, "I told you before that you have my complete confidentiality. Jürgen thinks you're landing in Guatemala City and I'm sure he'll find out you didn't get off this plane. Cesar will call him."

Viceroy said, "He will. And as for the rest of the people, they didn't see us board, just like we planned. Having them get on through the main door, and me and Regina through the cargo ramp was perfect. Nice touch on the curtains, too. I had my doubts when you described the plane, but this couldn't have been a more flawless execution."

The general reached out and firmly grasped Viceroy's shoulder.

"You're on the right path. I've bought into your stealth strategy. Someone in the Guatemalan government knows the truth, and I'm guessing a cover-up has always been in play. Apologies to you, Cesar," he added.

"None needed," Quintero said.

"Okay, so before you go, I've got something for you," Hammaren said.

He grabbed a small sack out of an overhead holding compartment and laid it on a seat, pulling out two things that looked to Viceroy like original brick cell phones.

"SAT phones. One for each of you. These are a few significant grades above the kind you'd find at retail level. You'll need it. If you find him, I'm your ticket out of town. These are programmed with two direct dials. One is me, two is Cesar. You and Regina are both three. That's it. All other numbers and combination of numbers won't work. Textbook simplicity. No possibility for error."

"Understood."

Viceroy was quickly run through a review of the procedure: power switch, antenna release, insuring it was on channel one, and instructions to just hold down the correct number he wanted to dial until the unit vibrated, then release. Call would then connect.

Hammaren said, "The battery is new and will give you plenty

of juice for a very long period; plus, it's charged through solar exposure. Water won't hurt it. This red button on the side is a location signal. Once you call me to come and get you, hit it. It's a toggle switch that you just push down with a little effort. It'll tell me exactly where you are."

Viceroy said, "I'll download Regina on this so she knows, just in case I get lost or stop breathing."

"Roger, none of that," Quintero said. "The journey ahead is somewhat already…um…I can't think of the saying. Ah, 'the skids are greased.' Another unique American saying. So, you have concealment, you have Gandy's tracks to begin with, whereas he had none, and you have me. I'm a call away. And I'll stay in the country until you reach the end. I'll also escort the church members around while they're down here and make sure they get back to the airport next week."

"Thank you," Viceroy said.

"And remember our chat on the Chizecs. I'll leave it at that."

"It's time," Hammaren concluded.

Viceroy got into his tandem harness.

"Ready?" Viceroy said to Regina.

"As I'll ever be."

Hammaren picked up the phone and checked their status. The pilot informed him the jump was two minutes away, currently at 10,000 feet and holding, ramp would open in one minute, weather conditions pristine. He also said he'd PA the civilians in the forward cabin not to worry about the noise and maneuvers the plane was going through.

Viceroy and Regina hooked in with their paratroopers and strapped on their helmets. He looked at her, a sheen of sweat on her face. Ox clasped his hands together as he caught Viceroy's eye, then disappeared behind the curtain. A rush of wind barreled into the rear compartment as the ramp opened, blowing Hammaren and Quintero a step back as they held onto side bars against the cabin walls. The thick, military curtain mid-cabin kept the noise and wind contained in the rear. The troopers escorted them both down the ramp. The land was pitch-black below with a small dot of light or two on the landscape. Regina found herself suddenly grateful for the nighttime jump.

"Here we go," said Emily. "In five, four, three, two, one...."

The troopers grabbed their bodies and spun them as they leapt into the nothingness, so they faced the sky. Viceroy felt the adrenaline rush and within seconds saw the plane get smaller and begin its upward climb.

Goodbye to all of you. Until next time. If there is one.

CHAPTER 24

Silk cracked open a beer from his refrigerator and resumed his position on the couch, staring once more at the information displayed on the laptop. The smell of sweet-and-sour chicken wafted from the opened top of the half-full, carry-out box sitting on the coffee table. His big screen TV was on, but muted.

The Mitch Mitchell stories on the web were scant. Basic news articles and a few photos. After a few more scrolls on the touchpad, he shut the whole thing off.

Despite his improved financial position, he had no plans of leaving the apartment, a one-bedroom in a moderately priced high-rise along the lakefront on Milwaukee's near north side. *Why leave?* It sat eight stories up with a panoramic view of Lake Michigan, underground parking, workout room, and a five-minute drive to downtown.

He yawned and arched his back to stretch out the muscles, at the same time interweaving his fingertips and pushing his palms straight up to the full length of his huge arm span, the pajama pants and t-shirt moving with his gesture. It had been a long day.

The morning was spent at the Sandt front gate recreating the exact movements of the mysterious person on the video. He had hoped for some epiphany or physical clue from replicating the actions, but none came. The bulk of the afternoon involved a lunch with his DEA contact to see what the guy knew of screed, which bore no information, followed by internet searches and research phone calls involving the Sandt empire, then studying Theo Gandy's behavioral habits from all the information available.

Of particular interest was the chat earlier in the day that Jürgen had arranged with a former Secret Service agent who had worked with Gandy. The nugget was Gandy's vice. As relayed by the agent, Theo Gandy liked to play the slots. He usually found the means of hitting up a casino when they took official trips since Gandy was always assigned to the advance team for the domestic presidential stops. If there was a casino in town, Gandy would find it. Immediately following the call, Silk made an appointment with the Potawatomi Casino's head of security; the only casino in Milwaukee.

He yawned once more and stood, opening the door to his small balcony to let in some winter air, then hit the floor as a small red laser skipped across his chest. The unmistakable sound of a fired bullet whizzed past his head, ricocheting off the ceiling and into a vanity mirror near his front door, shattering it into a thousand pieces. He scrambled to the coffee table on all fours, grabbed his gun from the couch, then spun towards the kitchen, staying low and away. Once there, he stood and reached around the corner back towards the living room, killing the lights. He flipped the safety off the gun and edged against the outside wall near the refrigerator, then lowered his body and peeked around the kitchen wall to the balcony door six feet away.

The still-powered TV lit up enough of the living room for Silk to spot the bullet ricochet mark in the ceiling. He calculated the angle of the bullet, comprehending it was fired from the small park across the street. It was the only plausible conclusion. His apartment being eight stories up, and with the mark in the ceiling having a straight trail leading in and leading out, the park was the only place it could've been fired from. He got down on his knees once again and crawled to the coffee table, hit the remote to kill the TV, then made it to the door, feeling the rush of cold air pouring in. Through the balcony railings, he spotted a vehicle in the park pulling away and out of sight two seconds later, the left taillight half-lit. *You missed.*

Staying down, he pulled the sliding door shut, crawling to the other side and pulled the drawstring for the curtains, then dog-walked to the couch; a safe place unless the gunman was hovering in mid-air outside. His inner calm immediately began to take over.

With precision, he began a mental checklist of what just happened, quickly moving to the wall where the mirror used to hang. When it shattered, the frame knocked loose and now lay in three pieces on the floor. He set them aside to clear the space, then used a pocketknife to bore out the bullet from the wall. He stared at it, lifting it up to the hallway light to his left.

Nine-millimeter, hollow point.

Dialing the number for Lori Coate, he resumed a seat on the couch.

"Hey Silk," she answered on the third ring.

"Hey."

"This is so weird. I was going to call you tomorrow because I've got some fresh news for you. But you rang me first, so you got the mic. What's up?"

"I just got done dancing with a bullet that broke into my apartment."

"*Holy crap.* Are you okay?"

"Yeah, yeah. It missed but found a home in the wall by my front door after destroying a mirror."

"Wow. Shit, Silk. Who, where, why?"

"Don't know, the park across the street, and don't know."

"You got our boys coming?"

"No."

"Silk, you need—"

"I don't need the police."

"You're sounding like a streetie."

"Listen, I'm involved in something that needs to stay off the radar. I called because I want you to run a ballistics test."

"Off the record?"

"Yeah."

"That's twice in two weeks. You trying to get me fired?"

"Like that's even remotely plausible."

"Okay, so that was dramatic, but geez…you're going to have to tell me what the hell's going on."

"Maybe, but for now I just need a ballistics test. I'll download you when and if I can at the right time. Agreed?"

He heard her sigh. "Agreed."

"Great. I'll drop if off in the morning. What time?"

"Make it the afternoon," she said. "I'm jammed up all morning, so pick me up at one-thirty."

"Pick you up?" Silk asked.

"Yeah, we're going for a ride."

"Why?"

Coate said, "Did you hear about that van that exploded off I-94 down near Kenosha?"

"Yeah. Somebody died, right?"

"Yep. And something else."

"What?"

"One of your damn misters was found at the scene."

CHAPTER 25

Viceroy and Regina had a rush of exhilaration and alarm as the land came into view and seemed to race upward towards them. The paratroopers handled the moment with ease and, once alit, they all quickly unhooked. Noiselessly, two U.S. Army vehicles arrived: one taking the paratroopers away in a southerly direction; the other, an off-road vehicle with two soldiers, armed, asking Viceroy and Regina to get in and then taking off in the opposite direction. Viceroy spied a pair of goggles on the driver, assuming he was equipped with night vision technology as the headlights were off. A partial moon provided some visibility of the Guatemalan plain, but all Viceroy could identify was scrub brush and dirt with an occasional silhouette of a tree. The vehicle made a few maneuvers as they rolled along, avoiding unseen obstacles. The second soldier kept looking through a pair of binoculars and every so often shouting something to the driver.

After twenty minutes they made a decidedly sharp turn, stopping at the edge of a wooded area. Viceroy and Regina were instructed to grab their backpacks before they followed the men into the trees. A third soldier met them and brought the small group to a dried-out creek bed in a ravine where she had prepared a campfire. No names were swapped, despite Viceroy's inquiry. "Best we keep that information confidential," was the reply he got. The female soldier instructed the two to make themselves comfortable.

"We'll be guarding you all night, so just relax," she said. The two male soldiers walked away and out of sight over the edges of the ravine. "There's two MRE's next to the fire. Sunrise is 6:30, so I'll be here again at that time. You'll continue to your destination during daylight hours."

Regina said, "Sorry to be naïve, but…MRE?"

"Meal ready to eat. I can't vouch for the tastiness, but it'll get you through. We've left another thirty there for you as instructed."

"Thanks," Viceroy said. "Much appreciated."

She gave a thumbs-up, then disappeared as well. After wolfing down a MRE marked 'Menu 8,' they settled in.

Regina excused herself, while Viceroy thought about how many campfires might be in their immediate future, then nosed around his backpack to locate some of the items he and Hammaren had agreed to include. First gadget found was rope. *Needed.* Wads of Guatemalan Quetzals. *Supplies, meals, and probably bribes.* A small Glock with ten boxes of ammo. *Asked for eight but ten's better.* A curious-looking, six-inch-long army knife with what looked like a dozen different utility implements ready to spring out when needed. *Perfect.*

Regina returned from behind a large rock.

"I haven't had to do that since I was a Girl Scout."

Their small campfire was dying out. The embers burned fire red with a few licks of flame occasionally erupting, emitting just enough light to keep the ravine aglow. Viceroy used a longer branch to gather the remaining embers into one pile, checking his watch and giving himself another fifteen minutes. *Asleep by one, wake up at six.*

"I didn't know you used to be a Girl Scout," Viceroy said to Regina as he took a seat on the ground.

"Yeah. Mom had all us sisters in it from kindergarten through middle school."

"Is that what started your 'do good' approach to life?"

Regina laughed. "No, I'll give that credit to Mom. What about you? Boy Scouts?"

"Oh, yeah. Reached Eagle Scout when I turned fifteen."

"That's the least shocking thing I've ever heard. And that's a good thing, because if you were relying on me to set up camp if we end up in those mountains in the middle of a jungle, you'd be taking your life into your hands. Just saying."

"Let's hope we don't have to."

"Yeah, well, maybe Gandy's still in El Ceibo living next door to Bertram Sandt."

"Where's the fun in that? This is a mission. I want danger and Chizecs and venomous snakes and a glorious moment of finding him, and then a parade in Milwaukee."

"Really?"

Viceroy smirked and shook his head as he stared at the fire. "No. I just want to find him as quick as possible and sneak out the back door."

"Your percentage still at one hundred that he's alive?"

"Yeah, it is. But after ten years he could be half a world away. But," he said, looking around the campsite, "we're here undetected, at least I hope, and our job is to keep it that way for as long as possible."

"We might stick out like a sore thumb. At least you will."

"Yeah, well, that's why I have my Latina girlfriend with me," he said with a wink.

Regina scooched herself closer to the dying fire. She looked over to Viceroy, his head hung between his legs. A hundred thoughts zoomed through her mind. Mostly, they all led to the obvious. The one thread of fact facing them down. Bertram…vanished. Mission team…vanished. Gandy…

She said, "The hunt begins, on this night, in this ravine."

"Yeah. Hoping Silk's hunt is underway as well."

"He'll find him."

"Yeah, I know. I just wish we were all hunting in the same place."

"Roger?"

"Yeah?"

"If I don't make it out of here and you do, I need you to promise me something."

"Regina—"

"No, please just listen for a moment. I told my sister and my mom I had some business overseas that I needed to attend to, and I wasn't sure when I'd return. I told them I'd be unreachable because of an investigation I'm on. They've lived with me and my career for the past twenty years, so that didn't bother them so much. And my father was always supportive. But that bullet I took in the neck two years ago changed things a bit. I need you to give them this," she said as she pulled out a small leather pouch, sewn up around the edges.

"What's that?"

"I hate being all sentimental and squishy, but I just need to get this to Mom. It was hers, anyway. It's her wedding ring that she had given me when I was seventeen. In honor of her, I carry it with me every day. I'd like her to have it back."

"Why did she give you her wedding ring?"

"I was supposed to get married."

"Wait…what?"

"I called it off before we got to the altar. He was my high school boyfriend, but I caught him with another girl the night before the wedding. I never told my parents. My sister knows but we agreed to keep that a secret. Dad would've killed him. Literally. I just told them instead that I wasn't ready and wanted to do more with my life."

"I'm in shock. Why've you never told me this? I had no idea. You hold onto your privacy so tight I just never feel comfortable asking you any details about your past."

"Yeah, well, it's one of those life moments I'm not real pleased about. Anyway, after that I applied to the police academy and the rest is history. It's just that Mom never gave up hope and she told me to keep the ring. She was confident I'd eventually find another guy."

"That never happened?"

"No. Not even close. My husband is my job, and I'm just fine with that," Regina said.

"One of the reasons you're so good at it. I'm a bit of the same way. At least now."

"I suppose. Losing Debbie was a horrible way to become single again. I'm really sorry you had to go through all that."

Viceroy nodded. She held out the pouch for him to take.

"What if I take it and I don't make it out of here? Or, we both don't?" Viceroy asked.

"Then it stays a Guatemalan treasure."

She held it out again and Viceroy tucked it into a secured pocket in his pants.

"I'm giving this back to you the second we finish the job and we're on our way back home."

"I would hope so. It would be weird if you kept it."

Viceroy grinned.

Regina said, "Hey, as long as we're talking about things we've never talked about, I have a question I've been wanting to ask you. Why did you pick me that day way back when? I know there were a ton of candidates."

"Why are you asking now?"

"Because we're in the middle of Guatemala on a dangerous investigation and if I go missing like all the others, I've always wanted to know."

Viceroy said, "For the record, that day I interviewed you and the ten others from Milwaukee PD for this job, you just stood out. It wasn't even close. I must confess the second interview was just for show. I wanted you without question, but MRSCU wouldn't let me do it without Strongsmith also interviewing. I told them I had the final two and he came up that day to talk to you both."

"Who was the other?"

"No one. I invented the second candidate, resume and all, and told Strongsmith the guy called and cancelled just before he was going to see him."

"Sneaky."

"What can I say? You were my number one, and only one, and I didn't want Chicago making the decision."

"Well, thanks for grabbing me. You know I'm indebted."

"Yeah, I know."

"You screwed up with Silk, though."

Viceroy laughed, the sides of the ravine elevating the volume. "It's all worked out, hasn't it? I can't imagine not having you both with me. I'm the one who's indebted."

"I know I can speak for both of us when I say that we're with you every step. Wherever that road leads."

"Same here."

"Too bad Jerry retired," she said with a yawn. "He was sort of like a trusty dog, and I don't mean that in a disparaging way. He was just someone we all could rely on for pretty much anything."

"Yeah, but I'm glad for him. Look, I think it's time we get some sleep," he said, checking his watch. "We've got five hours."

He set his new military-provided watch for 6AM, then rolled out the travel mat. Regina did the same on the other side of the campfire. The night air and the embers were enough warmth. Within a few minutes he watched Regina's breathing become sleep rhythmic. He laid his head back and looked up at a sea of stars—a mesmerizing sight of an unending palette of brilliance shining down on an unending plain of earth.

Alright God, you started this expedition, so you lead the way. And once we find him and get him home, you and I are finally going to have it out. If that's even possible.

The last small piece of firewood crackled and shot a spark up high, arcing across his vision before flaming out in mid-air.

Okay. At least we have an understanding.

He rolled onto his side and closed his eyes.

CHAPTER 26

At exactly 7:00, the three Army personnel climbed into the vehicle with the female taking the wheel. She put it in gear but kept her foot on the brake.

"I don't know what you're doing here, but whatever it is, be cautious. You're in a bit of a wild west this far out. The Mexican border is on the other side of El Ceibo and there are drug cartels in this region. Once we leave, you're going to follow the tree line that way," she said, pointing west. "When the trees diminish in about a mile, you'll see a road ahead of you. Follow that north for about another mile and a half and it takes you right into El Ceibo. Be smart and watch each other's back."

Viceroy asked, "Have you been there?"

"Once. Passed right through it at a decent rate of speed. Lots of huts, lots of dirt. A few houses and a public square. Mostly one-story buildings if I recall. Hopefully, you two aren't here on vacation."

"No, I wouldn't call it that."

"Well, that's good, because there are better spots in the world, unless you're looking for a few days to explore the sights and sounds of a poor Guatemalan village in the middle of nowhere."

"That's closer to the truth."

"Whatever wets your whistle. Duty calls, so we're hitting the road."

She gave a wave and hit the gas. They both watched the dust trail until it disappeared around a hill. Viceroy felt the two-day stubble on his cheeks and chin, purposefully unshaven to better align with their 'hiking through the country' story, then wrapped a kerchief around his neck.

Viceroy said, "You ready?"

Regina nodded.

"Here we go."

The temperature rose quickly once the sun cleared the horizon, forcing them to adjust their straps and perform other maneuvers as they learned how to walk with an ever-snowballing heavy backpack. The density of trees increased slightly once they found the road—a tight, two-lane, blacktopped ribbon in need of repaving. A beat-up and rusted-out white Volkswagen bus came up behind them with two men inside, slowed to eyeball them, then kept going without saying a word. The passenger looked back for an extra take as the driver hit the gas pedal.

"Friendly," Regina said.

A half hour later they caught the first sight of El Ceibo ahead on the plain. Regina set down her backpack and reached for her thermos, Viceroy did the same.

In the distance, to the northeast, the mountains they had read about from the research notes stood like sentinels guarding the secret forbidden zone of the Chizecs. El Ceibo's main town area was flat with small trees lining what seemed like the only road, the same one they were on. The western edge of town at the Mexico border transitioned to rugged hills. A tiny glint of the border crossing port building shined a short distance west of the village. Mostly visible were simple adobe buildings and corrugated metal huts.

"Ground zero," Regina said.

"Just remember, I'm your American boyfriend and we're on a journey to find your roots."

"Hopefully they'll buy that."

"Hopefully."

"But I'm Puerto Rican."

Viceroy shot her a glance.

"National pride. Stay calm. Today I'm part Guatemalan."

"We'll go with that."

Viceroy downed the last gulp as they neared the southern edge of town and paused to look at what lay ahead, the stark contrast of everything catching his attention.

As described, the town was mostly one-story adobe buildings clustered into the center two hundred yards ahead. Side roads shot off randomly east and west. Packed along the edges were some corrugated huts mixed in with open-air or wooden-sided markets. Movement was everywhere. Motorcycles and scooters blended in with older model cars and pick-ups. Children were plentiful, many of them barefoot, playing in the streets or otherwise involved in selling goods in the markets. Against this backdrop was color. The dust and heat and drabness and mountainous horizon of dull gray clashed with a vibrant palette of clothes and bazaar offerings.

It gave the impression to Viceroy that the town on the surface was trying to look the part, but behind the thin curtain lurked a gritty and deprived existence.

As they neared, some boys pointed at them; a few jumped on rusted bicycles and pedaled into town, while the rest scattered. A group of older women stopped chatting with each other and stared as they passed by

Viceroy said, "Let's just stroll, maybe stop at a shop or two like the good tourists we are. But I want to get the lay of the place, so we'll continue through to the north side."

They window-shopped as they walked. Viceroy snuck a look into a few of the huts, some had dirt floors and multiple beds. It became clear to him that the shoppers were tourists or Mexicans that had crossed the border and wanted cheap goods.

Halfway to the town's center, Regina stopped at a handbag shop. It was small, with bags hanging off nails on wooden posts cemented into metal stands. The heat was elevated with the shop's metal roof. Viceroy stood at the entrance and wiped down his forehead, watching her. She studied a few of the bags as she wandered through, then selected a stone-studded orange wallet and headed to the middle-aged woman sitting next to a card table towards the back, a cash box atop. They conversed for a longer time than they should've, and it ended with the woman pointing north.

"What was that all about?" Viceroy asked as they resumed their journey.

"I figured I'd buy something to get in her good graces and then ask her a question."

"What did you ask?"

"I explained that I like to take pictures of churches and asked if and where the town had one."

"Bertram Sandt's first verified position," Viceroy said.

"I left that part out."

They continued north.

Behind them, a young man followed on a scooter.

CHAPTER 27

Silk and Lori Coate parked in a designated police zone at the scene of the van explosion, a cordoned off area covering the field, freeway ramp, Bob's house, and extending out some amount of buffer yardage from the explosion's epicenter.

A blanket of single digit temperatures invaded Wisconsin with a predicted high of six degrees on a cloudless day. The upside was lighter traffic, the downside obvious.

On the way down from Milwaukee, Coate relayed the victim was an adult male from a neighboring home who had driven to the accident and was in the wrong place at the wrong time when the explosion occurred. The driver of the van wasn't found, and the victim's pick-up was missing. The assumption was the van driver took off with the pick-up. The possibility of others involved was eliminated. Only two sets of footprints in the snow. The van driver sustained a head wound but survived. Male. Determined by position and pooling of the blood in a ditch nearby. The victim's body was found in the cornfield eighty feet from the blast, badly broken, charred, and mostly unrecognizable. No known connection between the two people. No sightings of the pick-up or its license plate yet. The van and whatever its contents were blown into hundreds of pieces. Most small. Burned to the point of providing no meaningful clues. The one mister recovered from the scene had escaped damage by being buried in a foot of snow about fifteen feet from the blast. It was unused. No drug traces found in it. No fingerprints either.

Coate pulled at her thick woolen scarf, tightening it closer to the skin of her face, then tugged hard at the two hood strings on her parka. They had been out of the vehicle for all of thirty seconds and her eyes were already tearing up. Through her scarf, the plume from her exhales were visible.

Wearing nothing but a simple knit cap and earmuffs on his head, Silk yanked at his coat's zipper until it unsnagged and pulled it over his chin.

"This way," Coate said.

They trudged towards the epicenter, high-stepping through the snow now crunchy and squeaky from the frigidness making their steps sound like they were wearing Styrofoam boots. The spot where the van exploded was bare frozen ground. Coate gave him a slight tug to steer him around a spot towards the northeast and then stopped after six paces.

"Here," she said with a muffled voice, pointing with her mitten at the orange utility marking flag. "Here's where they found it."

Silk bent to a squat. He studied the angle of where the van was and the recognizable blast zone, then walked a line from the mister's position to the epicenter and turned back around facing the same way he just walked. Coate stayed put.

"What are you thinking?" she asked after a minute of watching him survey the line.

"Lots. How far was the search perimeter?"

"About two hundred feet. Past that, nothing really showed itself. Why?"

"Wasn't far enough."

Silk took off on a straight line deeper into the cornfield. Coate came alongside, slipping once and grabbing him to steady herself.

"Okay, you got something on your mind," she said.

"Just a tickle."

"What are you expecting to find?"

"Something."

She stopped and looked at him as he kept walking, the crunchy plops of his boots becoming less audible as he neared the edge of a narrow waterway cutting through the cornfield in a north-south direction.

"It's for runoff," Coate said as she neared.

Silk stood at the edge, then turned back, studying the van's path and spotting the flag where the mister was found. He walked north nine paces, then turned directly around and faced southwest where he stood looking for another full minute. His mind ran through angles and calculations.

"This is another Silk finding-something-that-no-one-else-could-find-moment, isn't it?" she asked.

"Maybe."

He bent down to the snow then did a slow swivel with his head in a northeasterly direction from the van's position, along a direct line of the flag to the waterway. His eyes skipped over the frozen trench and alit on an odd bump in the snow across on the same line. *Molecule.*

He rose and stepped back a foot, then easily leapt across. Coate stayed back.

The bump in the snow turned out to be a two-foot drift that had formed out of a field of flatness.

"Tree stump?" Coate called out.

"Drifts don't form without something solid underneath, so I'm about to find out."

With his back to Coate, Silk bent down and began a careful swishing away of the snow with both hands. Soon he rose and turned, holding a frozen translucent bag in his hands. It was undamaged. The liquid inside it frozen solid. He wiped off a final chunk of ice revealing a small, printed logo of a snake head with its mouth agape, holding a black circle.

CHAPTER 28

El Ceibo's plaza was a two-block inset square built of large, red-veined stones and ringed by a brown brick wall, five feet high around the entire perimeter, but for the short ramp at the south end. A small stage baking in the sun set against the north wall, and a rickety cart against the west, selling tamales and Pepsi-Colas in ice cold bottles as advertised by a decades-old metallic sign with rusty edges and paint noticeably missing in several spots. Despite its appearance, business was brisk.

The scooter pulled up to a parked line of similar machines under a row of trees on the south side. The young man coolly got off and leaned it against another scooter.

To Viceroy, he looked to be twenty-something—lanky, with overly broad shoulders, sporting jet black hair running away from his face to the base of his neck, accompanied by a mustache that couldn't quite fill itself in. His jeans were in need of a wash, as was the faded yellow t-shirt drooping off his shoulders making him look like a human hanger as he stood still in the shade.

The detectives watched him from their seat on the steps leading up to the church behind the eastern length of the wall and across the main road overlooking the plaza.

As Regina finished off a tamale, Viceroy drank a Pepsi, keeping a watchful eye on the tail while both tried not to appear so. After two minutes the tail flipped his sunglasses down and resumed his ride to a side street off the southwest corner, disappearing behind a building.

"You still think he's tailing us?" Regina asked.

"Yeah. He pulled up a block behind us when you were in that store and only moved when we did. He drove around the plaza while we bought our lunch."

"Next step?"

"Since the church is locked up, let's follow."

He took his Glock out of his backpack and shoved it in his belt, covering it with his untucked polo. Regina did the same using her blouse.

They followed the perimeter sidewalk towards the south end of the plaza, then cut right to the southwest corner. Regina purposefully squatted to retighten a lace and did a quick scan behind them. Ahead, a dingy-kept narrow street ran straight away. The first buildings on both sides were small open markets. Viceroy surveilled the left one, Regina the right, as they moved.

"Not here," Viceroy said.

"Not there, either."

Proceeding from the buildings on both sides were small, ramshackle adobe homes.

"Could be any of these," Regina said.

"Yeah. But I need a beer."

"Huh?"

Viceroy nodded to a point further down the street where it dead-ended at a commercial enterprise, an open-air entrance with a bar clearly visible inside. A weedy parking area of dirt and gravel served as a front apron to a wooden structure with a metal roof and a sign on a post out front. To the right were a few vehicles, among them the scooter and the Volkswagen bus from the morning.

"Pequeño Pete's?" Viceroy asked. "Am I saying that right?"

"Sort of. It means 'Little Pete's.'"

"Alright. Time to meet Pete," Viceroy said as he moved.

"Either we look way out of place or something else triggered a tail," Regina said.

"My guess is there's a power person running the show here and anything new gets a look. Remember what she said about drug cartel activity. I'm certainly looking American."

"Makes sense."

As they drew closer, Viceroy did a quick analysis with the clearer view.

"Listen, I don't want us to have our backs exposed to any position. See that table in the right corner?"

"Yeah."

"That's us."

The well-worn bar abutted the left wall in a rectangular shape, jutting out towards the middle of the interior. Wooden stools lined the counter, each with torn seat padding and many missing at least one support bar for the stool legs. Neon signs for beer and tequila and other spirits dotted the interior walls, only two with fully lit capabilities. Low-top tables sprouted up from the floor space in no discernible order.

Fifteen people stared them down when they entered. Viceroy counted six men sitting at a low-top table nearest the entrance plus the tail, two more men at the bar, a woman smoking a cigarette sitting solo at the bar with her back towards the sitting area, a couple at another low-top close to the bar, and three women sitting on a bench against the near wall to his left. Piped-in scratchy music served as background noise.

The detectives gave the bartender a nod as they made their way to the table, dropping their backpacks onto chairs, taking seats on the other two. He nodded back as he finished off the head of a beer and slid it down to the solo at the bar, then approached.

"Bienvenido," he said as he tucked a bar rag in his belt. "Qué puedo conseguirte?"

"Dos Equis, dos," Regina said.

The man spun back to the bar.

"Hope you like Dos Equis," she said.

"I do now."

Viceroy took in the surroundings, keeping an eye on the table of six. When the bartender delivered the beers, Viceroy heard the scrape of a chair along the wooden floor and looked over to see the tail get up. The eldest of the group, a bald man wearing a white wife beater and dusty boots, made a gesture then flicked his cigarette at the tail sending an ashy spark right at him. The tail jumped out of the way provoking a burst of laughter from the others before he walked straight to Viceroy and sat down.

"They want to know who you are." he said in perfect English.

"Nice to meet you," Viceroy said. "Roger," he added, extending his hand. "This is Regina."

The young man defiantly crossed his arms. There was a long hush as Viceroy drew back his hand and studied him.

"You're not from here, are you?" Viceroy asked.

Silence.

"Why were you following us?"

Silence.

Viceroy pulled out the Glock, wiping down the handle with the small napkin supporting his beer bottle, then put the gun back in his belt. He sensed the movement at the other table go still.

"Me and my girlfriend here are just passing through. She's got ancestors from Guatemala and we're on a trek through the country. Today was El Ceibo, tomorrow we're heading east."

The tail said, "Those men over there think you're narcs from the US."

"Why did you follow us?" Viceroy asked again.

Silence once more.

Viceroy reached for his backpack and pulled out an envelope, taking a swig of the beer as he opened it up, then tossed a photo of Bertram Sandt and Theo Gandy on the table. The photos stared at the young man as he uncrossed his arms and sat up, blinking quickly as he glanced over to the other table and then back to Viceroy.

Viceroy said, "You know, you're right. We're narcs. These two men are wanted for drug trafficking. We think they're operating some of the time out of El Ceibo. Do you know them?"

"No," he answered.

"Let me rephrase. Have you seen them?"

"Look, you need to leave. And you too," he said, turning to Regina.

Regina said, "We just got here and I'm enjoying my beer."

"No, I mean it. You need to leave."

"Why?" Viceroy asked.

"Because that table over there is ready to pump about twenty bullets into you."

Viceroy looked around at the floor and walls.

"I don't think so," he said. "Seems to me this is a well-run establishment. Looks like Pete doesn't stand for that sort of thing. I'd like to meet him."

The man shook his head. "Not now."

"Why not?"

"Because I said so. Just leave."

Regina said, "You know the men in these photos, don't you?"

He looked around, glancing to the bar, then over to the men.

"Maybe," he said in a hushed tone, turning back to them. "Tonight, on the plaza. Band starts at eight. Be there."

He got to his feet and made a hurried exit to his scooter. Viceroy looked over to the table. The bald man blew a puff of cigarette smoke into the air, threw back a shot, then leaned forward and stared them both down. Viceroy took a gulp of his beer, keeping eye contact the whole time, told Regina to exit, then walked over.

"I don't know if any of you speak English, but if you send another follower while we're here, you wish you hadn't."

He yelled out to the bartender gesturing for a round of drinks for the table and threw a bill down.

"Cheers," Viceroy said, finishing off his beer before tossing it to the bald man whose instincts kicked in to catch it, but fumbled, spilling backwash on his shirt as the bottle hit the floor and shattered.

The man let fly a cuss-filled rant, quickly trying to wipe a large spot of backwash off his chest. When he looked back up the two detectives were gone, along with the cigarette smoker from the bar.

CHAPTER 29

Viceroy threaded his way through the overflow crowd on the plaza as a mariachi band whipped up a frenzied but festive atmosphere from the stage. The weak spotlights provided the only illumination, making faces hard to discern. He walked a north-south pattern making U-turns as he made his way through the horde. Regina positioned herself at the closed tamale cart, guarding their backpacks while keeping a roving eye for the young man and the meet-up. Viceroy made a swing past her and they locked eyes. He gestured he was going to make another pass through. She motioned to her watch. It was now 8:40.

As he made the first turn, a hand firmly grabbed his elbow and steered him left. Reflexively, he yanked his arm away from the grip and turned for a confrontation. Above the noise, the young man from the bar pointed and shouted for him to follow. Viceroy glanced to Regina. She was gone.

He pulled his gun, following the bobbing head towards the east exit. When they reached the top step, he steered Viceroy and picked up the pace, heading across the street towards the church. Viceroy kept up, swiveling his head as he moved. The crowd was no less thin, but more mobile, making it harder to proceed. Once at the church they bounded up the stairs to the portico.

"She's safe," the young man shouted. "Stay here."

He took off on a run back across the street and towards the stage-end of the plaza along the wall. Viceroy battled the urge to follow but lost sight of him. Two minutes later, he returned with Regina and another woman.

As they approached, Regina flashed a thumbs-up sign. Viceroy turned his focus on the woman.

She was shorter than Regina with a tie-dyed head scarf that continued over her ears. Stringy, blonde hair spilled out in unkempt locks to her shoulders. Viceroy took note of the sheen of sweat on her face and the irregular gait in which she walked, drawing attention to the multi-colored maxi skirt hanging loosely from her skeletal body. When they reached him, the man again grabbed his arm and they proceeded to a small, unlit porch behind the church. The noise level was noticeably muted.

"Who are you two?" Viceroy asked.

The young man looked at the woman as if waiting for a signal or something from her in which to form an appropriate response. With labored breathing, she turned to Viceroy to answer him.

"We're soldiers," she said.

Viceroy said, "You're not Guatemalans; in fact, I'd argue American."

"Tell us who you are first," the woman said.

Viceroy looked at Regina, their silent connection communicating 'go for it.'

"We're here to find Bertram Sandt," Regina said.

"And, I'm pretty sure one or both of you know something," Viceroy added.

The young man looked around, his eyes widening as he swallowed harder. The woman spun to the church doors, unlocking them and pushing through as they followed. She quickly closed and relocked it, steadying herself against the hard wood. They stood inside a small vestibule with plaster walls. A short hallway extended straightaway to the back end of the sanctuary.

"Lights off, not safe," she said and moved down the hall.

The two detectives again locked in. Viceroy took his backpack from Regina and motioned to pull her gun. He mouthed 'trap' and raised his eyebrows in a questioning nod. They followed, with

Regina mostly walking backwards.

From the records, they both knew this was the church that Bertram Sandt's mission team had stayed at a decade prior. Two vertical stained-glass windows near the altar filtered a decent enough glow from the plaza to provide enough light to see. Nearest the left one, the two took a seat in the front pew while the detectives grabbed chairs from a stack against the wall.

"Okay," Viceroy began, "who are you and what do you know?"

Regina studied them, looking for facial clues to measure the temerity of whatever was going to come out of their mouths. As the woman began to speak, it hit her.

"Oh God," Regina interrupted. "You're Amy Peterson."

"*What?*" Viceroy asked.

"She was part of the mission team. You were on that mission, weren't you? You're from Milwaukee. I recognize you from the photos."

"I am and I was," Peterson said, adding, "And so's he."

"Joaquín," he said, extending his hand. Regina shook it.

Once he said it, Regina recognized him. Ten years older, but the cut of the jaw and the ears slightly turned out were the same from the photos.

"I'm Regina and this is Roger," she said to Peterson.

The stunning moment of their manhunt launch point inside a church was not lost on Viceroy.

You must be kidding me.

Regina said, "I...I don't know where to begin. What happened and how'd you get here? Where's the rest of the team? Do you know where Bertram Sandt is?"

Peterson stared them both down before clearing her throat.

"It's a long story but you don't have much time. Those men are hunting for you. Sooner or later they'll find you."

"We're ready," Viceroy said.

Peterson grinned. "Not for what's coming. They're not going to kill you."

"What does *that* mean?" Regina asked.

"It means you'd become part of his army."

"His?"

141

"Yes, just like everyone else in this town."

Viceroy said, "I think you're trying to help us, but you have to explain quickly if we don't have much time."

Joaquín cleared his throat, nodding his head back and forth, his eyes still worried.

"Screw him," Peterson said to Joaquín, who looked down and placed his hands under his thighs. "Everything you see is a show. We were placed here two years ago to run that bar. I renamed it Little Pete's. I serve as the proprietor, Joaquín as a scout for outsiders coming through town. You two were noticed, more so than usual. El Ceibo is the outpost of his empire."

Viceroy said, "You keep referencing a person. Who? And what do you mean by placed?"

"I don't know his name. He's just known."

The sweat beaded up on her brow. She pulled out a cloth, tamping it down on her forehead and behind her neck.

"Are you okay?" Regina asked.

"I'm heading to stage four. You have no idea what you're facing here. The drug. He's got the in and the out now."

Viceroy said, "Stage four? I don't understand. *What* drug? What does in and out mean?"

"Amy," Joaquín said.

"I know, just shut up," she snapped, then turned back to the detectives. "You both need to leave before it's too late. Get out while you can."

"Explain," Viceroy said.

"You want to find Bertram Sandt? If he's alive he'd be up there still. Look for a circle."

A heavy and rapid pounding from the back porch door reverberated into the sanctuary. Male voices screamed. The four jumped to their feet as Viceroy and Regina saddled their backpacks and drew their guns.

"Too late," Peterson said.

The thud of bodies slamming against the door came next, followed by more shouts.

"Follow me," she said.

They hurried to the altar and through an arch to its right. The crack of splintering wood down the hall pierced the moment, followed by a pause and gun shots. Through the arch they went to a set of stairs leading to the basement. The last thing Viceroy heard was the unmistakable sound of the door being breached and footsteps running towards the sanctuary. At the bottom of the stairs they passed through a metal door into darkness. Joaquín closed it behind them, sliding a deadbolt in place.

"That way," Peterson said in loud whisper. "Follow him."

Joaquín moved down a tight passage, flashlight suddenly in hand.

Peterson said, "I'm staying. Move. Follow Joaquín. He'll take you out of here and guide you to the center of the empire. But beware of the mist."

"Beware of *what*?" Viceroy asked.

The metal door rattled by someone trying to open it.

"Now," she said, in as loud of a whisper as she could muster.

The two detectives followed the glow of Joaquín's flashlight. After twenty feet the passageway cut right, then took them up a short ramp to a metal door above their heads.

"We just went through a saferoom," Joaquín explained. He punched in a code on a pad at the base of the ramp and the door above clicked. They moved up the ramp, Joaquín flipping the door open onto the ground. They soon all stood in a flowery courtyard on the property behind the church. He led them out of the area and past the plaza. In the festive partying they went unnoticed and soon were walking down a side street to a pick-up truck. They flung their backpacks in and headed north, keeping the headlights off.

Inside the church, Peterson sat in the front pew facing the group of men with her head down and arms resting in her lap.

"Well done," the bald leader said, extending his hand.

She took the berry and wolfed it down.

CHAPTER 30

Viceroy sat on a fallen tree at the edge of the rain forest with the SAT phone in his hands. He had just clicked off with Hammaren to inform him they were clear from El Ceibo after yesterday's close call. Viceroy wanted him to know they were at the trailhead and had a guide. In the course of the conversation, Hammaren also told Viceroy the church team had made it to their destination and Quintero said all was well. Viceroy thought of Ox and the mission and had a flash of something stir inside.

Not so fast. I'm not going there, he thought, looking up to the sky.

He observed Regina and Joaquín working together in the final stages of affixing their three hammocks to bamboo trees and covering them with mozzie netting, feeling bad about not helping but needing time to think about the recent events. Specifically, their escape the previous night and the ride to the base of the mountains, the few hours of sleep they grabbed in the bed of the pick-up, and the day's journey to this point after leaving the vehicle behind. The three empty villages they hiked through today and how eerie they were. Ghost towns. Joaquín said they were the same ones Bertram Sandt and the mission team had visited. Now they sat devoid of humanity and at the mercy of nature.

As they neared the rainforest, Joaquín paused and made them douse themselves in insect repellent and put on the leech socks that the Army had provided them in their backpacks. He gave them both a tube branded 'Shoe Goo' and instructed them to coat the soles and outsides of their shoes.

Throughout the day, both he and Regina had pummeled him with questions, but he refused to provide answers. *Keep asking. Something's strange. The feel of it all. There's a 'here' here. Something…* Viceroy's inner monologue kept prodding.

He put away the phone and joined them to hang the rope ridgeline and the rain fly over each hammock as the sun disappeared behind the tall canopy of the trees.

CHAPTER 31

The morning following Viceroy's call to Hammaren, Clay Czerwinski looked at his unkemptness in his home's bathroom mirror.

He pushed his scant hair around with his palms, ultimately deciding he could care less and instead threw on a sand-colored bathrobe and matching slippers. Slowly making his way to the stairs, he gripped the railing for steadiness and shuffled to the kitchen once he hit the first floor. A cup of water in one hand, he moved to the study just off the foyer and plopped down at his desk, adjusting his glasses and pulling out the tin from the upper desk drawer.

It was the sixth day since his return from the hospital. The doctors told him another four weeks of rest lay ahead but allowed him to recuperate in the comforts of his plush condo under the watchful eye of a visiting nurse. She arrived each day at noon and stayed through early evening.

The sun's angle had reached a point where it sent a shaft of warmth into the study when the phone rang. He pulled himself away from staring at the remaining seven green pills in the tin to answer.

"Hello?" Czerwinski said, his voice still weak.

"Clay," the voice said with enthusiasm. "It's Kendrick."

"Yeah, I know. An invention called Caller ID hit the market a long time ago."

"God, it's great to hear your voice."

"I'd say the same, but that would be a lie and my doctor told me to relax."

Kendrick laughed. "Welcome back."

"It's really good to hear from you."

"Jürgen and I came about a week ago, right before it started to look like you were improving. That was a hard visit seeing you lay there. We thought you were dying."

"Didn't know that. Thanks for the visit. But half the Senate wishes I did keel, and the other half wishes I'd stay away permanently."

"That won't happen."

"Oh, hell no."

"I understand you've got a nurse checking in on you?"

"Yeah. She's got curves in all the right places, so I look forward to that doorbell ringing every day. But if they wanted my heart to recover on a steady pace, they should've lined up a male nurse."

"Keep the focus, Clay. The Senate needs you back. When you're feeling up to it, I hope we can continue the discussion on our little project."

The two kept the conversation rolling until the doorbell rang. Kendrick finished with an indication that he'd like to visit towards the end of the week; Czerwinski quickly acknowledged his desire for that to happen and clicked off.

On his way out of the study, he glanced at the clock. *Too early for Nurse Curvy.*

He opened the door to an empty portico, except for an envelope with his name typed out in large font, black letters laying at the doorstep. Returning to his study, he took a seat in the corner chair to read where the sunlight was brightest.

DEAR SENATOR CZERWINSKI,

BY NOW YOU'RE HOME WITH SEVEN GREEN PILLS LEFT. YOUR NEXT SUPPLY IS WAITING. WE REQUEST ONCE AND FOR ALL YOUR CONSENT TO MOVE FORWARD THE APPROVAL OF OVALAR. QUITE LITERALLY, YOUR LIFE DEPENDS ON IT. YOU'VE BEEN TAKING THE DRUG NOW FOR THREE

WEEKS. SURPRISED?

WELCOME TO THE CLUB. AND WE AT MEDICAMENTO WISH YOU A SWIFT AND COMPLETE RECOVERY AND AN ENJOYABLE RETIREMENT IN THE NEAR FUTURE. WE ALSO KNOW YOU CAN ACCOMPLISH OUR REQUEST FROM THE COMFORTS OF YOUR HOME.

IN THE EVENT THE APPROVAL IS WITHHELD, START THINKING ABOUT WHAT YOU'LL DO EIGHT DAYS FROM NOW.

IF YOU PULL IN THE FBI AND GIVE THEM THIS LETTER, MIGHT WE SUGGEST YOU START WITH DIRECTOR DIXON. HE'S A HAPPY CUSTOMER OF OURS.

WITH KINDEST REGARDS,
YOUR FRIENDS AT MEDICAMENTO

He read the letter four more times. Courses of action careened around in his brain for the next twenty minutes before uncapping a large point black marker from the desk drawer. In large letters, he signed his name to his response, then placed it back in the envelope and resealed it with tape, scribbling MEDICAMENTO – YOUR EYES ONLY on the front, and placing it back on the portico.

An hour later when the nurse showed up and rang the doorbell, the envelope was gone.

CHAPTER 32

Silk sat across the desk of the Potawatomi Casino's head of security watching the man pin Theo Gandy's photo along the left side of the bulletin board above the rear credenza. It took some salesmanship from Silk to convince him to accommodate the request; it was only after he told him his employer was Jürgen Sandt that he received the commitment from the man to do so.

Silk was escorted out by an official looking employee to the security lobby to retrieve his phone, then to the floor and out the main entrance into the night.

"We'll watch for him, especially around the slots areas," the woman said. "If we spot him, we'll call you."

He headed for the parking structure across the street, hitting the elevator button. It had been eight days without a word from Cass. Impatient, he used the stairs and climbed the four floors to his Jeep, putting the heat on high, and dialed his number.

"Trev," Cass answered.

"Where you been?"

"Yeah, been meanin' to call. My son's friend finally coughed up the intel. She saw your man at Eddie's place. That bar. What the hell's he call it? That bar at that damn barn he calls a bowlin' alley."

"Brew City Bowling?"

"Yeah, that's it."

"Son of a bitch."

"She says—"

Silk clicked off, hit reverse, and squealed down the four ramps to the street. Exiting, he weaved through two blocks of cars, ran a red light, then another, and hit the freeway. Six exits later he ramped on 38th Street and took it straight up five blocks, pulling in, then holstered his gun and entered.

Friday night bowling leagues were in full swing. A thunderous mix of hip-hop music, crashing pins, and loud conversations. Bowlers and on-lookers everywhere.

He surveyed the scene, with a few looks shot back at him and his 6'5" frame. Taking three steps at a time, he reached the landing to the bar. The upstairs was as jammed as the first floor, with standing room only and a floor full of people at tables. Across the way, three bartenders were hustling drinks but no sign of Eddie. The bar area was lit only by a large beer sign overhanging the bar and tea lights on the tables. Silk spotted a twosome in the corner packing up to leave so he weaved his way through the crowd as quick as he could and grabbed it.

Now he watched. Intently. Everything. And everyone.

Fifteen minutes in, the office door opened against the furthest wall, behind the bar. A muscular Black woman exited. He guessed thirty years old; late thirties, max. She blended into the crowd, but he lost sight of her when she made her way around the other side of the bar.

A few minutes later the door opened again. Eddie backed out holding the door for a Black man with pockmarked cheeks and a Van Dyke beard. *Theo Gandy. Theo freaking Gandy.*

The two finished their conversation at the door before parting ways. Eddie back inside, Gandy into the bar. Silk sat forward with the balls of his feet pressed against the ground ready to move. Gandy meandered through the crowd without much purpose, edging or ducking his way towards the stairs. Silk rose and trailed.

At the landing, the crowd thinned and Gandy picked up his pace, bouncing down the stairs. Silk remained behind just enough to stay unnoticed. At the bottom of the stairs the crowd thickened again. Silk's pace accelerated when he thought he lost him for a split second, but Gandy reappeared on the other side of two large men having a chat near the front door. When Silk resumed line of sight, Gandy was buttoning up his black leather coat at the door before he pushed through to the parking lot. Silk moved, at one point not so gently displacing a young man's position in his path, and exited as well. Behind, the muscular woman followed, stopping at the front door and watching Silk through the glass.

The night was chillier than usual with the complete lack of cloud cover letting whatever leftover warmth from the day escape. Stillness always ruled in the winter cold, human movement conspicuously interrupting it only for the actual moments of activity before the setting froze once again.

He readily spotted Gandy walking down the aisle to the near left, stopping four cars in underneath a light pole, the same aisle as his Jeep. *Can't move now*. Gandy had his back turned away from the front door. Silk moved two steps down, pretending to be on his cell phone as he faced the same direction as Gandy. A minute later, a red Malibu came out from behind the building and stopped, letting Gandy get in, the passenger door making a cracking sound both opening and closing. As they pulled away, Silk sprang, run-walking to his Jeep, catching sight of the half-lit taillight as it crawled to the parking lot exit. Now he ran, not caring if they spotted him in their rearview mirror. He started the engine as the Malibu entered 38th Street heading back towards the freeway. Silk hit the gas, almost striking a car speedily turning in then having to wait for one to pass on the road. He floored it, having lost line of sight over the crest in the road, but spotted it again entering the ramp going back towards downtown. He sped up, taking the same ramp, and positioned himself six car lengths back.

The traffic increased as they neared the downtown area and Silk had to weave every so often to keep the Malibu in view, easier to track with its half taillight. At the waterfront, the Malibu exited into the warehouse district. Silk followed but slowed to take a right at the stop sign at the base of the ramp. Two blocks ahead the Malibu took a left, disappearing behind a poorly lit drab building.

Silk first decided to take a hard left to try and parallel the Malibu so he wouldn't be noticed, but switched his mind halfway through the turn and veered back to the same intersection two blocks down and began his left to follow, unaware of a trailing hybrid with headlights off. The driver of the hybrid hit the gas when Silk turned. The T-bone impact cratered Silk's driver's side rear door, sending the Jeep airborne about ten feet where it clipped a snowbank and side-crashed into a building, spinning it around and back into the street. The SUV lost control and hit the same wall head on, barely missing the Jeep as it rebounded. There it sat with steam pouring out of the demolished hood, the back end across the sidewalk, its entire front end resembling an accordion.

The Jeep, now totaled, came to a sudden stop angled against the curb on the other side of the street. The airbag deflated letting Silk open the door, unbuckle, and slide out. He looked down to his bleeding right knee. It had slammed against the console when the Jeep hit the building and ripped open his pants, imparting a quarter inch deep gash across his thigh above the kneecap. Blood soaked his pant leg immediately as the wound poured forth more, running down his shinbone to the ankle. He glanced at the hybrid, now half the size it used to be, and the muscular woman he had seen at the bowling alley in the wrecked driver's seat, her head covered in blood and slumped over.

The squealing sound of tires snapped his attention to his left. Careening down the street at him was the Malibu. Silk hit the ground, scuttling to safety beneath his Jeep. When it passed, he scrambled back to his feet as quick as possible, wincing as he stood, and fired four shots at the speeding Malibu now a block away. The last bullet must've landed as he watched the car ramrod a stop sign and smash into a parked semi.

Silk took off, gun at the ready, his right leg not allowing for full strides as he had to hop gingerly on it each time it pumped. The passenger side opened. Gandy got out and fled down another street to the next intersection. Silk took the corner a little slower in pursuit, glancing at the driver who was either unconscious or dead.

Ahead, Gandy looked back, but in doing so caught some black ice, flying his feet out from under him, landing him on his back and cracking his head against the pavement. The concussion enveloped him immediately. The edges of every solid object—the cars, the curb, the buildings, his own hands—got blurry. A wave of nausea washed over him. He couldn't move, could barely turn his head. A tall man appeared, standing over him, flashing a gun.

"Theo Gandy?" Silk asked.

Gandy just looked at him, trying to focus on Silk's face, finding it hard to do even that.

"Are you Theo Gandy?" Silk asked again.

"Eddie?"

"I work for Jürgen Sandt. Are you Theo Gandy?"

Gandy held up both hands as if to surrender. In doing so, Silk saw the letter 'F' branded into his palms.

The edges of Gandy's eyesight grew dark and started creeping towards the center of his view. Images stayed blurry, sounds muted by a new constant ring growing in his ears.

"Ruby, help me," Gandy said.

"My name's Trevor Moreland. I've been searching for you."

"April. He's coming."

"Who's coming?"

"First," Gandy said in a barely audible whisper.

Silk bent down to hear him better. "What does all that mean?"

"Mickey's dead," Gandy replied, snapping his head to attention on Silk, as if suddenly lucid.

"Mickey who?"

"They'll get it to me."

"Who will? Get what?"

"Trapper's Alley."

"What's Trapper's Alley?" Silk asked.

Gandy turned his head to one side and vomited.

"Screed," Gandy said.

"What about it? What about screed?"

"You know you can see the stars better from the second floor."

Gandy opened his mouth to speak again when the sound of a bullet cracked the air and embedded into his head. Silk wheeled around and saw a silhouetted figure in a full-length leather coat standing in the middle of the street, gun pointing directly at him.

"Hey, hey, I'm a cop," Silk said as he repositioned his pistol and pointed it back at the gunslinger, taking a few limping steps forward, but stopping when the figure didn't move.

Silk said, "Look, this isn't going to end well. Put down your gun."

Silk motioned to do so with his hands while he held onto the pistol. In that moment, the figure fired again, hitting Silk's collar bone area above his heart. The power of the shot at such close-range jarred Silk backwards, crumbling him to the street and losing the grip on his gun as it hit the pavement and bounced away. Silk heard the footsteps approaching.

"*Estar en paz,*" a voice said as it neared. *Be at peace.*

Silk lay, trying to get in a defensive position while blood emptied from his shoulder. He saw his gun, but too far away for a lunge to get it. *The end.*

Before the figure could pull the trigger a rain of bullets erupted from a speeding car headed right at them, ricocheting off the buildings. The figure took off, leaping over a guard rail and out of sight as the car screeched to a halt next to Silk.

As the blood loss ushered in a blackout, Silk turned his neck just enough to get a look. A silver Mercedes.

CHAPTER 33

Dawn broke over Port Isabel, Texas. Calm, warm, and with nothing unusual in its arrival. Except for a certain man wearing cowboy boots in a place he wouldn't normally be.

The Lisp sat alone in a pew at Our Lady of the Sea Catholic Church, a half mile from the warehouse. The phone call the previous evening told him to be there at 7:30 AM and which pew to sit in. He arrived at 6:30, just as a priest opened the doors to the sanctuary. He and an elderly woman entered. She disappeared into a confessional and left a half hour later. He stayed, awaiting the arrival of The Ghost.

The only moment he set eyeballs on the myth was two years prior. The Ghost had arrived one afternoon to the warehouse with a cadre of security for a spot inspection of the operation. One fool, a low-level forklift operator on the cusp of stage four in desperate need of a berry, attempted to bull rush the group as it toured the warehouse. Shot on the spot. The body was put in a crate and dumped in the Gulf of Mexico. In return, The Ghost withheld the berry ration for everyone an extra week. The suffering was ubiquitous. One employee died from the effects of the drug withdrawal in a broom closet where he doused himself with bleach and tried to light his clothes before guzzling the remaining half gallon. Two others committed suicide in their homes—one by gun, and one by jumping four stories from his apartment. When the berries were finally provided a week later, The Lisp vowed to find a means to strike back. One of the casualties was his little brother.

He checked his watch for the fourth time in fifteen minutes. The bouncing of his foot made a slight rapping sound where the heel of his boot contacted the wood floor. The empty room amplified it, but he didn't care. A bible and a hymnal sat in a rack affixed to the back of the pew in front of him, calling out his name to grab one of them and open it. He cautiously reached to the bible, then pulled his hand back and checked his watch again: 7:43.

A different priest came out from behind the altar carrying something, giving him a nod as he continued down the aisle and out the heavy wood main door in the rear of the sanctuary. Eyes ahead, The Lisp heard the creaking sound of it open, followed by a delayed hard slam when it closed. Two sets of feet audibly came closer, walking up the same center aisle. His foot stopped bouncing.

From his periphery, he saw The Ghost stop at his row while the second person took a seat directly behind him.

"Wonderful old church," The Ghost said, moving now to the row ahead and seating himself just in front but slightly to the left.

The Lisp took in his presence. The untucked floral print button-down and neatly pressed brown slacks deceptively concealed the magnitude of the man underneath. When he seated himself, he made sure the crease of his pants stayed aligned and pulled his shirt under him to minimize the wrinkling.

The Ghost said, "A perfect place to meet. The bounty on my head is a king's ransom. Stand please."

The Lisp stood for a pat-down from the guy behind, then reseated.

The Ghost said, "Some things have changed. We've had a series of unfortunate events happen in Milwaukee. Mickey's gone missing."

"Yes, I heard that. Maybe he'll turn up."

"Doubtful. But more troubling is Theo Gandy has died, along with two of my lieutenants."

"That I didn't know."

"It just happened night before last. I've got another ten up there, but Gandy was an integral component."

"I only met him one time. Sorry to hear he's dead."

"You're going to be his replacement. You know the plans as best as anyone and I can't trust others with the technical needs now that we're on the horizon of the operation. You leave late this afternoon and will assume the task. The final shipments will be arriving in two weeks for assembly and preparation."

"Yes, sir."

"The long, glorious plan is all coming together now. It's going to be spectacular. Your role is critical to its success and, rest assured, your reward will be high."

"Understood. Anxious to get there."

"Good. I didn't want this to be off-putting for you. A car will pick you up at three and take you to the airport. Upon arrival, you'll be escorted to our building where you'll live and finish the job. We'll be watching the entire time, protecting the building and insuring you are on task. I suggest you pack for a long stay, at least through the launch date, if not a week or so after."

"Yes, sir."

The Ghost finally turned all the way to him and gave him a friendly pat on his cheek, smiling as he did, then quietly left with his guard the way they came in.

When the wood door slammed shut, The Lisp let his body ease. It took a good few minutes to breathe normally. Feeling ready, he exited to his motorcycle and headed to the warehouse. There, he spun the combo lock to the numbers on the wall safe, the soft click cutting through the silence. With the safe door open, he paused to stare at the flash drive Mrs. Lobe had given him, sitting there like a sniper just waiting for the right opportunity to fire. He grabbed it, secured the office, and sped off on his bike to his apartment to pack.

CHAPTER 34

Three days had passed since the car chase and crash. Silk was released the previous evening and now sat in his office at Emilina with his left arm in a sling and a heavily bandaged shoulder, in pain and fending off the doctor's orders. Cass had entered ten minutes earlier with a cup of coffee and taken a seat, propping his legs up on the half wall.

"How fast were you going when you rushed me to the hospital?" Silk asked, keeping his eyes affixed on the reports opened on his screen.

"Shit man, I dunno. Ninety at least," Cass said.

"Well, again, thanks."

"You were critical, bleedin' all over my car and shit. Gettin' it reupholstered now."

"I owe you."

"Nah. Consider my debt from high school finally repaid."

Silk turned back to him.

Cass took a sip and continued. "It's been weighin' on me for twenty years."

"We're okay, man. We're okay."

"What the hell is it with me and you?" Cass asked. "Bullets and guns. That ain't a good mix."

"No, it's not. The bullet nicked my collarbone but tore open an artery. Doc told me an inch lower and I would've died on the spot."

"That's some messed up crap. Who *was* that dude?"

"I'm working on it."

"Your other man die?"

"Looks like it."

"Eddie too."

"Yeah. Eddie Browner. Never would've thought," Silk said, almost inwardly.

Cass gulped down the remaining half cup.

"Well, listen man. I'll leave ya to your biz. Just wanted to say hi after you called yesterday. Fancy place you're in here."

They hugged at the door and Silk watched him disappear before checking his watch. *Twenty minutes.* He reseated and read through the reports from Milwaukee PD.

The DNA test confirmed that Theo Gandy was indeed *that* Theo Gandy. The two others, Eddie Browner and Ruby Porfoy, the driver of the SUV that rammed Silk, also died. One of Silk's bullets struck Browner in the head behind his right ear when Silk fired at the Malibu. Browner held on for a few hours in a coma but eventually passed. Porfoy's fate was instantaneous and was revealed she had been sought for two other murders in Madison. The leather-clad stranger remained just that. Ballistic tests were underway on both the unfired bullets from Browner's gun and the stranger's bullets.

A knock on the door pulled him away from the screen. Silk favored his right leg trying hard to put the least pressure on it as he walked over and opened it up to the smiling face of Jürgen Sandt. With him was Kendrick Winston.

"You know, you really should be in a bed with your leg elevated," Jürgen said as they entered.

"Mr. Sandt, I appreciate the concern but I'm alright," Silk replied.

Each man took a seat in Silk's office space.

"Again, *Jürgen* please. You know, you detectives amaze me, and I've seen a lot in my lifetime."

"We just do what we do. Doc tells me I'll be just fine."

"Well, follow his order or you'll end up like me," Jürgen said, raising his cane up.

Kendrick said, "So, you wanted us to stop by?"

"Yeah. With the death of Theo Gandy, I'm at a moment where the trail gets harder. He was the target but was also supposed to be the resource for information on what happened down there in Guatemala and what he knew of Bertram."

Jürgen said, "Him hanging the satchel tells me he was communicating."

"I've watched that video at least a hundred times. I was skeptical at first. Truly didn't think it was Gandy, but now, well, I'm flipped, so no argument," Silk said. "But there's an element of the unknown. Plus, he clearly was connected to someone or some organization and I'm pretty sure his being in Milwaukee wasn't random. He *was* sending a message and wanted you to know, I'm assuming for the purpose of you finding someone to find him. That night he hung it on your gate was a call for help. And, I'm guessing it means the odds have increased that your son's alive, at least while Gandy was down there."

"That sounds reasonable. What can we add?" Kendrick asked.

"This is going to sound weird, but do either of you ever recall seeing him with any sort of branding on his skin?"

"Branding?" Jürgen asked.

"You know, like cattle get branded."

"Never," Jürgen said.

"Me either," Kendrick added.

"He was branded?" Jürgen asked.

"Both of his palms were branded with the letter 'F.'"

Jürgen said, "Mmm. That's disturbing."

Silk said, "He may have received the brands in Guatemala. He also said some things to me right before he was shot. Clearly, he had just been concussed so whatever he was saying would be suspect. But I can't connect them together, so let me throw a few words at you and see if something clicks from what he said."

"Fire away," Jürgen said.

"Alright. First one. Mickey. Do either of you know anyone by that name, either a first or last?"

"No," Jürgen replied.

"Kendrick?" Silk asked.

Kendrick said, "Nothing I can add. That name makes no sense to me or anything I would've interacted with him on."

Silk said, "How about Trapper's Alley?"

Jürgen said, "Not a thing. Not an iota of relevance. Perhaps it was code for something?"

Kendrick added, "Or a street somewhere?"

"I've thought of those angles, but right now I can't figure it out. He said some strange things in that minute or so, with Trapper's Alley being the weirdest. If something, anything, *any* idea on what that might mean comes to mind, call me. Even if you think it's not relevant or sounds irrational."

Jürgen got up and walked over to a trash can to blow his nose and drop in the tissue.

"We will. I'm guessing we weren't too helpful to you."

"Yes and no," Silk said. "Having no answers is somewhat helpful in an odd way."

The men chatted for a few more minutes, then left the gatehouse.

Silk sat in silence, replaying the chase in his mind one more time. The cars, Eddie, Brew City Bowling, Ruby, Gandy and his words, and mostly the mystery figure who shot him. *Porfoy knew I was at the bar. She also knew I was tracking Gandy. Cameras. Had to be. How did she know? Eddie. He was involved in something with Gandy. I stumbled into it when I visited him the first time.* He moved a bit and the stitches near his knee sent him a reminder. *Cass. Thank God he put two and two together. Can't believe he was the one I almost hit when I exited Eddie's place. Street smart. Followed. Who was the gunman? Someone in the upper ranks of whatever the hell we're dealing with.*

The phone rang. Lori Coate.

"Hi," she said. "You should still be resting, you know."

"Yeah, well."

"I'll cut to the chase. Oops, sorry, bad choice of words. I'll lay it out for you. Ballistics confirms the bullet from your would-be killer and the one that killed Gandy were both fired from the same gun. Whoever it was, was also your assassin that night from the park, and a damn good sharpshooter I might add. I had an assistant scour the park but she couldn't find a casing, so my guess is he or she picked it up before they drove away. You can do the math, but it was obviously the Malibu when it happened because of the taillight. As for Browner, Porfoy and Gandy, the autopsy report is back from the ME. They all had that mystery shit in their bloodstreams. Their hearts are all damaged as well, but like nothing they've ever seen before. Gandy's heart was the worst. And the frozen liquid from the cornfield is the same substance we found in that original mister. I also had someone try and determine what the hell the snake head on the bag was, is, or implies. No dice. We're clueless on that one. I've got a gal pal in the FBI and I sent it to her as well. I emailed you a pdf of the image in case you need it. Fleckenstein wants to get the PD involved. Police Chief chest-pounding. I strongly suggested he not do that at this time. He wasn't happy I said that. My reply included Jürgen Sandt's name and yours. He backed down, for now. So, that's the report. You're all caught up. How are you?"

"Your compassion is overwhelming me."

"I'll weep at your funeral someday. Until then, buck up."

"Just promise me you'll be in the front row."

"That would imply I care enough to be in the front row, but okay."

Silk laughed, emitting a stab of pain down his arm. "Ahhh."

"Collarbones suck. I broke one in elementary school and my whole summer was shot. Take some meds."

"I will."

"The good stuff; those large red ones I gave you. I'd identify them with their proper name, but I know that'd confuse you."

"Stop already. I can't laugh anymore."

"Okay. Back to business. You've got the latest intel. Seriously, I'm a call away. Anything you need at any time."

"Thanks."

He clicked off and reached for the bottle of large red pills, swallowing one down without a drink. Using both hands he lifted his leg onto a second chair and made a slight adjustment to his sling, trying to get into a position without feeling pain. The Gandy comments echoed. *Figure it out. Code?*

April. He's coming. First. Mickey's dead. They'll get it to me. Trapper's Alley. Screed. Gandy's final uttering resonated most in his mind. *The only real meaty sentence the man spoke.* '*You know you can see the stars better from the second floor.*'

Minutes ticked by. *Something's gotta click.*

He grabbed the computer keyboard and typed in TRAPPER'S ALLEY. The search engine served up two pages of information from the Detroit Historical Society about an indoor shopping center by that name operating in downtown Detroit during the 80's. The rest were one-off articles of a mixtape by an artist he never heard of. He looked up the lyrics to the songs on the track, but nothing screamed 'clue.'

I can't get my brain around any of it. Snake head mask. Snake head on the bag of screed? Screed. All three of them were on it. Somehow, it's all connected. First? Trapper's Alley? Where were they headed that night? What was their destination? Something's coming. Something big. When? Where? Who? And most important...What? He paused, grimacing. *Knee pain. Shoulder throbbing.*

He walked over to the couch in Regina's space and laid down, hoping the meds would ease the pain enough for him to recover his focus.

At the mansion, Kendrick watched Robert pull away, taking Jürgen to a meeting off property. He went inside and walked down the long, main hallway to his private well-appointed suite off the north end, a benefit from Jürgen since the day he was hired. He passed by the bedroom and strolled over to his desk, then drew up enough courage to place a call.

"You should've killed him," Kendrick said when the call connected.

A powerfully timed stretch of silence passed before the response came.

"Never let your position become so comfortable that you assume you have some power. Your motives are noble, but silence should always be your path. Soon, a major and essential move will be made. And while I still need you for the final maneuver, do not test the grace from which you are a beneficiary. And grace, Mr. Winston, is the free and unmerited favor of one to another. Remember this conversation and be careful. A graceless spirit I do not abide, and mercy is not my strongest trait."

Kendrick heard the click.

He bowed his head and put both hands to his face, unleashing a slow shake that started in his gut, followed by silent sobbing until he was spent.

CHAPTER 35

A woman seated in a Lexus reached across her shoulder, grasped the seat belt and buckled in, then backed out of her Hillandale at Georgetown row house to the street, heading to D.C. The early morning host blaring on the car speaker informed her it was going to be a nice mid-March day. Her million-dollar home sat almost at the top of a hill. A gentle incline took her down past Whitehaven Park to Reservoir Road, and out to the security gate.

Watching from behind a tree, a different woman resumed her trek up the hill after the vehicle's headlights cleared the bend in the road. Her strides crisp and purposeful but muted by black tennis shoes. She wore black monochrome.

At the top she found the address, a two-story brick row house cut into the hill.

It looked like all the others, with a street-level one car garage to the right, and to the left a small cement path and stairway leading from the short driveway to the inset front door and foyer. A set of first floor windows sat above the garage with a matching set directly above for the second floor. The architecture was plain, but stately.

She surveilled the possible attack points, opting to utilize the neighbor's house as scaffolding. A railing framed that walkway which she used to climb on top of the front door overhang. From there, her nimble physique provided the means to spider crawl up the corner where the front door overhang met the garage wall, getting toeholds on the mortar between the bricks and using her thighs and biceps to shimmy up. She reached the roof of the garage with ease and quietly walked across it to the further edge where it abutted the wall of the living quarters to the targeted house, a second story cut up window in reach.

She stretched her left leg over, getting a balance point with it on the small ledge and looked at the old-style window lock behind the lowest middle pane, then adjusted her right leg for a sturdier anchor. Using a u-shaped magnet, she pushed a button and the soft hum and emanating warmness within the metal quickly evinced. Once at full power a tight laser beam stabbed out of both ends. Skillfully, she focused the light beams on the small handle through the window pane, twisting and turning the magnet, maneuvering the movement of the magnetized lock to the open position. Within seconds she was standing in a small, unused bedroom.

The luxurious carpet provided soundproof movement as she made her way down the hallway to the master bedroom and straight in to the end of the bed. Taking a decorative pillow from the bench, she walked around to the headboard and looked down at a sleeping old man.

She watched his labored breathing, the chest rising and falling with a corresponding wheezing sound at each exhale. After a minute she sat. The man stirred and woke, going from groggy to alarm within seconds.

"What the—?"

The pillow came crashing down on him, leaving only his eyes visible as the intruder smiled. The old man flailed but to no avail.

"Senator, shh. Calm down," the woman said as she held the pillow over his mouth. Czerwinski strained to move. He formed a weak fist, all that his frailty allowed.

She continued in an elevated tone, "Your note you had delivered to Medicamento was received and read. I'm the reply. And I quote, 'Tell the honorable Senator Czerwinski that we have run out of time. Ovalar will move forward. Your influence is no longer needed. Stage four is awfully difficult, so to spare you the extreme discomfort of that horror, please accept our gift of euthanasia.'"

The intruder pressed down harder and watched as Clay Czerwinski suffocated.

She returned the pillow to its rightful place on the bench, then calmly walked to the first floor and exited out the front door.

CHAPTER 36

Silk grabbed the car keys off his kitchen counter and headed to the rental in the parking garage. The combination of cabin fever and injury restrictions were simply too much to take any longer.

Putting on his best outfit, letting the left coat sleeve hang unused, he arrived at Duke's Jazz Club around midnight. He called on his way down and found a bar stool close to the stage reserved for him when he arrived. A perfect perch for someone who just wanted to sip vodka on the rocks and enjoy a masterful few hours of jazz improvisation.

At the end of one particularly long set, the band took a break and Silk turned to the bartender for a refill as fill-in music piped in.

"Staying with Grey Goose?"

Silk nodded as the bartender gave him a fresh glass and started pouring.

"Good to see you," the bartender said. "It's been a while."

"Just busy and nursing this broken collarbone."

"I won't ask."

"That's good, 'cause I wasn't going to tell."

He finished off the pour and dropped in an olive. "You cops are the best."

Silk raised his glass in a nod to the bartender then turned back towards the stage. A screen had dropped down listing upcoming

THE COUNSEL OF THE CUNNING

events. He casually eyed the future performers hoping one particular band was on the schedule. When he reached the listing second from the bottom, he froze in mid-drink, carefully setting the glass back down on the bar.

MAY 10 – HEAVENS THROUGH THE ROOFTOP

In a swooping series of maneuvers, he found his money clip, threw fifty dollars on the bar and bolted out the door. Hitting the street, he flew down to the warehouse district.

CHAPTER 37

"Why we doin' this so late?" Cass asked.

"Because I need to. It's what I do," Silk said.

"Couldn't do this like three hours earlier?"

"Couldn't. Don't ask why."

Cass was driving the Mercedes while Silk kept his eyes peeled as they slowly rolled through the warehouse district. When the epiphany hit him at Duke's the previous night, he drove to the spot where Gandy had been killed and laid down in the same position to see if Gandy's line of sight somehow influenced the 'you can see the stars better from the second floor' comment. All that was visible from that angle was a decrepit billboard's scaffolding, with graffiti spray-painted around all the edges. *Maybe Gandy meant 'rooftop' when he said 'second floor.'* Silk resumed a drive around the area but eventually exhaustion won out. The next night he asked Cass to drive him as a favor, now underway.

Silk said, "If Gandy was speaking coherently, I'm guessing there's a building somewhere in this district with skylights. That's why we're doing this at midnight."

"Beer man going to pay me for this?" Cass asked.

Silk looked at him.

"Just kiddin'."

Cass took a turn, heading west away from the lakefront.

"What's the latest on screed?" Cass asked.

"Milwaukee PD's aware of it now. I asked a good friend to help me figure it out. It's a drug they haven't seen before."

"You got the *cops* involved?"

"Had to. I had to pull in a friend. She knows it's undercover so she's keeping it under wraps, but she's the best. Trust me."

"If you say so," Cass said.

"Any more hits on the streets?"

"Haven't heard any. They sorta' dried up lately."

"I hope it stays that way."

"That makes two of us."

Cass turned left, headed south. Silk had mapped out a continuous growing square from their starting point in the center of the district. The ward was old, with many buildings in neglect, making it easier to spot the ones that looked like they were yet operational. A few had chain-link fences guarding their perimeter. Whenever they drove past one that looked like it was still in use, they slowed to a crawl as Silk scanned the exterior. Any building with two stories earned extra scrutiny.

Silk said, "I got to ask you something."

"Shoot."

"Does the name Trapper's Alley mean anything to you?"

Cass hit the brakes hard, jarring the car to a stop.

"What the hell?" Silk said, putting a palm on his collarbone.

"Sorry."

"What was that for?"

Cass put it in park.

"Look, Trev, that name's not somethin' too well known. Why'd you ask that?"

"I'm trying to find out what it means. Gandy said it right before he was shot."

"Damn."

"Apparently it means something to you. What? What or where is Trapper's Alley?"

"Creepy fuckin' place," Cass said, mostly mumbling to himself.

"You know it?"

"Yeah. Look man, what I'm about to tell ya is part ghost story,

171

part reality, and most likely a whole shitload mountain of danger."

"What are you talking about?"

"Ghost story first. When the pioneers got here, there was a certain trail they all used for doin' business with the first fort back in the 1700's. Most of 'em were trappers, fur tradin' and all that. The trail supposedly sat between two long mounds down in this area where we're now sittin'. And when I say mounds, I mean like a block long or more. Anyway, what they didn't know was those mounds were ancient burial grounds for the local Indians. Story goes, the Indians had stopped usin' those for buryin' their dead decades before, but it was still some sorta' sacred ground shit. When they found out the trappers were traipsin' right through it, they arranged for a meetin' with twenty or so of 'em one day on that exact trail. Ambushed 'em and slaughtered 'em, leavin' 'em for dead right on the spot. That trail 'came known as Trapper's Alley."

"Okay, you're blowing my mind here. How the hell do you know all that? And why didn't that come up when I searched it on the internet?"

"Trev, there's lots of shit I could care less about, but history's my thing. Just is. That story is ancient, like long ago legend stuff, not fact. And from what I come to understand, the founders wanted it erased from history, 'fraid it would scare off settlers. Now it's just a wild-ass ghost story, prob'ly not showin' up on any damn internet search. It became somethin' parents in the hood would tell their kids to jolt 'em straight. 'I'm goin' to take you to Trapper's Alley and leave ya', my grandad would say. Surprised your parents didn't use it on you."

"Wow. My parents never spoke a word about it. What happened to that area, if it existed?"

"No one really knows. My grandad took me down here one time and showed me where he believed it was."

"Where's that?"

"Reality part," Cass said, turning to the lakefront.

At the southeast corner of the district, near an old shipping dock, he made a southward turn onto a dead-end street. To their left was Lake Michigan. The previous night's rain had melted off the vestiges of snow except in a few spots, exposing the large rocks and broken cement slabs serving as a retaining wall against the water. To the right was a wasteland full of scrubby trees and rolling mounds of nothingness. The cold air from the lake moving over warmer land produced a misty fog that clung to the area, now highlighted in the headlights.

When they reached the end, Cass parked. Without the headlights the view cleared. Ahead in the gloom stood a ten-foot high fence with razor ribbon atop. A short distance inside the fence sat an old industrial complex of three buildings, outlined against the dark sky. The security fence ran forty yards left to the shoreline, and then off to the right, creating a perimeter that encircled the compound. Thirty-foot tall unlit security lights were stationed every two hundred feet.

The two men both got out for a better view.

Silk approached the fence and stuck his face up against it to view the buildings without having to look through the metal weave. Two identical small buildings stood near the shore, both caved in and crumbled with beams sticking out. Any remaining windows were devoid of glass. The larger building off to the right looked solid.

Cass said, "I don't 'member this fence, but this was the spot. Those buildins' were here when grandad showed me this place and Trapper's Alley was supposedly just off the right edge of that bigger buildin' towards the far fence line. You see it?"

"Yeah, at least the general area."

"There was a long mound over there when I saw it, so I'm guessin' there was some truth to the whole thing. I can't tell from here but it's prob'ly still over there."

Cass looked over to Silk, his eyes affixed on something else.

"Hey Trev, over that way," he said pointing to a spot.

"Yeah. There's a reason you don't remember this fence. It's not that old."

"But the place looks dead, man."

"Except for that one little light off the far corner of that building," Silk said, pointing a finger at a spot further away.

Cass peered. "I don't see it. You got hawk eyes."

"You can see the top furthest corner of the big building, right? It's outlined against the sky. See it?"

"Um…yeah…. Oh yeah, I see that."

"Okay. Follow that straight down to the ground."

In the foggy gloom a small, dim glint of light appeared every so often.

"Oh shit. Look at that. There's a fuckin' light bulb on."

Silk walked towards the shoreline, seeing that the fence extended into the water a good ten yards or so, then did the exact same thing to the right. The snowy mud mix combined with the mounded terrain without proper lighting made it difficult. With an unusable left arm, Silk stopped, knowing one slip was a potential disaster.

"Can't do that in the dark," he said, returning to the road. "And from the looks of it, that fence goes around the whole place. There's an entrance somewhere. Let's go hunting."

He moved to the Mercedes and hopped in; Cass followed, but didn't start the engine.

"What's up? What are you doing?" Silk asked.

"This is where the whole shitload mountain of danger comes into play."

"You're not telling me something."

"I'm tryin' to protect your ass. And mine, too."

"What do you know?"

"I know you shouldn't be nosin' around here, is all. There's somethin' goin' on in Trapper's Alley, from what I'm told."

"Like what?"

"Look man, word spreads on the street. Sometimes it's bullshit, but damn near most times it ain't. Usually when word starts movin' through the hoods, it's truth."

"What truth are you trying not to tell me?"

"You know that van that got blew up a while back, down near the state line?"

"Yeah."

"And that guy's pick-up truck disappeared?"

"Yeah, I'm aware of the story."

"Well, Trapper's Alley's been whispered as involved. I didn't care since it didn't affect my enterprises, but when you said it so matter o' factly, I just had to slam on the brakes. The boys on the street are takin' it seriously. Somethin's brewin' here. Word is its big time, and it's 'parently somethin' pretty bad."

"You got any clue who owns this place?"

"No."

"Okay. Do you know of any other entrances?"

"This dead-end road was the only place I knew. Swear on grandad's grave. We parked and walked from here when I was a kid. But I'm guessin' you wanta' find the entrance."

"Yeah. Starting tomorrow."

Cass started the car but kept it in park.

"I'm not a runner, Trev. But this one's above my pay grade, ya know what I mean? I think I'm already too deep in. I got a biz to run, ya know?"

"Understood. Thanks for the help tonight."

"Yeah. Just stay cool. Don't go dyin' on me. But…call if you need me if you're in a spot."

He put it in drive and headed back the way they came.

Stationed inside a long-unused boathouse, a watcher observed them pass by then put down his night binoculars and called in the report. After the Mercedes cleared the area, the tall security lights flickered on…but stayed dim.

CHAPTER 38

Regina swatted an oversized bug off her arm and resumed her trek, quickening her pace to catch up with the other two.

Every day for the previous ten, they picked their way northeast through the rainforest. It became a ritual. Taking turns blazing a trail with Joaquin's machete, eating MRE's, purifying water to drink, the search for dry tinder for the nightly campfires, hammocks, and constant guarding against insects and lethal wildlife. The 'Shoe Goo' had kept their feet dry and comfortable, about the only body part that could make that claim. Joaquín had kept them tracking with first-rate compass utilization and his general intuition of where to go. The rain was almost daily and, at times, so intense they couldn't see three feet past their faces. Those moments were followed by sun and heat and oppressive humidity. In general, they were following a river, but Joaquín hadn't wanted to hug it too closely.

"The Chizecs are known to use it," was his response when queried by Viceroy.

The first day he informed them they'd entered Chizec territory and their route was a careful hike through it to their destination—a vast complex of ancient ruins—the heart of the empire. Also divulged was Bertram Sandt's foray a decade prior, taking the church team into the jungle in search of Chizecs only to be captured by them and brought to a horrid place, turning them over to the man that runs the empire. The detectives further digging had produced the opposite effect: Joaquín had become just a stoic guide.

After breaking camp on this day, Joaquín stated they were getting closer to a specific destination he was seeking. A brief, light shower had ended and soon after came the soft sound of a roaring waterfall. Joaquín cut a trail slightly north towards it while picking pathways of least resistance.

"Why are we going towards the river?" Viceroy asked, pushing aside a thick vine from his face.

"Because it's the only way to get to the ruins. We have to navigate the rocky descent next to the falls, but once we reach the bottom, we'll be able to walk the shoreline."

"*That'll* be easier," Viceroy said.

"Except for the crocodiles and alligators."

"Comforting news. What about being in the open?"

"Can't be helped," Joaquín countered.

The sun was ablaze as they crested a small rise in the jungle floor, the glow more visible through the thinning trees ahead. On the other side of the crest, the land ran steeply downhill to where the river cut through. The waterway was hidden, running slightly below the lush hillside, but they spotted it well off to their right much lower on the horizon. The sound of the flowing water had grown with each step.

Joaquín led them along the tree line for a little while longer, often looking to the river below before suddenly stopping.

"Here. Just trust me," he said as he launched himself into a slide down the incline.

"Are you *kidding*?" Regina shouted in complaint.

"Let's go," Viceroy said.

Regina followed what Joaquín did, pulling the straps on her backpack tight and taking a sitting position as if on a sled, pushing herself forward with her heels and hands until the wet ground and incline took control. She sped down the hill with ease as she leaned back. Viceroy trailed.

"Sorry about that, but it's the only way to get here," Joaquín said.

They had slid into a large swale of bushy ferns that served as a cushion. Each wiped off the wet muck from the slide as they peered over the edge to the river, now only six feet below. Its swiftness and power like an out-of-control freight train. The spray from the waterfall ahead dominated the horizon and soon they stood at the top of a rock ledge witnessing the breathtaking view that lay before them. Directly below their feet, the river transformed from a channeled surge of rage into a bright sheen of cascading waterfall infused with misty breakpoints where it intersected with rock face that jutted out from the cliffside on its race to the splash pool below. Regina snapped a few photos to add to her growing gallery as they sat on the ledge to take it all in.

The deafening noise blocked out the arrival of a Chizec behind them.

Looking up, Joaquín said, "Let's get moving. It's going to take some time to descend."

Before they could turn, the Chizec grunted and clanged his spear handle on the rock. The three scrambled to their feet to see him pointing it at them as if ready to lunge. Viceroy's first look was to the backpacks carrying their guns resting against a rock behind the man.

Of shorter height, he just stood there in a black cloth around his pelvic area with intricately carved wooden leggings, arm guards, and a small chest protector painted in vivid colors of indigo and rusty brown, leaving his paunchy stomach unguarded. The bridge of his nose and cheeks were covered in red streaks. Atop his head were animal bones of some species strung together with bamboo shoots to form a type of helmet that extended to the tops of his ears.

Missing half his right ear, Viceroy noticed.

A plume of long, green feathers was attached to the chest protector extending off each shoulder, giving him a birdman appearance. He held his spear straight at them, a simple wooden handle with a visibly sharpened arrowhead attached.

Viceroy asked Joaquín, "What's he want? What are we supposed to do?"

The Chizec grunted again and pointed his spear at Regina, then said something unintelligible.

Regina said, "What's that mean? Do you know their language?"

Joaquín said, "Just a few words. I don't know what he's saying."

Addressing the man, he said "Urcala."

"What's that?" Viceroy whispered.

"It's a greeting word. At least I think it is."
The Chizec replied.

Joaquín said, "That word I've heard before. I think we're okay. Regina, just bow and sit down. It's a custom of theirs."

"Are you insane? I'm not—"

Viceroy said, "Reg, just do it. Let's defuse this."

She rolled her eyes and did as asked. The Chizec seemed less tense, pulling his spear back a bit. As she sat, she quietly took a photo with her phone of the man, full length, as he stood against the rock and jungle backdrop.

"Let's try and approach," Viceroy said to Joaquín. The Chizec watched intently, then shouted something else unintelligible.

"That pissed him off," Regina said.

"Maybe," Viceroy said. "Joaquín, I'm going to take a step forward in a nice friendly way, and I'd like you to do it with me. Two is better than one. And if he freaks and lunges, I'm hitting the ground and rolling to our backpacks, so I can shoot him."

"You can't do that," Joaquín said.

"Watch me."

Viceroy slowly took a step forward. The man grunted but didn't move, keeping an eye on Viceroy. In slow motion, Joaquín followed with a step of his own.

In almost a whisper Viceroy said to Joaquín, "Move to your right; I'm going to edge left."

As they began the flanking maneuver, the Chizec erupted in a rage-filled discourse, then swung his spear at Viceroy who dove to the ground and rolled. Regina was quicker, springing to the rock and grabbing both backpacks. The Chizec pivoted, pushing Joaquín into a shallow pool near the river's edge, and let out a guttural run-on sentence. Answering calls came from beyond the rock.

Joaquín slipped but righted himself as his feet found their footing in the pool bed.

"Jump. The waterfall. You have to jump," Joaquín shouted.

Viceroy and Regina took one step towards the edge but paused.

"Now. They're coming!"

They looked at each other and, in a second, formed a silent understanding and ran. Viceroy grabbed her hand as they launched themselves on a dead run over the ledge.

Simultaneously two other Chizecs came into view from above. The skinnier one threw his spear, piercing Joaquín in the abdomen. He staggered backwards and went under.

The two charging Chizecs stopped at the ledge to see Viceroy and Regina's entry and waited until their heads reappeared in the splash pool far below as the swift current took them downstream. Further on, they saw the two pull themselves to shore and run.

"Mission accomplished," the skinny one said. "He'll be pleased." Turning to Joaquín, he said, "And he wants *him* dead."

He walked to the pool as Joaquín was attempting to drag himself to shore, the spear still embedded in his left side. Wading in, he pushed Joaquín underwater and held him there with his foot until the thrashing stopped, then grabbed the spear and pulled it out.

The two that had rushed the scene headed back the way they came. Mrs. Lobe walked to the fall's edge, taking off the bone and bamboo helmet, and watched the two detectives until they were swallowed up by the jungle before making his way back as well. During his walk, he rubbed his wrist and hoped for the best, knowing she had taken a photo.

CHAPTER 39

Pastor Oxenhaus and the mission team were a crew of sweat as they labored constructing an open-air church in a destitute sector on the outskirts of Guatemala City. The existing church was nothing more than a set of wooden poles holding up a worn canvas serving as a roof. The pews were rotted benches; the floor was dirt.

All in, everyone contributed, with some help from the existing congregation. It was a bountiful day in Ox's eyes, both physically and spiritually. The grimy "Bread of Life" orange t-shirts moving about brought him a smile.

Quintero spent most of his time on his cell phone. He had helped early on with introductions and relayed information to the mission team. The pastor of the church knew enough English to get his points across, but Quintero's easy interpretations made for a smooth launch of the day's project. Once underway, he hung around but was otherwise busy with his own doings.

An hour before sunset, the project halted. A quick prayer over the new, mostly complete building was orchestrated by both pastors before the Bread of Life team boarded their bus for the trip back to the hotel.

Ox took a front seat and watched Quintero through the windshield hold a final conversation with a few of the locals. He finished with a laugh, then walked backwards towards the bus staying in conversation with the pastor.

The squeal of tires preceded the visual of the shiny black van. The sound came from behind the bus and zoomed up its side. The van slammed on its brakes, causing the back end to slide slightly. Distinct pops from a fired gun sliced through the air. Ox watched in horror as Quintero immediately fell, a circle of blood quickly growing in the middle of his back like a time-lapse video of a blossoming flower against his white shirt. Three men jumped out: one flashing a gun at the church group in the bus; the other two putting a hood over Quintero's head, then carrying him into the van and flooring their exit. Before anyone could breathe, the van was gone.

Chaos replaced the crime, both on the street and in the bus.

CHAPTER 40

As the unfortunate event unfolded in Guatemala City, Silk looked out over Lake Michigan a short distance away from Trapper's Alley.

The previous two days and nights, he had surveilled the fence perimeter and the Trapper's Alley compound from a variety of angles, using binoculars and prudently chosen viewing positions. The first confirmation that the usable building was occupied became evident when a man exited the back door for a smoke.

Five other things became clear.

First, he discovered the main entrance and found that its steel doors were the lone gate into the place, making the water the only logical entry point for him.

Second, the building had skylights.

Third, a call had come towards the tail end of the second day from Coate who informed him the property was once owned by a company called Milwaukee Metal Works, but that they had gone out of business thirty years earlier. It was now in the hands of Park Bank, with no record of it being leased or in use.

Fourth, his need to communicate with Viceroy necessitated a call to Quintero or Hammaren.

Fifth, he required a boat.

The ice that had gripped Lake Michigan was melted enough that the first fifty yards out from shore had become a soupy mix of small ice blocks and freezing water, but navigable. Silk had walked the shoreline just north of the Trapper's Alley compound the afternoon of the third day, meeting the owner of a small marina, convincing the man to help him by providing a beat-up canoe and a long pole. The guy told him 'that place is disturbing, so just leave the damn thing there when you're done with it' before he closed up and drove away.

The sun was setting when Silk pushed into the calm waters of Lake Michigan, and had disappeared completely from the southwest horizon twenty minutes later, when he poled up to the seawall of the compound to a position just past the fence line nearest the first small building.

He tossed a gym bag the fifteen feet to the flat ground above, hearing it splat when it landed on the slush of the melted snow. Then he lunged, jumping from the canoe to the rocky seawall, landing awkwardly without the benefit of two usable arms for balance. He twisted his body towards the shore, but the momentum from the leap pitched him sideways onto a large concrete slab, frosty from the evening air and angled back towards the water. He slipped, falling to the slab, spinning his body to his right so it would take most of the impact to protect the stitches on his left collarbone. As he fell, he stuck his left leg out to catch the large rock at the edge of the slab. It spread-eagled him, but it worked. He used his legs and usable elbow to shimmy back up the slab to safety. There, he sat on a rock and felt his right knee, healed enough that it was okay. His shoulder screamed but the stitches held.

He unzipped the gym bag, putting a small flashlight and his cell phone in the two secure pockets of his coat, then grabbed the loaded gun. Carefully, he made his way to the small building in front of him, hugging the exterior wall facing the shore, then turned the corner. Ahead, the large, windowless building loomed about fifty yards away.

He sprinted across, coming to a halt at the midpoint of the wall facing back towards the shore. The target was around the other side, the fire escape stairs zigzagging from ground to rooftop. He hugged the wall until he reached them and began the climb, gingerly taking each step to mute any sound. At the top, there was one step down to a five-foot wide cement walkway framing in what he came to find.

The skylights. *'You know you can see the stars better from the second floor.'*

Two floors below, a small light against the south wall cast enough glow to expose the expanse of the first floor. He began a careful walk around the perimeter, noting the second floor's mesh walkway and guard rail, the bays, and the odd-looking boxes on stands in each one. The boxes cast a shine. *Metal?* The first floor was mostly empty except for a desk with a computer and the partial view of some sort of cage structure in the shadows behind. He continued to walk around in a clockwise direction. One bay on the second floor was empty.

Now at the corner furthest from the fire escape stairs, he caught the glow of an approaching light in the periphery towards the main gate. He hit the deck and watched from over the roof edge as the vehicle stopped at the gate. His view was cut off by the metal doors, but soon they were swinging slowly open, then closed behind as it passed. He moved swiftly, crouching around the corner to a spot where he could see the desk area better.

A man was there, taking off a coat as if he had just come in.

In the better light, Silk identified him as the guy taking a smoke the previous day. He heard the vehicle arrive at the building but was blocked from view.

Next, a neatly dressed Black or Hispanic man entered but he couldn't quite tell which, other than he was brown skinned. In his arms was another metal box. The first guy took it and went to the desk while the other one disappeared back through the door. Immediately, the first one disassembled the top.

Hinged.

Placing the rest of the box aside, he went to the cage and grabbed something. Too far away to tell specifically, but Silk saw him put a small item into the cover by utilizing some tools. While he was reassembling, the second one returned, wheeling in a handcart stacked with two large cardboard boxes.

They chatted for a few minutes, then the second one used a box cutter. He took out something from the box on top of the stack but had his back to Silk. The two gathered at the desk and when the second guy moved, Silk saw it.

No way.

In clear view on the desk was the now familiar translucent bag.

Cass echoed in Silk's ears. *'Somethin's brewin' here. Word is its big time, and it's 'parently somethin' pretty bad.'* What the hell are they doing?

The first one grabbed the box, holding it while the second guy opened the cover. He pulled something, and the inside of the cover flipped open exposing an empty space. The second man placed the bag in the space, clearly showing the first guy in an instructive way the procedure. It was hard for Silk to tell, but it looked like the guy was attaching something to the bag from inside the cover before he snapped the lid closed and let the cover hinge back to normal. The first guy nodded and walked a few paces away; grabbing a small object from the desk, he used a finger to punch what Silk guessed was buttons. All the sides on the box flew open. Silk could see the second man nod approval and make a sweeping gesture to the entire second floor.

Silk dove out of sight.

No lights, no alarms.

He breathed easier, even more so when he heard the vehicle start up. Then, the lights went dark below.

Silk gave it five minutes before making his way back to the fire escape and down. At ground level, he immediately ran along the building wall back the way he came, retracing his steps to the seawall. Almost slipping again into the water, he caught himself and eased into the canoe. Tossing the gym bag in, he froze, then whipped around with his gun drawn, quickly turning left, then right, then left again. No one.

He turned back to the canoe and stared down at the bow seat to the envelope pinned under a rock.

CHAPTER 41

Silk piled his black clothes in the corner of the closet holding his ever-growing laundry. Throwing on jeans and a zip sweat, he dialed the number again.

Another no answer.

He waited five minutes and for the sixth time, dialed Hammaren's number, then Quintero's. Same result.

He made his way to the couch, grabbing the lone sheet of paper from the unidentified envelope as it lay on the coffee table. The foray into Trapper's Alley two hours ago raced through his mind. *Screed. Metal boxes. Remote buttons. Gated entry. One guy, then two. Something's brewing. Something pretty bad.* His mind returned to the envelope.

That's why he took off his coat. He put the envelope in the canoe. Saw the footprints. Had to be him. He knew I was there.

Silk read the scribbled writing one more time.

YOU'RE SPOTTED. WE HAVE WATCHERS. MEET ME ON MARCH 23 - O'LEARY'S PUB ON CARFERRY DRIVE – 10 PM. I'LL APPROACH YOU. I'M ON YOUR SIDE.

Silk picked up the phone to dial Hammaren again when the phone rang. Jürgen Sandt's name appeared on the screen.

"Hello, Jürgen?"

His voice shaking, Jürgen said, "Cesar was murdered last night,

Mr. Moreland. In plain sight. Shot and carried off by a gang, somewhere there in Guatemala City." The man's voice cracked as he finished. "I just wanted you to know."

"I'm so very sorry to hear that."

"I've already sent a plane down there for the church group. I'm bringing them home."

"Are they all okay?"

"Yes. They're not harmed. Their pastor said Roger's not with them, though. That he left. That scares me. Do you know where he is?"

"I'm sure he's on the trail of locating your son. Not to worry. He'd find a way to call if he had to."

"Well, I'm calling General Hammaren next to let him know and so he can communicate to Roger somehow."

"Good idea."

"I can't express my grief right now. I'm too shaken."

"It's okay, Jürgen. My condolences."

As soon as they hung up, he called Coate.

Going to need some help on March 23rd.

CHAPTER 42

Days prior, when Viceroy and Regina hit the splash pool from the falls, the current separated them. Regina squeezed the straps against her chest to not lose the backpacks, then wildly kicked to the surface, breaking it briefly before the current took her under once again. She kicked harder and away from the center, hoping Viceroy was doing the same. The power of the river seemed to allay as she made her way towards shore. When she broke through, she spotted Viceroy ahead, already out of the river and standing on the bank looking to grab her. By the time she reached him the river had calmed, almost as if it, too, was grateful to be done with the terrifying trip over the cliff.

They looked back to the top of the waterfall spotting a Chizec, now silhouetted and small. Then they ran, not stopping until their lungs gave out. Abbreviated rest stops took up the remains of that day as they continued hugging the river. Viceroy kept an eye upstream every so often for signs of pursuit. None, it seemed. Finally, they stopped hours later and encamped.

In the forty-eight hours hence, they had carefully picked their way downstream, making for a slower go, but Viceroy had taken Joaquín's comment about crocs to heart and was using a long branch to ferret out any as they moved. Towards evening on the third day, Regina made her way over to a fallen tree, plopping down and unloading her pack. Viceroy took off his shirt and wrung out a copious amount of rain water and sweat.

"Feel free to do the same," he said to Regina, adding, "I need to make a call. I'll be out of sight right over there by that funny looking tree with the moss all over it."

Viceroy grabbed the SAT phone and disappeared behind the trunk.

Regina took the moment to completely undress, wringing out every piece of her clothing as best she could before pulling everything back on and joining Viceroy. As she neared, she heard him in conversation.

"Yeah, so I've got some unfortunate news. Cesar was shot in cold blood on a street in Guatemala City," Hammaren said. "We're in contact with the local authorities but the best they can tell us is it was probably a drug cartel hit. Cesar Quintero is a known public figure. They may be using him for ransom with the government if he survived. But from the eyewitness reports, he was shot in the back and went limp immediately."

Viceroy leaned against the tree and put his head down.

Hammaren continued, "Jürgen's not taking it well. He just returned from D.C. three days ago from a funeral for Senator Clay Czerwinski. He and Kendrick, well, they're both in a pretty depressed state. I was going to call you but, as we agreed, all communication comes from you."

Viceroy said, "The church team. Were they with him… Quintero?"

"Yes, I'm afraid so. But Jürgen sent his plane down there immediately and they all arrived safely back in Milwaukee late last night."

"That's a relief."

"Look, I'll move into action if you want to abort over this."

"No. From what we've learned, I think I know where his son may be, if he's alive. We're a day away from getting there. Jürgen hired us to find him and bring him home and that's what we're going to hopefully deliver for him. That said, just be ready. From this call forward, my next one may be an emergency evac."

"I won't ask where you are right now."

"Guatemala."

"Touché."

They clicked off.

Regina said, "Wow. Quintero."

"Yeah. Trying to process. Joaquín, too. I couldn't tell when we jumped what exactly happened."

"He was near the shore, that's all I recall. And now without Quintero…."

"I know. Let's just hope we don't find ourselves in need of needing him. We're alone and now without a guide or an ace to play. Just rely on each other and we'll make it."

She scratched at an itch on her neck with a grimace on her face.

"It's been a wild ride ever since the cargo plane and parachute jump." When Viceroy didn't comment, she asked, "What are you thinking?"

"Something's been bothering me since El Ceibo."

"What?"

"I don't know. That place had a strange vibe. Something was just off, like a duck in a robin's nest."

"Never heard you say *that* before."

"My grandpa used to say it when everything looks right, but your gut tells you it isn't. A bird, feathers, eggs in a nest, you know. But something isn't quite correct. A bird being there is right, but maybe the type of bird is wrong, or the nest is too small for the bird."

"I think I know what you mean. It all felt sort of too non-random even though everything that happened seemed random."

"That Chizec encounter was also strange. We just need time to pick through the pieces. But there's no time. We have someone to find."

Regina slowly nodded assent.

Viceroy said, "Assuming we get there tomorrow, let's hope it's not just a bunch of stone structures with angry gorillas running around."

"Well, assuming that's not the case, I doubt Bertram Sandt will be casually strolling the grounds either. What are you thinking?"

"Simple. We look for a circle just like Peterson described."

CHAPTER 43

The Lisp flicked off the warehouse lights, yawning and stretching for dramatic effect. The watcher had just left the building. He feigned going to bed shortly thereafter, closing the studio door and keeping a close eye on his watch.

When the moment arrived, he rapidly and quietly dressed, then used clothing and the extra pillow to recreate himself asleep under the covers. Deftly, he reached underneath the mattress and pulled out a travel toothbrush holder, popping it apart and taking the flash drive, replacing it before lowering himself to the floor. He laid down and then scooched himself underneath the bed.

One piece of information Mrs. Lobe provided before The Lisp left Guatemala was the secret escape route from the building; a removable faux block on the floor underneath the head of the bed. Gandy had believed it was part of the underground railroad from the 1800's when he originally found it and relayed the information through the back channels for usable intel to the inside resistance group. The tunnel ran eighty yards straight away, ending at a long-since abandoned building off the Trapper's Alley property. The Lisp had tested it before and found it just as described.

The large plaster block pulled out easily and he placed it aside, keeping it hidden under the box spring. Cooler air wafted in from the opening. He pulled himself through and stepped down the rickety ladder ten feet to the tunnel entrance. Only then did he turn on a flashlight and begin the trek to the other end.

A few minutes later he stood in the abandoned building, dusting himself off from the tunnel debris, and then hit the street to O'Leary's six blocks away. A northern strong breeze was ushering in a cold front producing cloud cover that blocked any moonlight. His walk was a dark, lonely hike through a dicey area without the benefit of a gun. He walked with purpose, knowing his heightened pace would radiate a degree of caution to someone who may want to do him harm.

O'Leary's was a landmark Irish pub on the northern edge of the warehouse district. Small, with wooden floors and beams and a grandiose bar. Irish drinking songs were emanating from a two-man band on the tiny stage in the corner with most of the patrons singing along.

Silk entered at 9:45. The shoulder was far enough along that he could finally let his arm hang with limited pain. He ordered a beer just to seem as if he was there for the same reasons everyone else was, but took small sips while he kept his eyes peeled.

Shortly after 10:00, a bald man approached him wearing cowboy boots and denim head to toe. He stood a good six inches lower. The man held his gaze for a second then nodded for him to follow.

When the man turned, Silk shot a glance to the undercover cops across the bar that Coate had arranged—two burly white guys that looked like they were regulars. The beefiest one gave him a slight nod.

The Lisp took Silk out the back door to the parking lot adjacent to a set of railroad tracks. Coate watched the two from her car as she sat directly facing the rear door and texted another who was covering the front that she had them in view. The music from inside was still audible so The Lisp led Silk towards the tracks and stopped near the bar's dumpster to talk.

The Lisp said, "I don't want to know your name. I don't want to know a damn thing about you."

Silk said, "I can't say I want the same from you."

"Listen. I'm here because I wanted to be. I'm watched round the clock. My employer is a nut job who'll kill you and me right now if he knew we were talking."

"Who is he?"

"A monster."

"Name?"

The Lisp paused and looked away. Coate reacted, grabbing her gun and opening her door, thinking it may be a non-verbal cue from the guy. They both looked over to her. Silk gave her a 'no go' nod without the guy seeing it, so she quickly pivoted, pretending to be on her phone as she walked slowly towards the back door.

"I don't know. Nobody does," The Lisp said.

"You're owned by Mitchell Industries."

"Good place to start, but you'll never find him out. He's not going to be connected. He's too smart for that."

"What is it you want then?" Silk asked. "You called this meeting."

"Our cameras spotted you while you've been taking pictures. I'm the only one who's seen them. I gotta believe you're a cop."

"Yes."

"That's good. I need you for back-up."

"Look man, I don't know who you are or what your operation is up to, but from what I saw you're dealing street drugs. I'm one phone call away from a raid."

"I wouldn't do that. He's got the whole place ready to blow if he's attacked. And his plans are way bigger than being a street dealer."

"What are you talking about?"

The Lisp reached into his pocket and handed over the flash drive, then checked his watch.

"On April first, at exactly one-fifteen in the afternoon, all hell's going to break loose. That right there's a duplicate. I got the original. If I'm dead by that day it means you're the only person on the planet who can stop it."

"Stop what?"

"Mayhem unleashed."

"Mayhem? What's this do?"

"There's a computer on my desk on the main floor inside the building. You can't miss it. It's the only one. You gotta plug it in and hit enter. The port's on the left side of the screen. The software will take care of the rest. Be there. I'll do all I can to help you. If I'm alive."

"Why?"

"To stop him."

"From *what*?" Silk asked.

"Changing the world."

"What do you mean?"

"He's going to enslave the planet."

"That sounds a little over the top. Why don't you just do that now then? Plug it in?"

"Because the man's a genius. He's got everything already wired for that exact moment. Any attempt to block it now would give him ample time to reload. Remember, I'm watched like a hawk, twenty-four-seven. Don't ask how I got here tonight. One escape route he don't know about. But the only way this is going to work is if you crash the party at one p.m. on the first. Either that causes a major interruption and gives me the cover I need, or you succeed and stampede right through to the computer. Bring some friends. A surprise attack's the only way."

Coate finished her faux conversation and went inside. One of the undercovers came out immediately and lit up a cigarette.

"Where? That steel gate doesn't look too crash-able."

"That dead-end road on the other side. Bring something to plow through it at a high rate of speed."

"And the bombs?

"I'll take care of that. Just get there at one on the first."

"What if I need to communicate with you?" Silk asked.

"Don't."

Silk ran through Gandy's final words in his mind.

"Who's Mickey?" Silk asked.

"Who told you that name?"

"Theo Gandy."

"Shit," The Lisp said to himself. "Mickey's dead. That's why I'm here."

"How'd he die and who was he?"

"Neither of the answers to those questions matter."

Coate walked out the back door and to her car, still pretending to be on her phone. Both men watched her for a quick moment, then The Lisp stared Silk down. Silk's eyes returned to the flash drive swallowed up in the palm of his huge hand.

The Lisp said, "Don't try and crack the code or give it to someone who can. If you mess it up, he wins. Use it only as I described. And when it's all over, I'd forget Mitchell Industries. That plug'll be pulled if it hasn't been already. That ain't the hot spot anyway."

"What *is*?"

A car abruptly pulled into the lot and stopped, then slowly moved as if looking for a place to park but bypassed a few open spaces.

The Lisp looked over to it, watching for a moment. "I've been gone long enough. There's no time to explain." He turned and disappeared into the night.

CHAPTER 44

The night noises emanating from the jungle were made spookier by the scene before them. Moonlit ruins combined with lit torches throughout the compound made for a scene akin to a Hollywood movie. *King Kong lives here*, Viceroy thought, as he and Regina looked through the entryway into the heart of the empire.

"This is what we saw from the river," Viceroy whispered as they crouched in the fold of a buttress root of an enormous ficus tree.

He peered over the top of it one more time to the entry where the stone path cut through the wall to a lone burning torch in the distance of what looked like a plaza or open space beyond the wall. He observed for a minute then crouched back down.

"Nothing," he said. "Only a lit torch across the way."

"Well, based on what we can see, that looks like the only entry," Regina pointed out.

They inched away from the ficus and through the stone entry to the inner wall of the plaza, immediately turning away from the torch and finding darkness after twenty feet.

He measured the plaza in his head, surmising it was approximately the size of a soccer field with a bit more squareness to it. There were six entrances including the one they just went through, each with a lit torch to the immediate right. They had entered at the east wall, the only entry along that stretch of the monolith. The other entries were at the southwest and northwest corners; two along the north wall at even intervals, the one directly across on the west wall that he had spotted earlier, and one to his left at the south wall next to a set of ancient stairs leading way up to a platform that he couldn't quite make out in the darkness. The entire plaza floor was constructed of square-cut stones, some obviously crumbled or uneven, and grasses growing in spots between. Two triangular obelisks stood on the plaza floor, each looking about twenty feet high. The nearest one was slightly to their left nearer the southeast corner; the other sat towards the opposite corner, but that one was missing its top third. In the exact center of the plaza was a raised stone platform that looked to Viceroy to be square shaped, but he couldn't be sure. It also looked extremely worn, with part of the exposed side missing a small section. *Erosion*, Viceroy guessed. Each corner had some sort of small pit with burnt bricks around their edges. *Used for fire.*

A distant noise of a door slamming suddenly resounded. From what direction, they couldn't tell, making both quickly crouch to a squat. They gave it a minute. Silence.

"We're dead down here," Viceroy whispered. He pointed to the platform high above. Regina gave a thumbs-up.

They sidled along the eastern wall to the corner, then slowed, turning along the south wall knowing they had to cross that wall's entry to the plaza while being completely blind to whatever may be on the other side of that exposure point. As they neared it, Regina got down on hands and knees directly under the torch and peered around the wall to a path leading straight south.

"It's a campus," she said in an urgent whisper, turning back to Viceroy.

"*What?*"

"There are buildings. Modern buildings."

Without hesitation he grabbed her hand and sprinted to the stairs, quickly bounding up them and making a beeline for the platform. When they reached the top they intuitively spread apart, Viceroy taking the plaza side, Regina the wall side, seeking for clues that they may have been spotted. No movement. They hit the ground and squat-walked to the middle of the platform.

"We needed to get up here fast. Best vantage point," he softly said as he stayed low and met her in the middle of the space.

Around them was a four-foot high wall encircling the half-moon shape of the large platform. To the rear was a small, roofed stone structure with three walls.

"This is where the ancients ruled," he said. "This is the temple mount."

"Eerie," was all Regina could muster as she looked around.

He nodded to move forward to the half-moon wall. There, they very slowly stood to take in the sight of the plaza. Viceroy stayed crouched, not extending to his full six-foot height, but enough to get a full view. He guessed they were standing about fifty feet up. The broad swath of moonlight across the ancient city and the tops of the jungle canopy beyond was riveting. A thousand images danced through his mind of what occurred long ago. *Who were they? Chizecs? Early ancestors of the Guatemalan people? What happened that it became deserted?*

After a few minutes of silence, Regina turned away and slid down, resting her lower half on the floor of the mount. Viceroy squatted next to her.

"What was that building for, do you think?" Regina asked in a whisper, pointing to the stone structure directly across.

"I'm guessing a staging area for the kings and queens, or whatever title they gave their leaders."

"Good call," she said. "Let's take a look."

Staying low once again, they walked the twelve paces and peered inside. It was bare except for a locked bin sitting against the back wall.

"Looks like the temple mount is still used for something," Regina said.

She stepped into the opening while Viceroy stayed out to watch for movement.

Another door noise echoed up, this time from below and behind the mount on the south side. Viceroy tensed, quickly sidling up vertically against the building's north exterior. He poked his head around into the corner of the building, getting Regina's attention and gesturing to be silent. Flipping his head back to the outside, he side-stepped towards the southwest corner of the building with his gun drawn, then stuck his head out just enough to see what he could.

Below his position was exactly what Regina described. A campus of modern buildings. Two were directly below him; the rest were off to the east. A wide path ran through the campus, looking like it connected everything.

Suddenly, movement.

Two individuals appeared at the far east end and were walking due west, soon to be below him. He moved to the temple mount back wall and lowered himself just enough to keep his eyes affixed on them. One was obviously a man of normal height with a rifle slung across his back. The other looked like a woman, rather small and of slight build. The man had his hand on her right bicep, steering her at a brisk pace. He watched as they crossed his position in front of the two buildings directly below, then lost sight of them. Moments later they reappeared, continuing their walk. At the end of the path was a flight of stairs extending west, but they hung a right to a path he couldn't see due to the vegetation. Their heads and shoulders stayed visible. Viceroy looked ahead to where they were going and saw a large torch light illuminating the top of the barbed wire fence. *I don't believe it.*

He spun away in the direction he came, hugging the temple mount building's wall, and poked his head inside to Regina.

"We gotta go," he said with conviction.

"Where to?"

"I just found our circle."

200

CHAPTER 45

The barbed wire fence and the bamboo hut it surrounded were both perfect spheres. The hut stood in the exact center of the footprint with a three-foot apron of manicured landscaping around it, and a ten-yard buffer of indigenous plants from there to the fence. The effect was a moat of fauna with the path serving as the only bridge to the castle.

Viceroy and Regina had taken the stairs off the west side of the temple mount, gambling that the southwest corner entry to the plaza led to something better than the south entry directly into the campus. It paid off. The path angled to the right as soon as they skirted through that portal and away from where they wanted to go, but another one appeared ten yards further up to the left. Guns raised, they took the left path and within thirty seconds were staring at the back side of the hut through the barbed wire fence.

'You want to find Bertram Sandt? If he's alive he'd be up there still. Look for a circle.' That's what you said. *Maybe we found it, Amy Peterson*, Viceroy thought.

Staying camouflaged as they squatted just off the trail, they surveyed what lay before them, specifically the hut and its structure, looking for a way in without having to consider the front door. The hut's wall stopped short of the thatched roof, creating a space for air flow. A beam of wood jutted out from the roof line at a sharp vertical angle every eight feet and extended past the wall two feet, so the roof hung over the edge of the hut. *Looks like a circus tent*, Regina thought. She took off her backpack and laid it next to Viceroy's.

A light was on inside, its dim emanation visible in the air flow space. They watched and listened for anything. Occasionally a shadow would cut off the light.

Regina whispered, "Someone's moving, maybe pacing."

Then a voice.

"I won't," a woman shouted in English.

"You have no choice. He wants *you* to do it. Only you," a male voice with a Hispanic accent responded.

"I don't care what he wants."

The detectives heard a gun being cocked.

"Here," the male voice said.

There was an extended silence, finally broken by the Hispanic man's voice.

"You heard him. His mission is finally completed, thanks to *both* of you."

Viceroy looked at Regina. "Did you hear that? He said, 'his mission.'"

"I said I won't do it," the woman shouted, this time louder.

Another extended silence as the shadow cut off the light twice.

"You're a religious man," the Hispanic said. "Perhaps you could enlighten the good doctor on the biblical meaning of 'Good men perish; the godly die before their time, and no one seems to care or wonder why.'"

Viceroy flinched. *Debbie*. Subconsciously he lowered his gun. Regina looked up at him, noticing the movement. His face was different, focused, but not on this moment. Something else. Then the man's words crystallized on where she knew he went. She reached over and gently touched the bottom of his forearm, pushing it back up to horizontal. He looked down to her, pulling his thoughts back to center, and nodded. The light returned to his eyes.

Another man's voice spoke from inside the hut—a soft, soothing timbre. They had to strain to hear each word as the jungle's sounds overrode his volume level from where they were positioned.

"Believers are saved from the wound of death, not from the

whip of it."

"What does that mean, Señor Sandt?"

The detectives bolted, jumping and running through the jungle's underbrush as fast as they could around the circumference of the fence until they reached the open gate. Viceroy ran through first across the ten yards of path to the hut entrance. Regina spun backwards to check their rear flank, then followed.

As Viceroy rushed in, the man with a rifle stood facing the opposite direction but turned at the sound of his entrance. Viceroy noticed the woman out of the corner of his eye sitting in a chair angled towards the rear of the hut, breathing hard and staring at him in the surprise of the moment. He knelt to one knee and aimed at the man, but the man hit the ground and rolled behind a table. The woman pitched herself to the floor, taking cover behind a desk as Viceroy stayed low and spun away from the doorframe. The sound of a bullet intended for him whizzed past his left ear. Regina heard the crack of the gun just as she entered and pivoted left through the doorway to a clear line of sight. She fired, striking the armed man in the neck as he turned towards her. His head snapped backwards, then he crumbled to the floor. Viceroy stood as Regina took a few steps towards the man. A pool of blood formed around his head as the bullet's entry and exit points opened the flood gates. She nodded to Viceroy.

Viceroy shot a look first to the woman crouched behind the desk, then lifted his head to the rear of the cabin. A lean man with long, blond hair in a t-shirt and jeans sat tied to a bamboo chair. The face was undeniable.

Bertram Sandt.

CHAPTER 46

"We have to fly," Regina stated.

Bertram Sandt stood up as Viceroy cut the ties.

"Who are you?" Bertram asked.

"No time," Viceroy said with urgency. "Your father sent us."

"My…father?"

"Yes, but we can't talk now. Just trust us."

The other woman stood next to the chair she had been sitting in when Viceroy entered. Her breathing still rapid.

"Are you here to…rescue us?" she asked in small voice, struggling to get the 'r' in rescue out.

Regina replied, "We are. But we're not going to walk out of here."

As she finished her reply the sound of intense shouts erupted from the campus, already starting to close fast.

"Shit," Regina uttered.

Viceroy said, "Do either of you know an escape route?"

Bertram shook his head.

"I might," the woman offered.

"Great. Follow me and then you lead. Now," Regina said.

The four moved to the door, onto the path and the gate. The sound of activity was nearing with more shouts and flood lights illuminating the campus. The voices were loud, moments away from visual contact.

Regina seized the woman's hand and ran back the way she and Viceroy had come, through the brush around the circumference to the path. Both detectives snatched their backpacks before they all started sprinting.

"Not that way," the woman said, trailing the other three.

"Take us," Viceroy shouted to her.

The woman hung a right onto the path leading to the corner entryway to the plaza. When they all got through Viceroy asked where to go. She pointed to the northwest corner almost one hundred yards away.

This time Viceroy led as they hugged the west wall and ran. Both detectives constantly turned their heads as they pumped their legs, looking for danger in any direction. At the corner he came to a stop and pulled the woman forward to lead. Before they could step through the entry, the glow of fire erupted further down the trail.

"What's that?" Viceroy asked.

The woman stood, almost frozen. "Chizecs."

"How could they—"

Before he could finish, she pivoted and raced across the plaza towards the east entry where the detectives had originally entered. Halfway there, a rain of machine gun bullets cut across their path. Regina spied the firepower coming from the temple mount and grabbed the collars of Bertram and the woman, yanking them to the ground behind the raised stone platform in the plaza's center where they all crouched, now breathless and pinned.

"Any other ideas?" Viceroy asked. "There's got to be another path."

Bertram pointed straight ahead.

"No," the woman said insistently.

"It's the only way," Bertram replied in a calm voice.

Regina asked in rapid fire, "What's he talking about? What's wrong with that way?"

"We can still make the east path to the river if either of you can use your guns to get us there," the woman answered.

Viceroy thought it through, looking at Regina, then said, "Alright, I'll cover for you. But when I say 'go' you have to run like all hell. Got it?"

Bertram again pointed.

"No way," the woman said, pulling his arm down. "Whenever you're ready," she added directly to Viceroy.

He looked to the east portal. Then his heart sank.

Growing ever brighter was another glow coming up from the path that led to the river.

"Oh no," Regina said, also spotting the light.

The machine gun fired, skipping bullets around each side of them and over their heads as they ricocheted off the floor of the platform.

Viceroy shouted above the bullet storm. "One shot. That path," he said, pointing to the portal the woman had vehemently objected to. "On my count."

"But—" the woman started.

Before she could get out her words, Viceroy stood, turned and emptied his Glock at the temple mount. Regina shoved the two forward, running to the exit while Viceroy ran backwards until his magazine ran out then dashed towards them and through as another round of bullets peppered the portal's framing.

Now they were on a new path but stopped.

"This leads nowhere," the woman screamed. "It's a dead end."

Bertram took off at a sprint, slipping once at the first bend by the statue of the half-man, half-bird figure. The others followed, having to go single file as the trail narrowed. The moonlight was all they had to help them avoid missing their steps, but once the glow of the floodlights and lit torches faded behind them, their vision adapted.

As Viceroy ran, he turned backwards every twenty feet to spot what may be following, which slowed him. By the time the others had reached the water wall, he was a good minute behind. When he came up, he saw them all just standing there, three across. The trail had widened at the last turn. He saw the falls pouring over the top of the cliff in front of them, but he couldn't hear any sound of a splash pool.

"What's the matter? Why aren't we—?"

A chasm. A five-foot-wide stretch of darkness going on forever in each direction.

"We have to jump across and through the waterfall," he said in a tone of obvious logic.

"It's a dead end," said the woman, defeated. "Like I said."

Viceroy looked left and right. The path went straight up the spine of an incredibly steep ridge. Off either side the land swept swiftly down at a death-defying angle. The vegetation was thick and unwelcoming, and he knew they couldn't just move into the forest. One or more could die or sustain a potentially serious injury if they tried.

Regina turned back to the path thinking they could retreat and find an alternate way. The growing light coming toward them changed her mind.

"This is it," she said, as they all turned to see the approaching torches.

"They're killers," the woman said.

When the first one appeared on the path thirty paces slightly below them, he stopped, clanging his spear on the ground. Within seconds, five more had gathered and began clanging in unison. One of them barked a guttural sound followed by a word. Like a well-oiled military unit, they all stopped clanging in concert. Another guttural run of sound and they pointed their spears in synchronization.

"You got enough bullets?" Regina asked Viceroy.

"Between the two of us we could take them, but they're just one wave. More's coming. We're trapped." Shoving a new magazine into his Glock, he added, "But what the hell."

The next sound was more of a screeching enunciation from the same Chizec, with a varied pitch, as he communicated to the others. Slowly, they broke off in pairs, positioning themselves left, right and center. Without another sound, they put one foot in front of the other in slow motion, advancing.

Viceroy and Regina raised their guns.

Viceroy said, "Take out the left. I've got the right. At least the flanks will be covered. If we have time for the center, just take a shot."

Two more steps from the Chizecs, then a genteel voice spoke.

"The Lord will deliver. He always does," Bertram said.

They all looked to him, shocked at the statement considering the moment, but more so the unfettered calmness in which he spoke.

He closed his eyes for a moment then flashed them open, turned back to the chasm, and jumped in.

"Bertram," Viceroy screamed.

The Chizec leader yelled something, spurring a charge. The woman and Regina both hit the ground and rolled into the chasm. Viceroy looked back to the onrush of warriors, then pivoted and jumped. The last vision he saw was the face of a tall snake, standing erect, towering over him and holding a large, black orb in its massive jaw.

CHAPTER 47

Free-falling objects do not encounter air resistance and will accelerate downwards.

Completely unwitting to the sheer expanse of the drop they had launched themselves into, and with a consuming darkness blinding them, the descent felt like forever until the sudden impact into the underground lake.

Viceroy wasn't sure how far he went under water, but instincts took over as he kicked himself towards the surface. A strong current tried pulling him in a certain direction. The backpack felt like an anchor as he struggled. He hadn't taken a large enough inhale and was rapidly burning through the small amount of air in his lungs. Finally, he broke the surface and gasped for oxygen. The air was quite cool, the water more so. He heard splashing around him from someone else and spotted Regina a few feet away swimming towards something off to his right. Still trying to recover his lungs, Viceroy swished himself around in a desperate search for Bertram and the woman. Ahead, Bertram was making progress in the same direction as Regina, so he followed suit. The current eased as he made his way to the edge of the lake. Behind him the noise of the crashing waterfall echoed; he just couldn't see it.

Bertram was the first ashore to a thin stretch of hard ground covered in a soft powdery substance. A mere fifteen feet wide and four feet deep, it was basically an indentation in a giant wall of layered rock. At either end the rock jutted back out into the lake.

In the throes of labored breathing, Bertram strained his eyes as he heard the splash of others approaching. First Regina, then Viceroy. When she pulled herself up to safety, Regina immediately unzipped her pack, found the flashlight and used it to search the water for the woman, shouting 'hello' and 'over here' for a good five minutes. No sound came from the lake, no movement in the water.

The three sat in silence hoping the woman would appear or give them a verbal sign she was alive somewhere. Regina kept scanning, pointing the light across the surface, back and forth.

"She's not here," Viceroy said, elevating his voice above the waterfall noise.

"How do you know?" Regina asked. "She may be treading water and we can't see her or she's ahead somewhere waiting for us."

They waited another minute as their eyes slowly adapted to the darkness. The waterfall area came into form and, despite the muted visual, the scene was astounding. A small mist clung over the lake at the waterfall impact point with a wall of rock behind.

"File that in your memory bank," Viceroy said.

Viceroy very quickly introduced the two of them to Bertram and gave him a lightning-quick summary of who they were and how it all came about. Bertram didn't even know it was ten years until Regina told him in response to one of his questions. He held his hands to his face as he wept, knowing his father and sister were alive.

Understanding they had to move, Viceroy grabbed the flashlight and stood at the water's edge, shining it down at the water.

"Look," he said. "Little particles are all flowing that way," he added, pointing off to the right. "That's the current. Let's follow it and see where it goes. We can cling to the rock wall as we move."

"That's right," Bertram said, wiping away the tears.

Viceroy asked, "Are you saying you know that's the way?"

"Yes. That's the way."

"How do you know?" Regina asked.

Bertram stood. "I did this once before. Shortly after I was taken. I jumped in hopes of escaping, but I was recaptured."

"Quite the story, I'm sure. But you knew when we leapt it was our only chance," Regina said.

"Yes. I knew. I'm ready when you are."

The three stood and waded in, clinging to the rock wall and pulling themselves along with the current. The lakebed beneath their feet disappeared quickly into deeper water. Viceroy led with Bertram in between. It took twenty minutes to reach the point where the rock wall angled to their left and soon the rocky lakebed beneath rose to a point where they could walk again. Behind them, the sound of the waterfall faded to background noise. On the other side of the cavern, that rock wall was also closing to the same point and soon the confluence of the lake and rock converged to the mouth of a small river.

"That's it," Bertram said.

As they neared, a gurgling sound echoed, like water being interrupted from its flow. Ten feet out, Regina shined her light. "Oh no," she blurted.

Face down, with her bare feet facing them and her face in the water, was the woman—half-floating and half-moored by her body weight to the shallow rock bed. Viceroy splashed his way to her and rolled her over. Her exposed face displayed a deep gash that cut through to her skull near her right temple, all the way down to the soft tissue of her neck and the torn jugular.

She had already bled out.

CHAPTER 48

As morally difficult as it was, they had to leave the body in the cavern. Just too cumbersome and too gruesome to take the remains with them.

The original leg of the river through the first cave tunnel took eleven hours, according to Regina's watch, with one stop to eat MRE's and an hour rest when they chanced upon a cramped but dry side cave. The water's depth stayed at three feet or so, deeper on occasion, with a steady current moving forward and just slightly enough downhill. The height of the tunnel roof was spacious. Both standing six feet, Viceroy and Bertram had to bend only a few times during the trek to avoid hitting their heads. The thought of floating rather than walking became an idea that was swiftly nixed for fear of careening into danger. The detectives' shoes stayed intact, but Bertram's feet were beginning to sustain cuts and bruises once his tennis shoes fell apart. When they finally reached the second cavern, he was having trouble putting one foot in front of the other.

They heard the next cavern before they saw it. The small waves of the river and hard knocking sounds echoed back to them as they neared. Stopping, they waited in silence for any clue the cavern was inhabited.

Viceroy carefully pushed forward with his gun drawn. Up ahead, at a slight bend in the riverbed, he spied an empty cavern with three skiffs moored to posts, their fenders bumping every so often against them. He shined a flashlight, waving up Regina and Bertram.

"What do you suppose these are doing here?" Regina asked.

Viceroy said, "I'm guessing they're for drug running, but I don't know. Let's see if we can borrow one and let's hope the owner doesn't mind."

He waded towards them, pulling himself up and into the closest one, surveying the small craft with his flashlight. The boat was built to hold no more than four people but had a decent-sized, flat-bottomed space for cargo. He thought the motor looked in well enough shape. A portable fuel tank sat in the bottom of the boat with the fuel line hooked to the motor. Viceroy nudged the tank with his foot, barely moving it but hearing the sloshy sound of a full tank of gasoline.

"All aboard," he said, assisting Regina then Bertram into the boat.

Within minutes they were motoring. The river's depth outgoing from the second cavern was significantly deeper and the current picked up speed as the cave walls narrowed. Not ten minutes later they broke through the mouth of the cave into open country. Bertram shouted a 'praise God,' as Viceroy increased the speed, skimming along the river until the gas tank was almost empty some hours later, then steered it to shore.

I have no idea where we are, he thought to himself.

They set up along the shoreline under a cloudless, starry sky with a campfire keeping them warm as evening took hold. The landscape had changed. Thin grasses and gnarly bushes with occasional tree groves clung to the terrain, now relatively flat in all directions.

After the campfire was underway, Viceroy walked to a brushy area out of hearing range to place a call on the SAT, something he wanted to do in private. Before he placed the first call, he toggled the red switch to send the homing signal, then called General Hammaren. The conversation was a little lengthy, but to the point. Bertram rescued, coordinates confirmed, ETA of evac chopper in sixty minutes.

"Just keep a fire burning until we get there," was Hammaren's final instruction.

The second call was to Jürgen, via a patch from Hammaren's phone. Viceroy walked back to the fire as the call rang, handing the SAT to Bertram. The old man's voice answered.

"Hello."

The sound of his father's voice spurred an avalanche of emotion. He could barely respond, asking, "Dad?" before the tears poured.

Viceroy and Regina walked away knowing the two needed time alone, finding a log to sit on near the river. Regina pulled off both shoes to clear out a few pebbles, massaging her toes and ankles before donning them again.

"Hammaren's got a chopper on the way. About an hour," Viceroy said.

"Well, congratulations to us, I guess. If there was a bar around here, I'd say let's go celebrate. I had my doubts the entire time. I still can't believe we got him."

"Me either. Couldn't have done it without you."

"My head's still swimming."

"Mine, too. Let's get this young man reunited and then you and I can download our thoughts on everything once we get back. I'm looking forward to seeing Silk, too. Hopefully, there's more good news coming from him. If he found Gandy that would be a tremendous upside. From Peterson to Joaquín to Bertram, they all referenced an individual. Someone who sounds like they're a dictator or head of a vast enterprise. Gandy will have answers. And whatever those answers are that man over there is a part of the story, and the Sandt family has earned a complete understanding of what happened and who or what is behind the curtain. Having said that, I get back to what I mentioned before. This entire experience is just…off. Something's not right, not lining up. We need time to process and comb through it all."

"I agree. Molecules?"

He smirked. "Yeah. Definitely a hunt for molecules."

Regina looked over to the campfire and nodded to Viceroy, pointing a finger in that direction. Bertram was off the SAT, softly rocking himself as he sat on the ground with his knees near his chest just staring at the flames. The two detectives made their way over.

"Hey," Viceroy said, taking a position opposite Bertram while Regina found a spot in between.

"Hi," Bertram replied. "I'm thinking I'm in a dream right now."

"Or, maybe you've awoken from a nightmare," Regina said.

"Yeah, maybe."

Viceroy said, "Can I ask you a few things, or would you prefer we just stay silent? We're getting out of here tonight. The Army is sending a chopper to evacuate us back home. Before they arrive, I had a few things on my mind, but if you're not up to talking...?"

"I'm okay."

Viceroy shot a side glance to Regina and raised his eyebrows.

Regina said, "We have about a million things, but let's just take a few steps. You can stop our questions any time you want. Is that all right with you?"

Bertram finally looked up; his gaunt features highlighted in the firelight. His blond hair that a decade ago was dazzling, now had gray interweaved. The gray-blond mix was also evident on his stubble that had sprouted over the past forty-eight hours. Viceroy rubbed his own face as he looked at him, brushing his fingers across what was now more of a beard.

"I'll answer what I can," Bertram said, his voice still trying to recover from the phone call.

"Okay. Let's begin with the woman. Who was she?"

Bertram looked to the stars as he began. "Her name is, um... was, Catarina Amador. A scientist."

"What was she doing there?" Regina asked.

"I think it's best if I just give you a holistic picture of what I know. It'll make it easier on me and probably on you."

"Sure," Viceroy said. "If you're willing to tell us your story, we would love to hear it."

Bertram picked up a stick and poked around the logs in the fire as he spoke.

"We were on a mission trip down here. One day we hiked up to a mountain to see some villages. It was there that we heard about the mysterious native tribe. The Chizecs. There were thirteen of us. I think only five are left, counting me. But I was the one who wanted to meet those people. I thought it was what God wanted us to do at that moment. I put everyone in danger, instead."

"Only five left?" Regina asked. "What happened to everyone?"

"I don't know," he said, taking a moment to wipe at a tear. "Anyway, the villagers told us the Chizecs lived deep in the jungle and we should follow the river. One of their elders led us. It took a whole day to get to a certain spot and then he left after we encamped. The next morning, we awoke surrounded by Chizecs. They took our belongings. One of our brethren tried to reason with them, but they killed him on the spot with a spear and dumped his body in the river, then forced us to walk."

"To where?" Viceroy asked.

"To where you found me. The ancient ruins."

"What happened then?"

"When we arrived, we were met by a man; the overlord."

"He was a Chizec, a king of theirs?" Regina asked.

"No. He was a modern man. Hispanic."

"Name?" Viceroy asked.

"Never referenced by name. It was always 'he.' But, over the years I did hear whispered amongst the guards a reference to him as 'The Ghost.' They said it in a way that I took to mean he was the same man."

The Ghost of Guatemala doesn't exist. A catch-all for criminals and bad actors of every sort. A convenient manifestation to explain away unsolved crimes and scare people. I wouldn't put any stock into chasing that fairy tale. Quintero's words reflected like an image in a fun house mirror as Viceroy remembered them.

Bertram continued, "We became his slaves. We were blindfolded and helicoptered to a different location and then put in jail cells in a disgusting building. No toilets, just hay, like we were animals. It was a long building with a walkway running along the entire length. We could communicate, we just couldn't see each other. It was terrifying, and I tried to keep everyone's spirits up by quoting scripture, but I'm not sure my efforts were working. I think we were in there for almost two months. Just daily food and water and allowed to take a brief walk every so often—but always individually, never together. I was praying so hard for rescue, but none came.

The guards were brutal and adopted our Joaquín as their personal interpreter. He was just a kid…a teenager; someone from our church who could speak Spanish. They treated him like a dog, beating or whipping him with jungle vines. One time, a woman from our group went for her walk but didn't return. Her name was Georgette. Georgette Holfelder. We never found out her fate."

Regina had tears well up and she tried to wipe them away without being noticed. Viceroy hung his head, listening and suddenly wishing Ox was sitting alongside them.

"Sorry," Bertram said almost inaudibly. "I just wanted you to know."

Viceroy added a branch to the fire. "It's okay. Glad you did."

Taking a deep breath, Bertram continued. "There was a moment that changed everything, though. One afternoon we all heard the helicopter arrive. We were yelling to each other, thinking that we'd be released. But then *he* stepped into the building. We hadn't seen him since that first day. He walked along the hall talking to us, telling us our time there was now ended and that we would be joining his army."

"What did *that* mean?" Viceroy asked.

"We were going to be moved back to the ruins. We would be harvesting, processing and packaging a special berry that only grew in some secret canyon. Then he told us to hold out our palms through the jail bars and he was going to treat us to one. We did what he said, and on the count of three we were all to eat what he gave us. I heard the reactions right away. The wails and screams seemed like they went on forever. I thought we were poisoned and were going to die. He was amused. He did a slow walk along the hall watching each person, sometimes laughing at what was going on. One by one he made his way down the hall until he got to my cell."

Bertram paused. A tear trickled its way down his cheek. He sniffled and wiped his face with his shirt sleeve.

"What happened?" Viceroy asked. "Something different when he reached you?"

"I, um…I ate the berry like everyone else, but it didn't affect me in that way. It didn't cause me to yell or scream. I found out later that everyone who consumes one is changed forever, but that didn't happen."

Regina said, "Well, what then?"

"Nothing," Bertram said, letting his words hang without explanation.

A few crackles from the burning wood as Regina pulled herself away from staring at him, enough to turn to Viceroy with a look on her face.

Viceroy asked, "Are you saying you didn't have a physical reaction?"

Bertram didn't answer. He looked up to the stars, then back to his cut and bruised bare feet crossed in front of him. He stayed like that for a long minute.

Regina finally said, "My God. You're immune."

"Yes," Bertram replied in a hoarse whisper.

CHAPTER 49

As the campfire burned in Guatemala, Silk and Coate sat in the FBI's offices in downtown Milwaukee waiting for the arrival of her friend, her gal pal, Maura Lunsford. A few hours earlier, Lunsford had called Coate with some information on the snake head image and wanted to show her in person but couldn't connect until six o'clock.

"You know I'm burning a date night with Andy for this," Coate said, adjusting the armrests of the conference room chair she was seated in.

The room wasn't all that large and rather mundane. A rectangular wooden table sat in the middle with six leather bound mesh-backed chairs around it. The end wall to their left held a large screen. In the middle of the table sat a computer port and a conference phone. The air inside a bit warm.

Silk replied, "Your husband's a prince, but besides missing out on McDonald's and a puppet show, is there really anything else you'd rather be doing?"

"Flossing arbitrary people comes to mind."

"Speaking of which, I need a large truck to ram through a metal fence. Any ideas?"

"That was random. Your weekend recreational pursuits are a little odd."

"Yeah, but concerts and sporting events are too cliché."

"In the interest of answering your question, I don't personally own one, but let me think on it. What about SWAT? I can make a call."

"Gotta stay under the radar."

"You know, at some point this investigation is going to have to see the light of day. I'm with you, but to keep stretching the boundaries is going to catch up, at least as it relates to me."

"You're never going to be named or mentioned, and I've got your back at all times. Whenever you want to say 'no' just say it."

"I guess I'd feel better if I knew what the hell you were investigating."

She's right. I'm asking her to put herself out there and risk her position. She's owed an answer, at least some information. "Listen, I'm going to give you a peek behind the curtain, but I'm only going to do that if you absolutely confirm complete confidentiality."

Coate gave him a look. One of *those*.

Silk said, "Okay. Good. If your friend walks through the door I'm stopping. It's all a bit of a deep dive, but about two months ago we agreed to a proposition from Jürgen Sandt after we found out MRSCU was closing down."

"*The* Jürgen Sandt? Proposition?"

Silk nodded. "To take another shot at finding his son."

"Are you serious? That's like a wow factor of eleven on a ten scale."

"Yeah. Like I said. Confidential. Fast forward, and the hunt for Bertram Sandt led us into territory that now appears to intersect with that drug. It's called screed and the operation behind it is still a bit of a mystery. But, a person of vital interest was also being pursued. Theo Gandy."

Coate's eyes lit up.

Silk continued, "Yeah. Before he died on the street, he said some things. I can't tell you all of it, but he clearly was involved in both the screed situation and our investigation into the disappearance a decade ago of Bertram Sandt."

"Holy crap!"

"A big holy crap. Like my boss would say, Gandy was a molecule.

A nuclear one. And that night at O'Leary's was another piece of the puzzle. That guy you saw me talking to is also connected, so thanks again for the back-up."

"My gratitude for filling in some blanks. Happy to be helping, seriously."

"I understand I'm asking things of you that are bending some rules, but now you know why."

She waved off his comment, then looked at the text that popped up on her cell.

"Okay, so Maura just texted; she needs another minute. A little background before she walks in. Her and I go way back. We both entered the police academy the same day and have become lifelong friends. Her name again is Maura, so don't go saying Mary or Maria or Laura, or some other embarrassing slip."

"Miranda, got it," he said, grinning and knowing he scored that point.

She rolled her eyes.

An athletic, red-haired woman wearing a sharp gray pantsuit entered. She put down a brown expanding file with a button and string closure and a laptop on the table before coming around the other side to greet them.

Coate gave her a hug and then introduced her to Silk. Light-hearted small talk was followed by Lunsford saying she didn't have much time, so she assumed her seat and plugged in the computer. The screen at the end lit up, displaying her laptop screen in large vivid detail.

Lunsford clicked a few buttons and then a file named SNAKE HUNT. The image of the snake head from the translucent bag filled the screen.

"Straight to the point. The FBI has software that can assist with searches, far more detailed and elaborate than your standard internet. But, as with everything, it takes some intricate direction from the technical side to find what you're looking for. So, I started with a domestic cross-check on this and initially came up with a few possibilities." She clicked a key and an image of four other snake heads appeared.

"First, there're street gangs in Chicago, Detroit, St. Louis,

Baltimore and Philadelphia that all use similar imagery as you can see, but after some analysis of their territory graffities, I just didn't think there was a credible connection."

"Next," she said with another click, "I looked for American corporate logos with the idea that something stamped on a plastic bag may come from a company. A few possibilities arose."

Several potentials were displayed.

"That first one is a company called Venum," she said, moving the arrow cursor across the image on the far left. "They make boxing equipment and wearables. Its close, but clearly not a match. That next one is an alternate logo of the Arizona Diamondbacks baseball team. It's used on a few hats, but I called and talked to their merchandise manager. The color schemes are different, and the head structure of their snake is larger than the one from the bag, not to mention the baseball in its jaws. Again, close, but not a direct match. The one beneath that is from Viper VaporCheck, a product for defense of damaging water vapor and soil gas threats from a company called ISI Building Products. It's a multi-layered polyolefin that serves as a barrier or retardant when buried below a concrete slab—you know, for commercial and residential construction. My first thought was 'Aha,' thinking the substance in the bag may well be this product, but after chemical analysis and a call to ISI that, too, was a dead end."

Silk said, "So, really only three corporate possibilities?"

"That's correct. None a match. But bear with me. I want you to know process so you have comfort with the answer."

"Yes, this is great stuff." Coate said.

"Okay, so I then went to the internet to look at clip art and creative graphics that are for sale online. As you can imagine there's hundreds of possibilities but, so I don't bore you with the bunny trails I pursued, in the end I eliminated all of them."

"That must've taken some detail," Coate said.

"You have no idea. Next, I scoured software games, online games, music acts, event logos, clothing brands, beverage brands, and about another dozen possibilities that I thought were logical. Dead ends, every one of them."

"Are you telling us we don't have any leads?" Coate asked.

Lunsford held up her finger in a 'wait' gesture. "What I'm telling you is I'm confident there's not a domestic match to that graphic."

"But...?" Silk said.

"But after expanding to an international search, I think I found your snake."

She hit a few more keys, keeping the original image visible but shrinking it and moving it to the upper left corner, hitting another key to make it seem transparent. Then she moved to another file within the folder but withheld opening it.

"I can't find out a damn thing about them, but there's a pharmaceutical company in Guatemala called Medicamento. No logo; no *official* graphic. But one of ours came across them a year or so ago. It was a footnote in his file report. A photo taken of a similar bag at or near the shipping docks in Port Isabel, Texas. Our contacts within the Guatemalan government won't confirm or deny. They're uncharacteristically tight-lipped, but it's a match."

She clicked the file and a snake head filled the screen, looking like the identical twin of the original still in the upper corner. She slid the cursor over, right-clicking on that image, then expanded to the exact dimensions of the current image.

Silk watched, amazed. *Perfect. Every detail exact.*

"You're probably going to say I can't, but would it be possible for me to speak with your agent?" Silk asked.

"No. Not possible."

"I figured."

"Only because he's dead. A heart attack killed him a year ago."

Lunsford took a call on her cell and quickly excused herself, having a goodbye with Coate and gently closing the door behind her, leaving Silk with the brown expanding file containing her report and hard copies of every image.

CHAPTER 50

Bertram's positive response to Regina's question of immunity hung in the air.

"I think it terrified him that I didn't react," Bertram continued. "Me, too. After that he treated me different. When they moved us back to the ruins, he put me in that hut away from the others. I was considered untouchable. When the guards found out, they feared me, at least most of them. For a long time he took an interest in Christianity, visiting me for hours at a time, sometimes over dinner in his mansion, asking lots of questions. I thought he was starting to believe but…then he changed."

"Did something specific happen?" Regina asked.

"Well, that's where Dr. Amador comes in."

"She arrived and convinced him otherwise?" Viceroy asked.

"No, not really. Dr. Amador arrived years after we got there. He brought her to my hut one day. She was a molecular scientist of some sort. There were other scientists, too. I liked them. They never hurt us. Please go back and save them when you can."

"What did Dr. Amador do specifically?" Viceroy asked.

"A lot of bloodwork on me. She was trying to figure out my immunity."

"For what reason?" Regina asked.

"Something to do with his business."

"Do you know what his business is?" Regina clarified.

"No. Well, just hold on. I...I recall something about...um..."

The distant sound of whirring helicopter blades crept into their ears. Each stood up and looked in the general direction, to the north. A lone, dim light was hovering in the air, becoming larger as the chopper neared.

"Hammaren," Regina said.

Viceroy calculated about a minute until landing.

"Bertram," Viceroy said, peeling Sandt's eyes away from the sight. The younger man turned. "Do you know what Dr. Amador was doing?"

"That's my freedom," Bertram said to himself, pointing in the air and returning his gaze to the sky, now wholly engaged with the chopper's approach.

Viceroy positioned himself between Bertram and his line of sight, gently but firmly putting his hands on his shoulders.

"Bertram, I just need to know."

As if being pulled back from another world, Bertram shook his head to recalibrate his mind to Viceroy's question. The chopper descended, whipping the air as it alit, the noise now deafening.

"Know?" he shouted back.

"Yes, I need to know," Viceroy said at the top of his lungs.

"About Dr. Amador?"

"Yes."

"She made pills."

Viceroy let go of the man's shoulders.

An Army paratrooper jumped off the chopper, asking the three to move with haste.

Regina boarded first, but before Bertram put his foot on the stair to climb in, he turned and shouted to Viceroy who was standing right behind.

"I just remembered something else. She was doing something with a liquid. He was really excited about it."

Bertram shrugged slightly and bound up the stair.

El Ceibo. Peterson. 'But beware of the mist.' One thing was clear to him: Bertram Sandt was never supposed leave Guatemala.

Never.

CHAPTER 51

The helicopter was a Sikorsky UH-60 Black Hawk, a machine capable of performing a wide array of missions, including aeromedical evacuation. Black, sparsely outfitted, and fast.

Bertram and Regina sat in two cushioned seats in the rear, resting. Viceroy was in a jump seat nearest the pilots wearing a headset connected to the communication system.

"Where are we?" Viceroy said to Ben, his escort from the parachute jump.

"Mexico," Ben replied. "You were camped inside the Guatemala border about two miles."

"You guys were close. You must have a base around here?"

"Near enough. Made for a quick evac. We're headed to base now. I understand you'll all be on a plane to D.C. late tomorrow. There'll be an ambulance waiting for you at Andrews to take you to Walter Reed. They want to get all three of you to the hospital for a medical check. I'm also to inform you that Senator Sandt will meet you there as well, along with a gentleman named Trevor Moreland."

"Great. Thanks."

"Who'd you pick up down there? Last I saw, there were just two of you."

"Just someone we met that needed to get home."

Ben turned around to look at Viceroy and was going to ask

again, but gave him a friendly wink instead. He then settled back into his pilot's seat, hitting the off switch for the communication.

Viceroy joined Bertram and Regina in the more comfortable seats for the remainder of the ride.

Bertram was finishing a comment. "Really, it's hard to talk about it. It was one of the more horrible experiences."

Regina turned to Viceroy as he settled in.

"Bertram was just telling me there's a building there that The Ghost uses as a bit of a torture chamber. New slaves are all branded with a letter 'F' on their palms."

"That's awful," Viceroy said.

"And, well, I'll let Bertram tell you," she said.

Bertram said, "I was just saying that I would be called upon to go in there. People were hung in shackles after getting branded. They would stay in there—sometimes for a week, sometimes for a month. He had me go in and try to speak with them to help their mental state. But I couldn't speak much Spanish or any Chizec, so he allowed me to bring Joaquín with me. We tried to help them, but we weren't very effective. Some died."

"I'm sorry you had to experience that," Viceroy said.

Sensing Bertram was still talkative, Regina said, "Can I ask you another question?"

"Sure."

"Did you meet a man named Theo Gandy? Was he ever there?"

"Yes. I know him. I haven't seen him in a long time, though."

The two detectives sat up, quickly glancing to each other.

"Did you ever give him anything?" Viceroy asked.

"Well, he wanted something that I had on my nightstand. It was a bookmark my father had given me, but he, Mr. Gandy, was so forceful about it I couldn't refuse. So, I gave him that. Now that you brought it up, I think that was the last time I ever saw him. Do you know if he's alive, or where he is?"

Regina thought, *Which way you going Roger? What are you going to tell him?*

Viceroy said, "I don't know if he's alive. We're also trying to find him, and any clue would've been helpful. That's why we asked."

"Someday I hope to see him again."

Bertram sat back without saying another word, suddenly closed in thought. He shifted to look out the small window and soon enough his heavy eyelids took over. Regina took the moment to rest herself.

Before Viceroy closed his eyes, he quietly opened his backpack and pulled out the wooden box, placing it in the seat facing Bertram. Then he unzipped the secured pocket of his pants and lifted out the pouch that Regina had given him the night at the ravine. He tapped her arm, rousing her. She looked at him and saw he was trying to catch some sleep, then spotted the pouch on her leg.

A grateful smile swept across her face as she clutched it.

CHAPTER 52

When the call came from General Hammaren, Jürgen had gathered Liesl, Kendrick and Silk at the mansion and had Robert speed them to the hangar where they boarded the *Niña*. An hour later they touched down at Reagan National Airport and were whisked to Walter Reed Hospital.

After ninety minutes of pensive waiting, Bertram walked through the door of the VIP care room, escorted by Hammaren with Viceroy and Regina in tow. A moment of disbelief evaporated into reality. Jürgen broke down in seconds, crying non-stop for fifteen minutes. Liesl's tears were flowing so hard she was having difficulty controlling her physical shakes. The three held each other in the middle of the room and wouldn't let go.

Two doctors and a few nurses were there as well, standing off to the side, beaming as they watched the Sandt family reunion. Hammaren bear-hugged Viceroy and Regina, displaying a rare personal emotive moment.

Silk stood with his arms crossed, leaning one shoulder against a wall. When the detectives were done being congratulated by the General, they turned to him.

"Hope you two had a great vaca. Nice tans," he said. Regina leapt over and gave him an embrace, followed by Viceroy. "Helluva nice beard," he added.

"Thank you. Just…thank you," Kendrick said in a throaty whisper as he sidled up to them.

All three detectives were standing against the wall nearest the door of the spacious room, a well-appointed suite with a living space and bedroom designed to accommodate high-ranking military members, special patients from the federal government, and foreign ambassadors.

Viceroy said in a low voice, "We're just glad we got him home. I'm sure your docket will be full of media requests once they find out Bertram Sandt is alive and has returned. His story is going to shock the world. Trust me."

Kendrick escorted all three of them out into the hallway, joined by Hammaren; a nurse followed, staying near but not close enough to interrupt.

"I didn't want to say anything in there, but we're going to keep this under wraps for a while," Kendrick said. "He's going to need time to re-acclimate and begin the process of reclaiming his life. I'm sure Jürgen will want to talk with you at length sometime soon."

"How's Liesl?" Regina asked. "She always seems like the forgotten child."

"She loved and missed her brother very much. Maybe now, with him back in her life, she can…straighten a few things out."

Viceroy said, "One other thing. We left behind someone in our flight from the ruins. She died during the escape. Her name was Dr. Catarina Amador. Maybe someone can search that and find out where her family is. I'm sure they'd like to know and hopefully find closure."

Kendrick acknowledged he'd follow up.

"And there's many more up there," Regina added.

Hammaren cleared his throat. "The nurse is going to take you two downstairs for checkups. After that…." He gestured with an open hand to Silk.

Silk said, "After that, we're getting back on the plane. I'll download you when we get wheels up, but we need to get back to Milwaukee tonight. This story ain't over."

"It's actually tomorrow already," Regina said.

Viceroy said, "It's alright, I'm anxious to hear everything."

"I'm going with you," Kendrick said. "I can begin to craft the story and coordinate the upcoming press onslaught much more effectively from my office. I'm going to need time to pull it together, so flying back now works well."

They all agreed to exit as soon as possible. Hammaren turned back, re-entering the Sandt suite, while the detectives followed the nurse.

When all was clear, Kendrick slumped down on a bench in the hallway waiting area. He held his hands over his face, leaning on his thighs with his elbows. *My dear friend Clay Czerwinski, Garrett Newcastle, Theo Gandy, and who knows how many others. The Sandt family. All they stand for and all that's at stake. The motive was undeniable. The decision was correct. For him, for her, for the future.* The collective weight of his life's mosaic congealed into a physical reaction around his chest and stomach.

He dashed to the restroom down the hallway just making it in time.

CHAPTER 53

Silk wasted no time.

The detectives were in the four-seat passenger area. Kendrick chose to sit by the pilots to allow the detectives privacy.

Silk unloaded in a concise, chronological recap covering everything from being shot, to finding Gandy and the night of his murder, the connection to screed, the discovery of the apparent hub at Trapper's Alley and on to the night at O'Leary's, and finally the unnerving warning of doom on April first and all that the insider had said.

Viceroy let him lay it out. With each revelation, Viceroy's pistons were firing, shifting the focus of the entire Sandt commission into a higher gear. He finished the conversation, saying, "Let's get these dots connected before it's too late."

When they landed, a limo took them to the estate, dropping off the detectives at the gatehouse and then onto the mansion for Kendrick. Viceroy instructed Regina and Silk to get some sleep but to reconvene at Emilina at 10:00. Silk pulled away with Regina to take her home.

The lifeless atmosphere of the gatehouse enveloped Viceroy when he entered, the smell and texture of the place extraordinarily foreign. He had to pause just inside the door trying to reverse engineer the reality of where he now stood. Film clips of the morning at the condo when he first met Jürgen and what ensued thereafter played out on his memory screen. He stood unmoving as minutes ticked by. Eventually he made his way to the bedroom, shedding every piece of clothing that was provided to him at the hospital, and sliding between the sheets.

Kendrick went to his suite upon arrival and unlocked the floor safe he kept in the den next to his desk. He shuffled through a few files until he found the correct one, putting it into his briefcase. Hanging on the inside door of the safe were the keys to his Bentley Continental. Hurriedly, he walked through the mansion to the rear exit of the north wing where his white beauty was kept in the pristine carriage house. He hadn't driven it in seven months and hadn't planned to do so again until May, at the earliest. It was for pleasure driving during summer evenings after all.

The quiet but powerful hum of the engine fired, the car almost purring, begging to be driven.

Medicamento. They're piecing it together. It's eminently clear to me now. I've been just a chess piece in the grand scheme this entire time.

As the Bentley idled, he wrote on the front of the envelope: *Open only if Kendrick Winston is dead or missing.*

Not so gently, his foot hit the gas pedal.

CHAPTER 54

A watcher dropped off the female covert operative at Miller Park, pulling the car into a turnabout adjacent to the massive fenced-in parking lot surrounding the baseball stadium.

"Just like Czerwinski," the watcher said before the operative closed the door. "Get in, get out, and don't get caught. Our plant is expecting you at the south side security entrance. I'll be right here when you return."

The operative pulled a black stretch-fabric mask across her face, tucking in her short hair, and gave a thumbs-up. She easily scaled the cyclone fence and took off on a sprint, out of sight from the watcher. Her path was veering as she avoided the pools of light from the tall street lights dotting the lot. A blanket of clouds blocked out the moonlight providing extra cover.

At the south security entrance, a figure stood waiting. Specifically, a stadium security guard.

No words were spoken as he opened the gate, letting her slip in. Silently they walked to the nearest elevator, taking that to the service level—a cement-blocked corridor with low-watt security lights stationed every twenty feet. Jumping in a golf cart, they headed around to the other side of the stadium. The guard slowed to a stop as he steered the cart to a set of double steel doors, unlocking them and flipping on the lights.

The operative stepped into the room, quickly locating the electrical box housed along the inner wall to her right. The grid schematic took her a while to discern before she pulled an item out from her fanny pack and affixed it to a precise set of wires. The guard relocked the door, giving it an extra pull for peace of mind, then u-turned the cart and returned to the elevators, parking it in the exact same position.

The hum of the elevator was the only sound as they climbed. At the main concourse level, they got off and walked back to the security gate. He reopened the lock, shoving it aside just wide enough so the operative could exit.

Before she did, she reached into the backpack and gave him a mister, which he immediately inhaled. Stage three effects instantaneously ebbed away as he leaned against the gate. His breathing eased; his posture taller.

She took the used mister and began her run to the watcher. The guard returned to his station inside and flipped the security cameras back on five minutes later.

CHAPTER 55

In the three days since they returned to Milwaukee, the detectives undertook an exhaustive deconstruction of both Silk's investigation to date and the Guatemala rescue of Bertram Sandt. Some progress made, dead-ends arose, paths to nowhere followed, and a focused picture of it all stayed mostly blurred. A lot of time was expended on what Silk knew of Trapper's Alley and the logistics of the raid in two days, compliments of a gravel hauler he had secured.

And just before Viceroy was set to call it a day, Regina asked a question that caused a prolonged discussion on its merits. Of the hour it took to make a decision, the final ten minutes were spent in silence. Viceroy had to make the decision on whether or not it was time to pull in the FBI and DEA. Viceroy knew the known facts and breadth of the case was why Regina had brought it up, and that she probably was right. What they knew of the Sandt saga now covered two continents, an ostensibly major drug operation, murder, kidnapping, and most likely billions of dollars in the mix, among a few other reasons. Regina and Silk contributed their answers but the final one, the only one that would count, was Viceroy's. Head down, arms crossed, he sat while the other two waited.

"No," he announced; his voice just above a whisper. "No, we're not going to do that. Regina," he added, looking to her, "while you're probably spot on correct, we can't. It's Jürgen Sandt. It's his family. It's his life. And, we're beholden to him. No one else. His long nightmare has come to a close and we need to keep that intact. There'll be a time for those agencies to be pulled in. But not until this is over and we've won, or until we're out of options to solve this ourselves. I will protect him and his family until the end. As official employees, I would hope you're in step with me on that. If you aren't, that's okay, but you need to voice it right now."

Regina just gave him a slight grin. "I'm in. Always. Just wanted to raise the obvious question is all."

Viceroy looked over to Silk.

"We're cool. Never doubt it."

Viceroy smiled.

Brains on empty, Silk and Regina exited into the night to rest up for one more round tomorrow. Viceroy watched out the gatehouse windows until they cleared and turned out of view. He texted the gate's entry code to the one man he wanted to see tonight and sat at his desk. Spinning his chair to look at the interior wall, he stared at the analytical medley in front of him, subconsciously rubbing his fingers through his beard.

Viceroy had written on the huge dry erase wallboard a combination of words, places, names of individuals, chronologies, and other notations connecting Guatemala facts with the Milwaukee investigation into Gandy. Green and blue colored markers drew quasi-links of connectivity among the red-colored ideas, and yellow circles around things he thought landed on possible answers. The eraser was used often as the three detectives tried to weave together the threads. He used the upper third of the board to write down the best notions; black marker on white board. Stark conjecture based on the rainbow of possibilities below.

The "masterpiece of muddiness," as Silk had named it, was magnified by the unrelenting gnawing sensation he had felt in Guatemala. It hadn't left him. Regina either. Something wasn't right. The answer was in the soup in front of his eyes. Whatever was going to occur the next day, April first, was linked to Silk's Milwaukee events and all that transpired in Guatemala. Elusive connective tissue.

He knew the words on the board had the answers. Somewhere.

Viceroy went upstairs and cracked open a chilled drink from the small fridge and wolfed down some trail mix.

As he finished off the final gulp, the phone rang. General Hammaren.

Viceroy said, "General, good evening. Wasn't expecting to hear from *you* at this hour."

"Well, I just left the Sandts and I wanted to let you know they're planning on flying back this Friday, the second. I think I heard them say they'd leave mid-day."

"Okay, great. How's Bertram doing?"

"I've stopped by every day and, from what I can tell and from what Jürgen says, he's doing as best as could be expected. Bertram has had a few moments, but all-in-all he's ready to finally go back home."

"I'm sure being here will help all three of them."

Hammaren said, "Yes, it will. One other thing. I'm flying to Milwaukee on the third and bringing Ambassador Pachuca with me. Kendrick has a plan to let the world know about Bertram, but he wants to coordinate first with the Guatemalan government. There's going to be a hell storm of media for the foreseeable future. I understand there's extreme sensitivities around the Chizec's involvement. Jürgen agrees. I'm just the escort, but I need to head back to D.C. as soon as I get him to Emilina. And we're coming in under the radar, of course."

"Of course."

They clicked off. As he headed back down to the offices, he heard the gate's motion sensor ping. Viceroy watched the vehicle park from the office windows and the big man's shadowy form emerge.

Alright. Time for a chat, the three of us. You know the topic. The tale of Bertram Sandt and a bookmark.

Before the knock, Viceroy swung the door open.

Standing on the landing with open arms was Pastor Greg Oxenhaus.

CHAPTER 56

Silk wolfed down the two-egg special at the chain restaurant across the street from his condo. Not his favorite spot, but the only one open at 6:00 in the morning. He hoped Viceroy and Regina were similarly prepping in whatever fashion worked for them. Their rallying point was 12:40 at the marina where Silk had previously commandeered the canoe.

At 6:45, he called his old friend, Tom Schultz—a grizzled, buzz-cut retired Milwaukee cop he worked with during his tenure as a detective in the department. Schultz answered on the first ring and confirmed he was picking up his brother's gravel hauler at noon and would be there on time, adding that he wasn't going to sit on the sidelines 'if any shit started flowing.' Viceroy used his vast network to bring in seven additional detectives from around the area.

Silk gulped the last of his coffee, then slapped down a ten. The forecast was favorable, with partly sunny skies and a high of fifty degrees. He walked. To think, to theorize for the nine hundredth time the meaning of what the guy with the lisp said, to breathe, to find a hole in the scenario, to rake over his thoughts seeking a hidden clue, and to simply move and get the blood flowing. With each step he felt the adrenaline crying out to break free, like a thoroughbred racehorse stuck in a small paddock for too long. The doomsday moment was another seven hours away. He continued to walk, head down, inward.

Across town, the skin on Regina's fingertips was starting to wrinkle from staying too long under a hot shower. She hadn't moved for fifteen minutes. The pulsating shower head shot gentle splashes of warmth across the back of her neck. The jungle seemed like a distant memory. Today, however, was for mayhem. Another day on the frontline. She slowly turned the handle off and let her body air dry, absorbing the steam that hung in the air all around her, then toweled down before putting on a robe and heading to the kitchen for a cup of black coffee.

At Emilina, Viceroy sat at the end of his bed. Alone. Ox's visit the previous evening was short. The Quintero moment in Guatemala was discussed. So was God. Viceroy's position stayed unchanged. When Ox left, he was alone again. Similarly, the gatehouse sat like an inanimate object in a still life painting. No movement, no noise. No Debbie. The fulfillment of rescuing Bertram Sandt was already dimming from the eclipsed sun of his severed life. He looked at the picture on the dresser of the two of them. Embracing, smiling. Her dimple. Her hair. Her face. The jacket she wore was opened just far enough to expose a portion of her pink t-shirt. One word was visible: *Move*. He stared at it for a long while, then rose and turned the whole of his thoughts to what may lay ahead.

CHAPTER 57

At 12:20, the owner of the marina met Silk and led him upstairs to a man cave-style room where he could wait for the others. Viceroy called and confirmed the additional detectives were on their way.

With time to kill, he switched on the large screen TV and took a seat.

He pressed down on his collarbone and then the knee; both were relatively pain-free. The thought of Theo Gandy laying in the street and the mystery man that shot him flashed like a subliminal ad in his brain.

After a segment on some national news, the local morning hosts came back dressed in Milwaukee Brewers hats and jackets launching into a piece about Opening Day. The final piece was an interview with the head of stadium operations confirming there was an electrical fire late yesterday that broke out on the service level. The guy relayed: "No structural damage occurred to the stadium, but all the hot dog hawking boxes were destroyed in the fire. The good news is, we quickly found a local company to replace them last night, so all is good for baseball fans today."

Silk shot out of the room, bounding down the stairs. It was 12:31. Forty-four minutes to mayhem. He called Schultz. Two minutes out. Viceroy and Regina next. Driving together, five minutes out.

Silk shouted into his phone at Viceroy, "Forget here! Go to

Miller Park. The boxes are for hot dogs. It's Opening Day. Forty thousand people in one spot. He's going to set them off at the game. Get to the stadium."

Viceroy acknowledged, wheeling his vehicle in a sharp turn on the freeway to cut across the median. Two accidents unfolded in his rearview mirror. Regina set the siren on the roof as Viceroy floored it, weaving in and out of vehicles. She called her contacts at Milwaukee PD, then was patched through to the captain on site at the stadium with her contact at HQ still on.

"Kollman," the guy said.

The contact said, "Listen quick. I got Regina Cortez on the line. She's got an emergency and she's legit."

Regina flooded out the information. Kollman clicked off and sent an APB across the channel to his team of thirty cops, most of them positioned outside the stadium. They rushed to the gates, desperately trying to muscle their way through the throng of fans still in line. Kollman jumped on his cell to activate another ten personnel. Eight of those peeled off. The other two raced to the commissary of the concessionaire on the service level. Pandemonium started bubbling up at the gates as a terrorist attack became the buzz.

Inside the vehicle, Viceroy slammed his fist on the steering wheel at the line of red taillights bumper-to-bumper as they reached the outer limits of the ballpark's footprint.

"Hang on," Viceroy said.

He took a ramp down, riding the shoulder, almost clipping cars as he flew by. At the bottom he made a sharp right U-turn onto a grassy area and gunned it onto railroad tracks paralleling the freeway.

"Oh, shit," Regina screamed as the vehicle went airborne, the driver's side landing on the interior of the track.

Viceroy let up just for a moment then hit the gas again; the bumpy ride took them adjacent to the large parking lot surrounding the stadium. The lot was jammed, every one of the twelve thousand spaces filled, and fans were streaming to the gates. He slammed on the brakes at a visual breach point. They scaled a cyclone fence and raced towards the nearest gate, picking their way and shouting at fans to "clear" as they ran with guns held high.

***

As Viceroy and Regina were nearing the gate, Silk boarded the passenger seat of the gravel hauler while the eight other detectives piled into the dump trailer. Schultz pulled out of the marina and onto the road straight to Trapper's Alley, gunning it to full speed as they neared the dead end. The truck handled the impact without a problem, then hit a depression in the ground, sliding to a stop halfway between the shoreline buildings and the big one.

Silk opened the door as a rain of bullets ricocheted off the vehicle. He spotted the sniper on the roof and in response positioned his body on the cab step using the door as cover, then fired three times, hitting the guy on the last shot. The sniper disappeared. All eight detectives jumped out and took positions around the truck. Schultz stayed behind the wheel, ready to rescue them or ram the next obstacle.

Inside the building, The Lisp and four others looked up as the sniper dragged himself across a skylight pane leaving a trail of blood behind, before he stopped and went limp. Two additional sentries came into view, rushing to replace his position. On the floor, a female grabbed a detonator switch off the desk and flicked it on, then again, then once more. Nothing. She and two others scrambled for guns lined up in a rack against the wall and ran to the exit door. The Lisp stayed seated at the computer with the flash drive in his pocket.

The Ghost calmly sat next to him.

***

Viceroy and Regina had made it to the gate, barking and pushing upstream as they maneuvered to the entrance with fans trying to turn back to their cars. The cop at the entrance waved them through. Inside, the pandemonium level was less. Most fans were already inside the stadium when Kollman activated the security. Regina called him, telling her where to meet. They sprinted, weaving and shouting as they ran down the first base side concourse to the small security office. He shouted to her, but the noise level was deafening as the crowd cheered the end of the National Anthem and the transition to energetic music blaring out the stadium speakers. Regina pointed off to her right where the concourse straightened. Viceroy counted at least twenty cops. Kollman saw them and pulled them into the middle of the group.

Viceroy spoke to everyone, turning clockwise as he yelled above the music. "We got four minutes. Every hot dog vendor you see, take them down, get their boxes and get them outside. Toss them if you have to! Don't shoot the boxes. Move."

Kollman barked out orders. Half the group ran towards ramps to take them to the upper levels of the stadium, the other half split, going left and right on the main concourse with another group covering the seating bowl. Viceroy and Regina separated to go do what they could. He stayed on the lower level while she followed the upper level group.

***

Trapper's Alley was a gun battle. The three from inside, plus the two additional roof snipers, had the team trapped, unable to do much except fire off a shot when they could.

Shultz shouted, "Everyone get back in and ready to roll. Silk, buckle up."

The men scrambled to get back into the dump trailer. Schultz hit the gas, steering straight for the three ground-level attackers near the exit door. Bullets careened off the side of the trailer from the snipers. One bullet pierced the windshield and embedded itself in Schultz's seat. He didn't notice or didn't care. The three other shooters scrambled away, each one picked off by a detective with full cover from the trailer. The roof snipers stopped shooting and disappeared. The hauler kept going, ramming into the warehouse's exit door, destroying it and the door jamb, creating a small space in which to breach the inside.

***

Viceroy checked his watch. Two minutes. The group he trailed disappeared around the bend in the concourse. Fans everywhere. Hawkers everywhere. Amid the crazy, he heard a faint "hot dogs here" voice. He stopped, turned, seeking, surveying. Across the concourse and up a way stood a chubby man wearing the food hawker uniform holding a box above his head. Viceroy ran right at him.

***

The detectives jumped out and rushed to the damaged doorway as Schultz hit reverse. Silk tried to get through the opening created by the truck, but his large frame made it impossible. The door itself was a twisted hunk of metal. Four of them pushed the mass with all their strength and shoved it back another two feet. They heard Schultz's revving and backed away. He floored it again, this time blowing the whole door and jamb back into the warehouse. The team moved in; guns drawn. Silk motioned five of them up the stairs to track the snipers. The other two and Silk stepped carefully forward. In the dusty air from the impact, he made out the guy from O'Leary's facing a computer at the desk. Silk began a slow walk with his gun pointed directly at him, while the other two fanned to either side in the same mode. Four steps in, two shots were fired from above. They spun and watched a body fall to the floor, landing with a thud. A sniper.

***

The blind-side impact of Viceroy's body slamming into the hawker was more than enough to dislodge him from his box. Viceroy stayed on top of him, shouting to fans that had quickly gathered to get away, pointing his gun in the air to impart them to follow orders. Screams and chaos erupted around him.

***

High above the field in the upper level of the left field corner, a woman sat in the last row watching everything but the baseball diamond. The music was loud, the sell-out crowd retaking their seats following the anthem. An odd movement to her right caught her attention. A police officer appeared in the vomitory two sections over, causing a stir with fans as he frantically tried to run up the stairs. She knew what he was looking for, but that he also had

245

guessed wrong. Directly below her another man appeared in white pants and a red-striped shirt holding a metal box high above his head and shouting his sales pitch. She watched the policeman spot him, then point and shout to deaf ears before flying back down the stairs. The hot dog vendor proceeded towards her, and when he reached the halfway point, she hit the send button on her phone. The sides of the box flying open and the appearance of the policeman at the bottom of the stairs happened simultaneously. Seconds later a fine, clear mist shot out from the box in multiple directions.

***

Viceroy rolled off the guy, grabbed the box and ran for the nearest exit. Something clicked inside as if it was just turned on before he could clear the stadium. He knew of no other action he could take than to run faster.

***

Silk shouted at The Lisp. He didn't move, so he edged closer and shouted again. Same result.

A call from above. One of the detectives. "We got him. We got the other one."

Silk turned back, now just three feet away from the desk. The proximity gave him the clear picture of The Lisp through the density of the dusty air. Plainly visible was a bullet hole at the base of his neck and a line of blood running underneath his collar. On the computer screen was simply the word ACTIVADO. Spanish, but he understood what it meant. The side of the computer was without the flash drive. He saw it sitting on the floor, crushed as if someone had stepped on it. *Oh my God.* Silk grabbed his flash drive, plugging it into the port. When the pop-up came on the screen, he hit enter and waited; his breath was now coming in short, quick gasps. Another pop-up message. CONFIRMAR. Silk hit the SI button.

***

Viceroy had reached the exit and was going to fling the box into a patch of landscape near a walkway when the humming stopped. The box felt dead, silenced. He squatted down, hesitant to do anything, but with the chaos of innocent people all around him his protective instincts kicked in. He hustled over to the landscaping and opened the box. The sight and smell of hot dogs wrapped in foil filled his senses. The rest of the box just sat there, inert.

***

In an abandoned building, The Ghost exited the secret tunnel. He looked out the window to Trapper's Alley, his eyes scanning the property.

"You were perfect," he said out loud, then spotted the limo, cross-checking its arrival with the time on his watch. A deep, satisfied inhale followed.

As it drove away, the U.S. Army General seated across asked, "Success?"

The Ghost beamed. "Beyond all measure. The one off-line box was executed with precision. The other boxes were never going to open to activate. I didn't need two thousand victims, just enough to send the message of what we're capable of. Now, the ingenious and masterful final stroke can be achieved."

The General grabbed two stem glasses, giving one to The Ghost before popping open a chilled bottle of Krug Clos d'Ambonnay and offering a toast.

CHAPTER 58

"Eighty-seven," Viceroy said under his breath as he jogged through the rolling forested hills of Emilina. 'Eighty-seven fans at the game inhaled the odd mist sprayed from a hot dog box on the stadium's upper level,' the reporter had said.

He had been running for thirty minutes through the rain, having just arose late morning after a mere three hours of sleep. The jog was more for clearing his head than anything else. On his feet were the shoes that once held the note from Debbie. He looked down to watch them splatter water with each step, as if to push back from the event that had taken her life.

The mania from two days ago was still raging. The interim forty-eight hours was a tornado of police work, calls, meetings, and on-site investigations from the events at the stadium and the related raid at Trapper's Alley, all of it still in process. Viceroy had supplied as much information as he could hoping to maintain the buffer between the atrocities and the Sandt family for as long as possible.

The Sandts had flown back yesterday as well, and Jürgen had reached out when they landed, inviting him to dinner with the family. At that moment, Viceroy was inside Trapper's Alley and had to take a rain check, telling him that he and team were assisting law enforcement with the stadium investigation, withholding telling him there were likely ties to Bertram's ordeal.

Silk was keeping him abreast of information as he worked alongside Milwaukee PD. He had called three hours prior to tell Viceroy the authorities in Port Isabel, Texas, had confirmed that Mitchell Industries offices and warehouse were vacated there as well. They didn't know when.

Regina had left earlier, driving to Chicago's O'Hare airport to catch the noon non-stop to Texas. Viceroy had ruled out the *Niña*, wanting to avoid any involvement from the Sandts. The plan was for her to stay in Port Isabel for as long as the investigation required and possibly get to Guatemala if the events now unfolding would require one of them there.

A bend in the trail took Viceroy over a small hill, circling him towards the mansion, now two hundred yards to his right. Through the trees he admired its beauty and old-world stateliness as it sat in a natural bowl among four small hills. The trail cleared an opening in the trees, hugging the vast lawn of the mansion's grounds, bringing him within fifty yards. He spotted just one vehicle, a black sedan parked on the brick apron, and remembered that Hammaren was bringing Ambassador Pachuca in for that meeting. *Guess they've arrived.*

His path took him back into the woods, over a postcard-worthy bridge spanning a small stream before spilling out to the gatehouse parking area. The rain picked up intensity as he slowed from jogging to walking. When he reached the front door, he sat on the step, letting the downpour cool him before taking on the tasks ahead: a shower, food, and another crack at studying the wallboard.

He ran his fingers through his beard thinking the only reason it sat on his face was his inability to shave during the hunt for Bertram, and the whirlwind of activity that unfolded once they returned. *Get rid of it. Fresh start. Maybe that'll jump start things.*

Upstairs, he stood in front of the large sink mirror looking over his entire body. Several scratches were still in the angry red stage on his hands and forehead, but the two bruises on his right thigh were finally turning greenish and less painful. He studied the beard. The hairs mostly matched the brown color on the top of his head, but mixed in were red and gray ones. He seized the razor, fingering around the bottom of the drawer to find the beard attachment, and began running hot water in the sink. "Plugging you in," he voiced to the razor, "and taking you out," nodding to his face in the mirror.

He flicked on the switch and brought the razor up towards the left ear to begin. Before he made contact, he froze. Gradually he lowered his hand, and in slow-motion turned off the water, then the razor.

'Plugging you in and taking you out.' *Peterson. He's got the in and the out now.* 'Would hate to see what I look like in a photo.' *So did the Chizec.*

Dropping the razor, he threw on jeans and a sweatshirt at hyper-speed, fumbled to put on the same tennis shoes, then launched himself down the stairs, taking two at a time to the office.

Using Regina's computer, he pulled up her Guatemala photo gallery file, clicking it open and started scrolling, searching... searching. *Got ya.*

The full body vertical photo of the Chizec at the falls. Viceroy studied it, starting at the head and scrolling towards the feet. He stopped at the mid-section of the photo capturing the stomach and arms from the elbows down. *Something's wrong. A duck in a robin's nest.* He continued to scroll south to the legs, stopping at the knees. *Wait a second.* Scrolling the cursor back up, he stopped again at the mid-section, zooming in to the left hand, the one holding the spear. The Chizec's index finger pointed straight across his body. What's he doing? Viceroy grabbed the photo with the cursor, zoomed closer and deftly moved it along that direction, stopping at the man's other hand. He blinked twice, trying to make sure he was in fact seeing what he saw. *I'll be damned.*

He vaulted over to the wallboard, picked up the eraser pad, and wiped out half the words and sentences on display. In rapid fire the connective tissue started to form. As the new words and concepts disgorged from his brain, he furiously wrote them down.

At one succinct moment, he abruptly stopped and physically stepped back as if he had slammed into a wall at full speed, then dropped the black marker on the floor. He pivoted to his desk, calling up the file for the video that launched the hunt for Bertram Sandt. When Gandy turned to depart the camera shot, he hit pause. There it was. *All this time in plain view.*

Viceroy glanced over to the wallboard. Floating words that were previously untethered sprouted tentacles, connecting to other words, forming understandings and clarity. Misters, screed bags, Bertram's 'We'd be joining his army,' and Peterson's 'You'd become part of his army,' pills, Medicamento…the bag, Gandy's mask. *They're all the same. The snake heads. All four.*

Staring at the images, he punched in Regina's number.

"Please pick up," he said out loud. One ring, two rings, then three, four, "Damn…"

"Hello," Regina said in the middle of the fifth. "Roger?"

"Reg! Gandy. What's 'ghost' in Spanish?"

"Fantasma."

F. Oh my God! He's…here.

Without clicking off, he flew upstairs and grabbed the Glock and magazines, then ran out the gatehouse front door, sprinting through the rain across the parking lot on his race to the mansion.

Left behind in the solitude of the office, the right wrist of the Chizec stayed enlarged on the computer screen, displaying a perfect tan line that only comes from a wristwatch.

CHAPTER 59

Without any other reference point to guide him, Viceroy chose the front door.

The mansion boasted three enormous wings off the main quarters, which was a two-story circular structure of five thousand square feet. Viceroy had only been inside once, early on when he accepted Jürgen's offer. All he could recall now as he ran was the huge atrium. It followed the contours of the main quarters. Circular, with half-moon grand staircases against the outer walls uniting at the second floor to a pillared balcony overlooking the space. A marble floor reflected the artwork on the walls.

Rain-soaked and breathing hard, Viceroy gripped the gold-plated handle and turned it. To his surprise, the door was unlocked.

He stepped through to a rather unassuming carpeted vestibule with a view to the atrium straight ahead. Muffling a small cough, he deftly closed the door, listening.

Silence.

He moved forward, each step firm but staying on the balls of his feet, towards the atrium and marble floor. A plan rapidly formed in his head to take the left staircase up to the balcony and see where that led, but his first step onto the marble emitted a piercing squeal from the wet rubber sole. He immediately backed up and waited to see if anything reacted to the noise.

Safe.

He took off the shoes and ran to the staircase, itself graced with a plush red-carpet stair runner with small logos of the old Sandt Brewery weaved into the fabric. Sitting on the first step, he re-laced, then moved up the flight to the balcony where the carpeting continued down a wood-paneled hallway leading away from the atrium.

Step-by-step, Glock in position, he walked. Three closed doors spaced out every twenty feet lined the left side. As he passed each one, he stopped and listened before moving to the next. At the end of the corridor hung an extraordinarily large portrait of Volker Sandt. Viceroy stared at the founder for just a moment then turned right as the corridor continued, and then shortly, a left. When he made the second turn, he heard muffled voices.

He squatted, trying to center the source. Two options lay ahead fifty paces. To the left, a large wooden door, slightly ajar. To the right, a stone arch leading to wherever that would take him.

Knowing he'd figure it out when he reached the end, he simply stood and walked with purpose, gun pointed. At the juncture, he knew the direction of the voices and turned to face the stone archway, which opened to a small semi-circle shaped balcony overlooking a large room. Viceroy could only see the top half of the room from where he stood. Straight ahead in his sight was the upper reaches of a two-story fireplace and what he could see of the crown molding. To the left, he spied the edges of a chandelier. He crouched again, listening to the voices below.

"Prayers won't help you." *Male. Deep-toned.* Viceroy couldn't recognize the voice, so he concentrated on the man's cadence.

"Leave him be." *Jürgen.* "My goodness, please put it down."

"Then let me repeat," the male said. "All we need is you to make one phone call. That's all it will take. And what you saw two days ago at the baseball game will become commonplace. Milwaukee will be mine within a month." *Hispanic accent.*

"How could you do this?" Jürgen implored. "And you two, your betrayal will never be rewarded. Not by me, not by any Sandt."

"Enough, Jürgen. Just, for *once*, be quiet. This is one situation you have no control over." *Hammaren.* "I signed on because of these two. Your only son a religious nut and your only daughter a drug addict. Your wealth and the Sandt name would've been squandered. At least now there is a path forward."

A woman's voice shouted. "You pathetic bastards." *Liesl.*

The male laughed. "Which one should we kill first, Jürgen?"

No response.

"I think it should be you, Bertram," the man continued. "Are you going to rely again on your Jesus? Because so far, He's greatly forsaken you and your family."

In a voice stronger than Viceroy had ever heard him speak, Bertram said, "He frustrates the devices of the crafty, so that their hands cannot carry out their plans. He catches the wise in their own craftiness, and the counsel of the cunning is brought to a quick end."

The crack of a skin-on-skin slap cut through the air.

"Bertram," Jürgen shouted.

"Time's up," the male said. "I'm handing you my phone. Just punch the send button. It's a direct dial to Dr. Yarling's cell phone. And while you do that," he added, with the sound of a gun being cocked, "your long-lost son awaits the outcome."

Viceroy launched.

He took two running steps to the balcony rail, guessing he could reach the chandelier by using the railing as a springboard. But the railing was a bit higher than he had calculated and it took some momentum away from his leap. Now on a higher and sharper downward arc, he extended his left hand and caught the bottom of the chandelier instead of the higher point he had intended. His grip on one of the arms held, but the entire structure ripped off its mounts in the ceiling, sending him spinning towards a corner. He let go before it crashed into the side wall; he broke his fall on a chair near a window, first hitting it and then crashing to the floor.

Hammaren's military training moved him instinctively to a forty-five-degree angle towards and to the right, but Viceroy was quicker than the elder General and fired a bullet, landing it in his chest.

As if in slow motion, Viceroy spun, eyes sweeping across the room, charting the situation in a flash of his mind's eye. Seated in a chair in front of the fireplace sat Jürgen, face contorted in a moment of fear and surprise. Next to him in another chair was Liesl, but all he saw was the back of her head with her arms handcuffed behind the chair back, as she was diving to the floor. On a couch across from those two, straight ahead of him but slightly back, was Bertram; he was also moving to the floor. And, as he finished the sweep, Viceroy spotted the male almost with his gun barrel pointing in his direction.

Viceroy pitched himself towards the couch, using the one side as a barrier between him and the shooter. Three bullets fired, embedding in the couch as he heard the man shout at him in Spanish. Viceroy placed both hands under the couch's frame near the small legs and lifted with all his might. He rose with it, knowing that Bertram was off. At the apex, he shoved the entire mass towards the spot where the man was, then dove towards the fireplace while firing four straight rounds at the other end of the couch as he stretched parallel two feet off the floor.

He rolled towards Jürgen, coming to rest near his feet. The couch had done its job of making the man move to his right, forcing him into the same line as Viceroy's bullets. Viceroy looked up from his position on the floor to see the man writhing in pain on his back, holding his abdomen and screaming things in Spanish. Viceroy shot glances everywhere on the ground looking for the man's gun, seeking it, taking three long strides in a desperate search for the weapon.

Viceroy stood there now, in the middle of the room over the bleeding man on the floor. Hammaren lay still on the window-side. Liesl stood, having wriggled herself free of the chair back. Bertram stayed down, somewhat in a fetal position, softly talking to himself and inaudible to everyone else.

Still seated was Jürgen Sandt. He saw his son and then his daughter, both alive, both seemingly unharmed. His eyes turned on Viceroy.

Viceroy pulled his gun up, pointing it at the man on the floor, wanting to say a thousand things. The sum of it all lay at his feet, sweating profusely, in pain and, finally, in custody. The damage-maker, murderer, horror-creator, life-destroyer—the person thought for so long to be a figment of everyone's imagination—now in the flesh, bleeding and at his mercy. The Ghost of Guatemala.

"Don't," Jürgen said, calmly and with compassion. "It's over now."

Viceroy very slowly peeled his eyes away and locked in with Jürgen.

The unspoken moment said everything. Viceroy knew the task, once thought to be an impossible undertaking, was finally complete and a miracle reunion the fruit of his team's efforts. A broken family could begin to heal.

As for Jürgen Sandt, the pride in knowing he was right, welled up. That Roger Viceroy *was* the man for the job. Not because of his brilliant detective skills, but rather, his broken character. It was his secret ingredient even if Roger never recognized it. Sandt knew before he ever rang Viceroy's doorbell months prior. Two shattered families. One mutual event. Healing.

Jürgen voiced one final thought.

"Kendrick," he said.

The crack of another gunshot split the air. Viceroy reacted in the direction of the sound, to a side room off the interior wall. He cautiously pushed the door open further with his feet, holding both hands on his gun, ready for whatever was inside. The room was entirely empty, except for the body of Kendrick Winston on the floor.

CHAPTER 60

Inmate #22576-E sat across the table from Viceroy, his shaven bald head sticking out of his gray and black striped uniform. His arms chained to a chair bolted to the floor. Real name unknown. The Ghost of Guatemala.

Viceroy sat relaxed, his left leg across his right, wearing gray slacks, button-collared black shirt, and a black corduroy blazer. A beard still graced his face, finely trimmed and a new permanent addition.

Minutes passed in silence as the two took each other in. Finally, The Ghost spoke. "Why are you here?"

"I needed to see you one last time," Viceroy said.

"Why?"

"To tell you that a cure is looking possible. A permanent reversal of the damage screed had on its victims."

"How?"

"Bertram. His DNA. But of course, you knew he was the key all along. It's too bad Dr. Amador isn't here today to see the results.

257

All her research was recovered, including her secret experiments to find a cure. Jürgen is setting up a research lab. The Sandt Center for Molecular Health Science, now under construction on the grounds at Trapper's Alley."

"Inspiring. How *is* Bertram?"

"Fantastic. He's working with the Guatemalans on developing clinics across the country to be ready to cure the people you enslaved. And there's a good many."

"And Jürgen?"

"Older. Same energy, same outlook. You wouldn't know he's eighty."

"Not surprised."

Viceroy uncrossed his legs and sat forward, leaning his elbows on the table. "Liesl voluntarily became the alpha patient, and while there's been a few harrowing moments, she's blazing the trail with the doctors. She's becoming a hero to a degree."

"Good for her. But I'm going to miss Kendrick more. He was a friend."

"Despite your scheme to use him?"

The Ghost flashed Viceroy a surprised look.

"No, no, don't pretend you're shocked. It took a while, but I got the jigsaw puzzle put together. I know how you engineered the entire thing. You're a study in blind ambition, evil calculation on a grand scale, complete disregard for all that is good, and corrupted motivation. A story like no other. What you did was gruesome."

"What I did was rise from the ashes to become a fairy tale."

Viceroy just stared back. A look of tranquility on his face.

The Ghost continued, "Tell me, Señor Viceroy, how you completed your jigsaw puzzle."

Leaning back, Viceroy said, "This tale began a long time ago, to the discovery of a berry with the most powerful addictive properties the world has ever seen. A young boy of twelve or thirteen goes on a logging trip with his father, who is murdered in the middle of the jungle for reasons unknown. But the boy, assumed dead, survived unbeknownst to anyone and ended up at some ancient ruins no one knew existed and discovered the secret canyon. There he stays for a good number of years. By age twenty or so, he crafts a plan, a gateway to emerge from the jungle and establish an empire. The vehicle is a berry that he, himself, has a lifelong addiction to. And the boy, now a young man, seizes on an opportunity to reap a consistent flow of cash by creating a user base that needed the product to stay alive. And, most important, do it in a way that kept him invisible. Become a ghost."

He shrugged acknowledgement.

"Step one was to leave the ruins. You made your way to Guatemala City and hooked the government leaders to give you cover and power to execute your grand scheme. Fairly easy task. Eat a berry, receive instructions on how to stay alive by following your orders."

"It wasn't easy at first. It took a few deaths by withholding the berry to convince them," The Ghost interjected.

"Sorry to hear it was such a hardship. Step two, you needed a labor pool for harvesting and distribution. One of your more imaginative strategies was the invention of the Chizecs. A people born from enslaving the villages at the base of the mountains. The berry was your weapon. The government went along. After all, how could they not? You held their deaths in your hands. They granted you an entire rain forest in which to operate, free from inquiring eyes. The creation of the Chizecs was the brilliant, calculated protection you needed to operate without interference. No one allowed in, granting you a zone of absolute safety and security."

"Every general needs an army."

"And an enemy to battle. Step three was to eliminate the competition. The drug cartels. It took several years, but again you did it with screed. Yet, you were intelligent enough to understand that keeping those enterprises afloat was good business, so you made the gangs an extension of your own empire where they continued dealing street drugs, with all profits flowing to you. The gang members swelled your army to thousands of pretend Chizecs, sentinels, watchers, and enforcers. And El Ceibo, well, that served as sort of a company town where you allowed them some rest and relaxation, like any good employer would do."

"The whip is good. But once loyal, it was in my best interest to keep them that way."

"Wonderful foresight. By this time, you're in your mid-thirties, and you're asking yourself, how are you going to grow? What move would launch you from a Central American fairy tale to the most feared force the world might ever see? Bold decision, but your answer was to conquer America. Your new gang extensions already had distribution here, so why not use it? America was the pinnacle, the summit. A large customer pool and the world's greatest wealth. Target the super wealthy and charge them half a million dollars per year to stay alive. But you were missing a *significant* major puzzle piece. Namely, securing cover with the U.S. Government. How to accomplish *that*?"

"It was a challenge to be met."

"Step four. Enter Cesar Quintero. Your second greatest invention. Someone to facilitate your plan at high levels. An individual who could maneuver through a tangled web. An insider, so to speak. Glib, with charm and connections. This man would be everything you needed. A Guatemalan who speaks English, has Ivy League schooling, but most importantly is connected politically and economically with both countries. You gave him a bum arm, but that added to his influence. It made him a sympathetic figure." Viceroy veered a bit. "Where did you learn English, by the way?"

"I kidnapped a teacher from the American School of Guatemala. I gave him five months. He did it in three."

"And then you killed him."

"You'll never know."

Viceroy paused, trying to peer behind the man's eyes, into his soul. Nothing.

Viceroy continued, "Besides Quintero's arm, the man's look was vitally important. Always impeccably dressed. Interestingly, he never went to Princeton. Instead, he arrived on that campus with one express purpose: find the chancellor and give her a berry. A day later he leaves New Jersey with an agreement the records would be falsified. He now exists forever as a graduate in exchange for a lifetime supply of the very thing that kept her alive until she passed away some years ago."

"Chancellor Judith Merrill."

Viceroy tossed a gym bag onto the table, unzipping it. The Ghost stared at it before shifting his eyes to Viceroy.

"Cesar Quintero had a few other identifiable attributes," Viceroy said as he reached into the bag and pulled out items. "Wire rim glasses, a gold-edged tooth, alligator shoes, a large mole which you simply attached to this piece of paper when not in use, cufflinks, a mustache, and a ponytail that was easily interweaved into your otherwise normal length hair. Oh, and another added feature was the voice. It had to be distinct and quite different than The Ghost. Cesar Quintero was high-pitched."

The Ghost looked over the items on the table, skipping from one to another, then smiled to himself.

"We found these in your Washington apartment. Soon, you weaved your way into the political scene in D.C. A Guatemalan national with plenty of money and connections to more. Over the next five years or so, you work the system. The politicians, the federal agencies, the contractors, and whoever else would be a path of influence. And, you supply them with the same for Guatemala. A tidy position to be in, and all the while building relationships and embedding your influence all over town because you knew, one day, you would launch your attack on the United States. And in that window of time, you begin your friendship with perhaps the most powerful politician of them all: Jürgen Sandt."

"A perfect plan, you must admit."

"Well-executed, I'll give you that. With your alter-ego Quintero entrenched, it all could be activated. At that time, you were closing in on your late forties and at some point, you launched step five. Common street drugs for common Americans; screed for the select few able to undertake that kind of payment annually. You grew screed users, adding eight to ten customers each year. Always careful on who it was. Our estimate is you had close to four hundred customers, representing two hundred million a year, and that was growing. A lot of Hollywood types, tech titans, entrepreneurs, and the rest made up of heirs to fortunes."

"Four hundred and eleven, to be exact."

"So, I was off by five million."

The Ghost sneered.

"All was going so very well until one fateful day your world was hit with a catastrophic event. Unexpectedly, a missionary team from America stumbled into your Guatemalan kingdom. It wasn't a large group, but they had crossed into the forbidden zone. Using your Chizec front, you had them captured and brought to the ruins. The only problem was, you were unaware that one of the people on the mission team was the son of the billionaire senator who you had befriended. Bertram told us where you took them."

Viceroy noted a slight flinch in The Ghost's face.

"And then, you fed them, each receiving a berry they hadn't seen before. You knew full well Bertram Sandt would be hooked, and then he would have to stay silent. But something happened you couldn't fathom as a possibility. His immunity. Now your head is spinning. Your universe hangs in the balance. Kill them and the weight of the nations will come crashing down on Guatemala. Jürgen Sandt's son, after all. And under that spotlight you assumed that someone in the system would crack and squeal. But, if you keep them alive, they live to tell the truth. What's the path forward; the compromise position? And then it hits you. Externally, let the world think they've simply disappeared. Perhaps they met their fate at the hand of the Chizecs. And since the Chizecs were off-limits, well…that became an easy out. It was a theory, but really anything could have happened to them. The world will never know. But internally, it's a different story. You chose to, in fact, keep them alive. Bertram was given special treatment because he is who he is, and he's immune. The others, simply workers.

"You and the Guatemalan government make sure the first hunt for Bertram goes nowhere. Then things stay somewhat easy for a long time, years in fact, until one day an idea comes over you. A wild, ingenious scheme forms in your head. What if Bertram's DNA could be tapped into to create a counter-drug to screed, one that was a control substance and not a cure? You would reap the benefits of both ends of the business. Better yet, take it to the masses. Get the population hooked on screed, and then be the sole owner of the only medicine on the planet that can control it. A cure means a one-time customer, but a controlling drug means a customer for life."

Sniffling before speaking, The Ghost said, "Brilliant, don't you think?"

"Evil is what I think. So now, step six. You build a world-class laboratory in your jungle kingdom begging for a world-class scientist in biomedical engineering and, hopefully, a passion for molecular manipulation. There were a few to choose from, but you plucked the cream of the crop from the streets of Baltimore. Dr. Catarina Amador. She ultimately delivers you the drug you now call Ovalar. Your new-found plan is beginning to take shape. But you need to weaponize screed into mist form because you need mass quantities of customers. Dr. Amador comes through yet again."

"She did."

"In between all this, you knew you needed a legitimate pharmaceutical company to distribute Ovalar to the public. One that solely owns the patent. And to get it into the U.S., you'll need Congress and the FDA to grant your drug orphan status, otherwise you'd have to partner with an American-based pharmaceutical. That couldn't be allowed. So, step seven was Medicamento and an international shipping company under the alias of an American businessman named Mitch Mitchell. Mitchell Industries out of Port Isabel, Texas, serving your operational needs. Your cover for distribution of screed for the masses was Guata-Fruto, the import-export brand of Mitchell Industries."

Silence.

"The final step was getting Kendrick Winston hooked, Jürgen's right-hand man, compelling him to be a very powerful advocate for Medicamento's entry into the U.S. market with his influence in Washington. And that led to hooking Liesl and getting seventy-five million from her in the process. Clever. But politically, there were three people you needed. Garrett Newcastle, Dr. Alicia Yarling, and most importantly, Senator Clay Czerwinski. If they all fall into place, you're off to the races. As Quintero, you use Kendrick Winston like a marionette, manipulating him to press the politicians to move along with the approval of Ovalar's orphan status for Medicamento's sole benefit. But it doesn't quite go as smoothly as you need it to. The politicians aren't playing along and your efforts stall."

"They were fools."

"Or, maybe they were upstanding. But it hatched two chess moves. Chess move A was orchestrating Bertram's return, for it would cement your ultimate checkmate. Get him home, rally around the miracle with the family, then Cesar Quintero—the public character you played oh, so well—can show his true self, The Ghost of Guatemala, and force the end game.

"First to go find Bertram was Theo Gandy. You help him with his strategy and he unwittingly fell into your trap. I don't know what happened down there, but clearly Gandy messed up your plan somehow and you had to tack in a new direction. You make Gandy a screed slave and got him to befriend Bertram. Over time, Gandy finds an item he can use, per your instructions. A bookmark and a wooden box. Once he has it, you send him back to Milwaukee, housing him at Trapper's Alley. One night, he receives instructions to hang the satchel at Emilina's front gate, knowing all along it will motivate Jürgen to send another detective to find his son. Namely me. The rest of the story we all know."

"It worked perfectly."

Viceroy ignored the comment.

"Chess move B was to streamline your political risks on a parallel path with the third search for Bertram. You had to kill off Newcastle to ensure you were dealing with only one powerful influencer, Senator Czerwinski. With Newcastle gone, Yarling would do whatever Czerwinski tells her to. Only Czerwinski could make everything happen. Somehow you get him to swallow a berry, but the man never turned. He surprisingly resisted you to the end, telling Medicamento to take a hike. You had him killed in such a manner as to look like natural causes, and focused all your attention on Dr. Alicia Yarling, the last person who could officially green light Ovalar. You knew she might crack under that pressure, so you played the final hidden ace you had tucked in your sleeve, or better stated, tucked in Guatemala. The return of Bertram."

"That is my greatness. Manipulation and decisive action."

"You out-maneuvered yourself. The final play was to withhold pulling the trigger in exchange for Jürgen placing a phone call to Yarling. And to put an exclamation point on it, you needed a mass addiction of innocent people in Sandt's hometown to raise the stakes to a height where even he couldn't resist your demand. For everyone knows the Sandt name and legacy is wholly intertwined with the well-being of Milwaukee. Perfect timing. The baseball home opener. Lots of bodies."

The two sat in a stare down, each waiting for the other to make the next verbal play. Over a few minutes, The Ghost's outward demeanor became more and more defiant until he broke the silence. "You went down there, and it all came to be as I had planned. From that first meeting at the embassy, you just didn't strike me as a threat. I miscalculated your intellect."

Viceroy said, "No, that's not it. You just never considered that a broken man's views are through a different lens. You see, the entire time I was in Guatemala, I knew something was off. The rescue was just a little *too* easy, a little *too* coincidental. We're there a few hours and meet two people who have a story about your kingdom in the ruins, and by nightfall we're heading to the jungle with a young man who's been there and who's taking us in a pick-up already outfitted with the right gear. In the jungle, he takes us to the falls where we meet a pretend Chizec who acts in such a way that causes me to think twice. We escape. I'll acknowledge leaping over the falls was a bit harrowing, but we were herded there. We're getting close now and you need Cesar Quintero murdered, for public consumption. You knew once we rescued Bertram, he'd be able to ID you as both The Ghost and Quintero. So, you arrange to have him gunned down in front of the church missionary team so there are direct and trusted American witnesses. And then Regina and I reach your ruins and within an hour we have Bertram Sandt rescued and we're again being herded to the chasm. You knew we were going to jump, but you knew what lay below. A nice underground lake without much danger and only one exit. Then we make our way to a cavern that just so happens to have a boat with a full tank of gas and keys in an easily opened compartment. We speed out of there and General Hammaren just happens to have a helicopter in the neighborhood to evacuate us home. All very orderly. But not natural."

"The plan was executed flawlessly."

Viceroy leaned forward. "But for three misses. You were blind. You didn't know there was a resistance within your army."

"What are you saying?"

"They all became clear to me right before our moment at the

mansion. The first one," Viceroy said, tossing on the table a photo of a Chizec missing half his right ear, "was the Chizec at the falls. I don't know what brand of watch he wears, but it was nice of him to point me to the outline of it on his tanned wrist. By the way, we've not found him yet, but we're searching."

The Ghost's breathing became heavier as he stared at it.

"The second was Theo Gandy. The night you sent him to Emilina's front gate. He wore a costume."

Viceroy noticed him flinch and he continued. "When we saw the surveillance video, it didn't make any sense. On the sleeve of his shirt were two images. Gandy knew there could be dangerous eyeballs viewing the video, so he had to communicate in code. He used masking tape to place a number five and an arrow on his clothing and angled correctly to get that on camera. Five and an arrow. Quint...ero."

Wildly trying to squirm out of the shackles, The Ghost screamed in Spanish.

"Ah, but hold on, there's one more," Viceroy shouted above the rant.

Now breathing hard, his brow furrowed, The Ghost jutted out his chin. "What?"

Viceroy reached into his bag.

"Gandy was wearing this mask," he said, placing a photo on the table. "We screen captured that from the security video. Which also matched this image," he added, placing the translucent screed bag next to the mask, "and in more of a schematic, artful adaptation, this here belt buckle." Viceroy gently placed the belt The Ghost wore, while being Quintero the day at the embassy, right next to the bag. "Oh, and my drawing of the snake head from the statue that stared me down as I leapt to my possible death at the chasm that night."

He put a piece of paper alongside the other items, on it was a crude drawing generally matching the other snake head images.

"Four matches. All pointing to one individual on both sides of the equation. Quintero for the belt and mask; The Ghost for the bag and statues. They screamed 'same man.' You almost had it. The in *and* the out. Both ends of a sadistic drug operation with global plans to keep on spraying until millions of people would have to buy Ovalar for the rest of their lives in order to not die. All in all, a perfect scheme. The Ghost played the part of the drug lord, and Medicamento's Ovalar the only option for the world."

The Ghost's demeanor shifted. He sat back in the chair and turned his head away, no longer engaged with Viceroy. Instead, staring off into space, his mind somewhere else.

"Before I go," Viceroy said as he grabbed the items off the table, "there's just one other nugget I'd like you to be aware of as you live out your days here. I received a call from the owner of the *Wisconsin Lantern* asking me to come down to his office not long after I shot you at the mansion. When I arrived, he handed me a very bulky envelope full of documents. They were the property of Kendrick Winston with a note to contact me in the unfortunate event of his death, or if he went missing. Kendrick was on to you; he just didn't know the how or what. And of all the shocking information in the envelope, the most intriguing was finding out that the owners of Medicamento were Kendrick Winston, your insider and part-owner compliments of Liesl Sandt's seventy million dollars, the President of Guatemala, Octavio Del Santos, Grady Hammaren, and a name we haven't been able to confirm identity as of yet. Efren Zupaya. *My* guess? Zupaya's a Guatemalan native, an orphan, the son of a logger, who went on to be a self-made billionaire with one simple and exclusive product grown nowhere else on the planet. Call me if the name ever rings a bell."

Viceroy winked, gathered his belongings, and quietly exited the room.

The Ghost was escorted back to his isolation cell, an austere space about the size of his former limousine. He didn't move, just stared, blinking at the white walls and white floor.

In the parking lot, Viceroy threw the gym bag in the back seat and soon entered the freeway. A mile later, he hit the 'PLAY' arrow displayed on his cell phone's screen. The podcast with Pastor Greg Oxenhaus began.

"Good morning, everyone. Welcome to Bread of Life. This morning I'd like to share something that's moving my heart. It's a God story involving a friend of mine. My friend's journey is a metaphor for what I want to explore, and even though he's not quite ready to return to his faith, I hold out prayerful hope. I'm going to begin with a statement that I think summarizes where we'll be going today. Simply put, in the rubble of our life's ruins, God ensures every one of us an escape route to healing and freedom. Let's unpack…"

A tiny, imperceptible grin moved one of Viceroy's cheeks as he very gently turned up the volume.

*

ACKNOWLEDGMENTS

I must start by giving thanks to my awesome wife, Lori. From always being a first draft beta reader, to the hours spent helping market the finished product, and for her unfettered support of my quest to accomplish something in my writing, credit for this book is due her as well. My deep thanks, my love, for helping me chase my dream.

Thanks also to my beta readers—Cathy Jolly, Mary Gay Jolly, Mark Crockford and the individuals from my fantastic publishers at Suspense Publishing. Your feedback and questioning crafted a stronger, more well-written story.

To John and Shannon Raab of Suspense Publishing, I cannot express enough my gratitude for taking me on as an author. Even with a few bumpy moments, you never wavered in your belief in me and my talents, and you've been an incredibly deep resource and tutor on how to break through to success. A special call-out to Shannon for your flair in book cover design. I'm still thrilled every time I see this cover! I'm now a more refined and well-rounded author, and I credit you both for elevating my game. You two are an amazing team.

My everlasting thanks as well to Liza Fleissig, my agent with Liza Royce Agency. I wouldn't even be writing this if it wasn't for you plucking me out of the haystack six years ago and telling me I'm more than capable, and then inviting me to join the LRA family.

A huge nod of thanks to the support I receive from my immediate and extended family. My daughters Lauren and Joelle and the sons-in-law Zack and Collin, you're always there to cheer me on. And Jo, what would I do without your help on my digital marketing? Siblings Scott, Gary and Diane: thank you each and the support I receive from your spouses and children. It means more than you know.

One final thanks. I lost my mother, Billie Jeanne Harms, in October of 2020. She loved reading her entire life and had told me once that she also wanted to have written a book in her younger years. So, Mom, this one's for you.

ABOUT THE AUTHOR

Steven C. Harms is a professional sports, broadcast and digital media business executive with a career spanning over thirty years across the NBA, NFL, and MLB. He's dealt with Fortune 500 companies, major consumer brands, professional athletes, and multi-platform integrated sports partnerships and media advertising campaigns. He's an accomplished playwright having written and produced a wildly successful theatrical production which led him to tackling his debut novel, *Give Place to Wrath*, the first in the *Roger Viceroy* detective series which earned awards from Killer Nashville and American Book Fest. The second book, *The Counsel of the Cunning*, is due out in fall of 2021. He's a member of Mystery Writers of America, International Thriller Writers, and Sisters in Crime. A native of Wisconsin, he graduated from the University of Wisconsin-La Crosse. He now resides in Oxford, Michigan, a small, rural suburb of Detroit.

AUTHOR'S NOTE

Dear Reader,

I hope you enjoyed reading *The Counsel of the Cunning* as much as I enjoyed writing it. Support from readers like yourself is crucial for any author to succeed, particularly in this e-book era.

If you enjoyed this book, please consider writing a review at amazon.com and if you are inclined, follow me on Facebook at https://www.facebook.com/authorstevencharms. You can also go to my website at stevencharms.com.

The reviews are important and your support is greatly appreciated.

Thank you,
Steven C. Harms

GIVE PLACE TO WRATH

A ROGER VICEROY NOVEL: BOOK 1

**Killer Nashville Silver Falchion Award Finalist – Best Mystery
American Book Fest American Fiction Awards Finalist –
Mystery/Suspense**

Detective Roger Viceroy, divisional head of the Midwest Region Special Crimes Unit, awakes one morning to a bombing in a wealthy suburb of Milwaukee. As he and his team dive into the investigation, a mysterious clue launches a manhunt with scant other evidence to point them in the right direction.

Over the coming weeks, the related murders unfold, each with a unique twist and the same clue left behind. Viceroy uncovers one other common thread—a seemingly random association with the small north woods town of Curwood, Wisconsin.

As the death toll mounts, Viceroy has to connect the dots and stop the carnage before it reaches the final target, Governor Kay Spurgeon.

"I was on the edge of my seat and couldn't turn the pages fast enough."
—*Readers' Favorite*

https://amzn.to/3y0Cecr

CPSIA information can be obtained
at www.ICGtesting.com
Printed in the USA
BVHW040504231121
622229BV00013B/360

9 780578 933795